PRAISE FOR EILEEN GOUDGE AND THE CYPRESS BAY MYSTERIES

"Eileen Goudge writes like a house on fire, creating characters you come to love and hate to leave." —Nora Roberts, *New York Times*–bestselling author

SWIMSUIT BODY

"Clever, fast-paced, and filled with as many laughs as twists and turns, *Swimsuit Body* is sure to delight cozy fans. Eileen Goudge breathes life into her lovably flawed and fearless heroine Tish Ballard and all the quirky characters that populate this killer tale." —Lisa Unger, *New York Times*–bestselling author of *Ink and Bone*

"Eileen Goudge does everything right in this new mystery. The amateur sleuth is irresistible. . . . The dialogue crackles with wit. The plot is twisty and surprising. The northern California small-town setting is fun and charming. You'll delight in reading this master storyteller's master work." —Jane K. Cleland, author of the Josie Prescott Antiques Mysteries

BONES AND ROSES

"Expect to become immersed with the indomitable heroine, Tish Ballard, the cast of colorful secondary characters, and Eileen Goudge's trademark storytelling." —Sandra Brown, *New York Times*–bestselling author

"A sophisticated, cleverly crafted mystery with complex, intricately drawn characters . . . I was fascinated by everyone in this story, and never saw the ending coming." —Donna Ball, author of the Raine Stockton Dog Mysteries

Swimsuit
Body

Swimsuit Body

A CYPRESS BAY MYSTERY

EILEEN GOUDGE

OPEN ROAD
INTEGRATED MEDIA
NEW YORK

This is a work of fiction. Names, characters, places, events, and incidents either are the product of the author's imagination or are used fictitiously. Any resemblance to actual persons, living or dead, businesses, companies, events, or locales is entirely coincidental.

Copyright © 2016 by Eileen Goudge

Cover design by Mauricio Díaz

978-1-5040-2873-8

Published in 2016 by Open Road Integrated Media, Inc.
180 Maiden Lane
New York, NY 10038
www.openroadmedia.com

To Karen, my sister in life and in crime

Swimsuit
Body

CHAPTER ONE

In my line of work, surprises are never good. That's why, as I'm unlocking the door to the Mediterranean-style beachfront villa on Sand Dollar Lane, I freeze at the sound of movement from inside. It's midmorning, so I'm not expecting company. My last guests checked out yesterday, and the next one isn't due until later today. Whoever they are, they have no business being here.

Suddenly, I'm wide awake, where a minute ago I'd been yawning after another late-night Skype session with my boyfriend. I lower my black Tumi messenger bag and the wicker basket laden with goodies that I'm toting onto the Saltillo-tiled porch. I bend down and pull out my iPad and the .38-caliber Smith and Wesson I'm licensed to carry. I slide the revolver into the waistband of my size-ten Jag jeans. I use the iPad to access the Excel spreadsheet in which I keep track of arrival and departure dates and the maintenance and housekeeping schedules at the dozen properties I manage.

Casa Blanca, in the exclusive gated community of Casa Linda Estates, is the largest and most luxe of my vacation rentals. It sleeps fifteen, so bookings to date have been large parties. The current one is my first single. Also, my first celebrity guest. I consult the spreadsheet, which shows her arriving today, June 1, well after the 3 p.m. check-in time. I return the iPad to my bag. Now the only sound is that of breaking waves from the beach below. The noise

I'd heard a minute ago was probably nothing, a mouse skittering or a breeze blowing through a window that had been left open a crack. I tend to spook easily, a holdover from my near death at the hands of an assailant last summer. Now, anytime I hear a car backfire, I think it's a gunshot. So I keep my gun on me just in case and ease the door open as I enter.

No sooner do I step inside does it come flying at me like a projectile-vomited hairball, startling me into almost dropping the basket. A blur of black-and-tan fur materializes into a small dog, a Yorkshire terrier I see when it launches itself at me, pawing at my pant leg and yapping maniacally. I recognize it from the cover story on Delilah Ward in the current issue of *People* magazine. There's a photo of the dog curled on her lap, wearing the same rhinestone-studded collar.

The bitch has arrived. And I don't mean the dog.

I knew she would be trouble from my dealings with her personal assistant, Brianna Sweeny, a scarily efficient young woman with whom I'd spoken over the phone. I'd envisioned Brianna as the secretarial equivalent of a hired gun, packing weaponry in the form of a laptop and multiple handhelds synced to a Bluetooth device glowing evilly in her ear as she bedeviled me with her employer's endless list of requirements, which included her desired brand of toilet paper (Quilted Northern), pillow (down, medium-firm), and coffeemaker (a Jura Capresso I'd had to order from Williams-Sonoma to replace the Mr. Coffee). To add insult to injury, Brianna had told me I was expected to sign a legal document agreeing not to reveal the location of Miss Ward or so much as breathe her name. I almost called it quits at that point, but in the end I couldn't refuse. I owed it to my clients, the Blankenships. The booking was through the end of August, which amounted to a tidy sum.

After payment had been made in full, I emailed the set of instructions with passcodes for the key lockbox and house alarm.

Standard operating procedure. I expect guests to show me the courtesy of arriving and departing on schedule. Occasionally, there's overlap at either end, but never had a guest shown up an entire day in advance. Why hadn't Brianna or her boss requested an early check-in? Did they think I existed solely to serve at the whim of Her Royal Highness?

I shake the Yorkie loose from my leg. "Down, Cujo. I come in peace." My soothing tone has no effect. He continues to boing up and down like a kid in a bouncy castle, barking his furry little head off.

Normally, I carry treats in my pocket—dogs frequently mistake me for an intruder, an occupational hazard—but I'm fresh out on account of the Rottweiler that nearly took a chunk out of my leg at the Andersons' Cape Cod on Cliff Street earlier in the day. At the moment, however, I'm less concerned with any threat posed by Cujo's Mini Me than I am with the beeping sound emanating from the alarm console. I dart over and punch in the passcode, breathing a sigh of relief when the blinking light goes from red to green. The last thing I need is for the cops to show. As it is, I'm on thin ice with Detective Breedlove after my arrest for breaking and entering last summer. (I'd been after clues in my mom's murder investigation, not valuables, but try telling him that.) But that shouldn't have surprised me given our history. When you've lived in a small town your entire life, you don't need class reunions to remind you of bad shit that happened way back when—your former classmates are the folks with whom you do business or serve on committees or vote for (or against) in local elections. Or, as in my case, who are arresting you.

"Hello! Anyone home?" I call in my loudest voice. No answer. She must have stepped out. Fine. I'll leave the goodie basket and be on my way. Filled with locally sourced comestibles—coffee beans from the Daily Grind, blueberry muffins from Paradise Bakery, a selection of cheeses from Fog City Dairy—the basket is my way of welcoming new guests, and I make sure it's the first thing to greet them when they arrive. The bottle of Bonny Doon chardonnay I normally provide is the only item missing from this one. I don't want to tempt Delilah, who is fresh out of rehab, into falling off the wagon. From the stories I hear in AA, I know that it's a short fall.

I head deeper into the house, Mini Me trotting docilely at my heels, having apparently decided I'm friend and not foe. I'm nearing the end of the hallway when I spot a figure lurking in the shadows up ahead. I let out a yelp before I realize it isn't human. It's a foam-core cutout of Delilah, part of a freestanding lobby display advertising her soon-to-be-released action flick, *Category Five*. I gaze upon her doppelgänger—sultry eyed and pouty lipped, butter-blond tresses blown back as if by hurricane winds—and wonder if she could possibly be that gorgeous in person.

She's more than a pretty face. From humble beginnings—she grew up in foster care—Delilah Ward skyrocketed to fame at age nineteen with the low-budget slasher flick *They Come Out at Night*, which grossed over two hundred million worldwide and went on to become a cult classic. She costarred in several more pictures after that, before her life and career were derailed by personal tragedy. Ten months ago, she lost her husband, former stuntman Eric Nyland, when his private plane went down in the ocean off Catalina Island. She went into seclusion following reports of a breakdown, resurfacing a couple months later to confirm in a press conference that she had been in rehab, after the tabloids ran a blurry shot of her outside the Betty Ford Center. Since then, she'd gone on to make another picture. Now she's here in Cypress Bay, where her next picture is being filmed.

It's a big deal in our small community. Excitement has been building since the film crew set up camp along the coast twenty miles north of town. Our sleepy Northern California seaside town hasn't seen this much buzz since Brad and Angelina were here to look at a property a few years back.

I step from the hallway into the great room. Usually, the ocean view showcased by twelve-foot floor-to-ceiling windows is the first thing I notice when I walk in. But that's not what draws my attention now. I come to an abrupt halt and look around in disbelief. The room is in shambles. Dirty plates and glasses litter every surface. Cigarette butts overflow from saucers used as makeshift ashtrays—never mind this is a nonsmoking residence. A red-wine stain mars a fawn sofa cushion, and the residue of white powder on the glass surface of the wrought-iron coffee table tells me booze wasn't the only substance abused. Delilah Ward didn't just arrive a day early; she partied all night.

I've spilled more alcohol than the average person drinks in a lifetime, so normally I don't judge. I've been sober four years but still have dreams from which I awake disoriented and drenched in sweat, wondering where I was the night before and who I had sex with, verbally abused, or inflicted bodily harm to. But this is beyond the pale. Typical of a drunk, Delilah has trashed the place when she wasn't even supposed to be here.

I make my way into the open-plan kitchen where the granite countertops and butcher-block island are awash with empties and half-eaten deli platters. There's wet garbage in the recycling bin and, inexplicably, a man's wallet. The soles of my sneakers stick to the tiled floor where spills had been left to dry. My disgust mounts as I move from room to room surveying the wreckage that extends throughout the house. The master bedroom looks like the post–Hurricane Katrina New Orleans Astrodome, bedcovers torn apart and the cream carpet strewn with items of clothing. Beer bottles sit in pools of moisture on the cherry night tables. Towels are heaped on the travertine floor of the en suite bathroom, and in one of the double sinks, an upended container spills lavender-scented lotion. A close look shows it to be from the set of Molton Brown toiletries I'd supplied upon Delilah's request. I'm mad enough to wring her pretty little neck.

Mini Me whines piteously as if to say, *It wasn't me*. I'm bending to give him a reassuring pat when I see what he left on the Turkish runner in the hallway. "Bitch," I growl. "Not you," I say when the Yorkie yips in response. It's not his fault that his owner didn't let him out to do his business.

I so do not need this. I have two more stops on my morning rounds, one of which involves an ant invasion, the other a dead tree limb. I could leave this for Esmeralda, my housecleaner who was hired by Delilah to come in every day, but I don't. With a sigh, I push up the sleeves of my turquoise Hang Ten Surf Shop sweatshirt to tackle the worst of the mess. I'm itching to phone Brianna—her Bluetooth device will be buzzing like an angry hornet in her ear when I do—but it can wait.

Dripping with sweat, I dump the last of the three large garbage bags I've filled in the trash bins. I'm heading out the door when I remember the goodie basket that I left on the kitchen counter. I retrace my steps, mentally scratching out the words *Compliments of the Management* on the handwritten card tucked inside and substituting *Bite me* as I retrieve it. I'd sooner give it to a stranger on the street.

If I were nicer, I'd cut Delilah some slack, if only because she was recently widowed. But I'm not nice, so to hell with it. I'm headed to my SUV with the basket tucked under my arm when a midnight-blue Lexus sports coupe pulls into the driveway. A blond woman, dressed in short-shorts and a tank top, climbs from the driver's side. A jolt of recognition has me halting in my tracks. I stare at her as she walks toward me. Even with the huge designer sunglasses that partially cover her face, I instantly know who—or rather what—I'm looking at.

The supernova that is Delilah Ward.

She really *is* that gorgeous in person. Slender and perfectly proportioned, she has legs that go on forever and boobs that bounce in a way that tells me they're not the store-bought kind. Her hair is naturally blond—I know from the pictures I've seen of her as a child—and falls in loose curls around her shoulders. If someone told me she was from another planet, it would make sense. A planet where there is no such thing as cellulite, and you can party hard without appearing the least bit hungover the morning after.

She smiles, dazzling me with the whiteness of her teeth as she extends her hand to shake mine. "Hi, I'm Delilah! And you must be . . ." She frowns as though trying to remember my name.

"Tish." It's short for Leticia, my grandmother's name. It's a moment before I remember I'm mad at the woman with whom I'm shaking hands. "I wasn't expecting you until tomorrow."

"Oh, God." Her smile gives way to a rueful grimace. "I knew I was forgetting something. I promised Brianna I'd call and it totally slipped my mind. Karol"—she names the director of the picture—"wanted us to meet to go over some script changes, so I flew in a day early. I'm sorry. My bad." Her gaze drops to the goodie basket. "For me? Oh, now I feel even worse. I'm such an idiot!"

"It happens." I can overlook the fact that she failed to inform me of her change in plans, which seems minor compared to her having trashed the place. "But I have to charge you for the extra day."

"No problem. I'll have Brianna take care of it," she says blithely.

"There's something else we need to discuss." I say, adopting a firmer tone.

She pushes her sunglasses onto her head. Her eyes are the blue of a tropical lagoon fringed with dark lashes. I become transfixed as I gaze into them. "Is this about the neighbor lady who complained? She calmed down after I explained we were rehearsing. I'm surprised she said anything."

Mrs. Cooley is the closest neighbor. She's in her eighties and hard of hearing, so it was more than loud talking if she'd called to complain. "From the looks of it, you were doing more than rehearsing."

"Oh. Right. About that," she says, catching my meaning. "I was going to tidy up, but it was late by the time everyone left, and . . ." She trails off at the stony look on my face, and I brace myself for a blast of who-do-you-think-you-are star displeasure. But she smiles instead, a dimple forming in one cheek—the dimple that fixed her place in the Hollywood firmament from frame one. "I bet you think I'm one of those Hollywood types. I'm not, I promise. I'm usually very considerate."

I soften toward her. "Well, you might want to review the rental agreement. I wouldn't want your stay spoiled by any . . . unpleasantness. Also, keep in mind the housekeeper, Esmeralda, works a tight schedule. If you need full-time help, I can recommend a service."

Delilah waves her hand in an airy gesture, the diamond engagement ring she wears on her right hand, signifying her widowhood, flashing in the sunlight. "That won't be necessary. I can manage. Between you and me"—she drops her voice to confide—"I'm no stranger to scrubbing toilets."

"It'll be our secret," I reply with a smile. She glances down at the basket that's tucked under my arm. *Am I forgiven?* her plaintive gaze seems to say. I relent as I had earlier with Mini Me when he licked my hand. I hand her the basket. "Enjoy."

She beams as if I'd just awarded her an Oscar. "Thank you, I will." She plucks the card from the basket, scribbles something on the back with a pen she produced from her teal Prada bag, and hands it to me. "My cell number," she says casually, as though it hadn't been as tightly guarded by her assistant as the pin number for her bank account. "Call me if Brianna gives you a hard time. I pay her to be scary because I'm the world's biggest softie," she adds in a hushed voice, eyes sparkling like those of a naughty but adorable child who pulled one over on the adults.

I walk away confused. Was that the spoiled creature who'd insisted on two-hundred-thread-count Egyptian cotton sheets and who couldn't possibly drink coffee that wasn't brewed in a machine that cost more than what I make in a week? The woman I'd just encountered had seemed . . . sweet. A word I never thought I would use to describe Delilah Ward.

CHAPTER TWO

The Voakses' Spanish colonial sits high on a hill above the bay, a mile or so from the Roaring Brook Camp where I was a counselor the summer before my sophomore year of high school. Amid the serene woodland setting, I wage war on the ants that have invaded the kitchen. I strafe them with bug spray and set out traps, then do a sweep of the pantry searching for any open food containers, which are crack to critters small and large—I once chased a bear from one of my other properties—before I head over to the Russos' midcentury modern by the university to meet with Brandon, the tree trimmer.

The dead tree limb that hangs over their neighbors' garage is the proverbial sword of Damocles in more ways than one. The neighbors in question, the Hendersons, a retired couple in their sixties, offered to split the cost of having it removed, and while I like to think they're simply reasonable people, I can't help wondering if their friendly gesture has anything to do with the fact that my client, Victor Russo, owns a casino in Vegas. Maybe the Hendersons are afraid he'll have them whacked, along with the tree limb, if they don't play nice.

It's almost 1:30 by the time I break for lunch. Leaving Brandon to finish up, I climb back in my Ford Explorer, the green Eddie Bauer model with the red stripe that tells you how old it is—the speedometer has more miles on it than Bonnie and Clyde's get-away car—and head over to Ivy's. My best friend, Ivy Ladeaux, lives down the street from me, so when she's not pulling a shift at the Gilded Lily, the collectibles shop where she works part-time, we eat lunch together. On the way, I stop to pick up sandwiches at our favorite vegetarian eatery, McDharma's. The parking lot is full and I'm lucky to find a spot. I pull in as a circa 1970s Volkswagen bus, painted with peace symbols and plastered with political stickers, is pulling out. The driver, an old dude with graying shoulder-length hair, wearing sunglasses the same vintage as his vehicle, gives me a friendly wave.

Cypress Bay is the land of old hippies who didn't fade away. Take the owner of McDharma's for instance. Austin Atkins is a former sixties activist who burned his draft card back in the day. More recently, when the McDonald's corporation threatened to sue for copyright infringement, he took action and became a cause célèbre after he went to the press. McDonald's backed down within days of the story about the David-versus-Goliath battle going viral. Austin threw a party to celebrate, a meatless barbecue if you can imagine, and we all raised our glasses, business owners and counterculture types alike, in a toast to his victory over The Man.

When I pull into the driveway of Ivy's gingerbread house, I'm greeted by the sound of hammering. Jax, the handyman, is replacing a section of rotted railing on the front porch, his golden retriever, Buddy, stretched out alongside him. Jax's hair, tied back in its usual ponytail, is the same red-gold shade as his dog's fur. The two have become a fixture since Ivy inherited the house from her grandmother. There's always some repair going on. The two-story Victorian is a money pit and far too big for one person, but Ivy has lived in it since she was twelve and has a sentimental attachment to the house. I think she would sooner donate a kidney than sell it. I walk over to greet Jax and Buddy before making my way to the garage that Ivy converted into a studio.

I find her hunched over the workbench, peering into the retractable magnifying glass clamped to one end as she puts the finishing touches on the diorama she's been toiling over all week. She wears bib overalls and a smocked peasant blouse with puff sleeves, an outfit no one over the age of ten could pull off except her. Ivy resembles Meg Ryan in *When Harry Met Sally* with curly black hair instead of blond. You might find her unbearably cute, with her big blue eyes in a heart-shaped face, until you get to know her and discover she's a woman of substance with the heart of a warrior. She's also quirky, another thing I love about her. She doesn't just march to the beat of her own drummer, she dances the funky chicken and makes it seem cool. Which is why we've been best friends since we met in sixth grade.

Next to her, I look like the giantess in *Attack of the Fifty-Foot Woman*. I'm five foot ten with dirty-blond hair, cut shoulder-length, gray-green eyes and dusky skin of my Cherokee ancestors—if there's any truth to the Ballard family lore about the raid that resulted in the birth of my great-great-grandfather. My grandma used to say I had an hourglass figure, which, in modern-day parlance, means you could stand to lose a few pounds. You'd think it wouldn't be hard with all the running around I do in my line of work, except that for every calorie I burn, there's always another one lying in wait ready to pounce. I think guiltily of the party leftovers that I ate for supper last night, after they were pressed on me by one of my clients. I don't want to know how many calories are in a gougère.

Ivy looks up, blinking, at my approach. "Don't tell me it's lunchtime already?"

"Past."

She peers at her diver's watch, which looks cartoonish on her dainty wrist, and makes a surprised noise when she sees what time it is—a quarter past two—before remarking, "Well, that explains it."

"What?"

"I suddenly realized I was starving."

"I left you a message. Which you'd know if you checked your voicemail."

I bend to examine her latest creation. Ivy's dioramas are one of a kind in that they're made from dead insects, which she buys from an honest-to-God insect emporium in L.A. It sounds gross, but it's not. Her dioramas are works of art. The one before me is of a shoe store, featuring a daddy longlegs spider and a longhorn beetle as customer and clerk, detailed with dollhouse miniature-size furniture and objects. I watch as she bends a spider leg no thicker than an eyelash, using tweezers and a moistened Q-tip. When she finally sits back, all eight of the spider's appendages are perfectly positioned and shod in teeny-weeny sneakers. I smile at the whimsy.

"Sweet. But my favorite is still the ladybug picnic."

"That's because ladybugs aren't on your hit list." She can smell Eau de Raid on me.

"Ladybugs eat aphids. They can live."

With a tired sigh, I sink into the chintz armchair, a castoff from the house, whose seat is permanently molded to the shape of Grandmother Ladeaux's bottom.

"Rough day?" Ivy turns her swivel chair around to face me.

I tell her about my diva in residence, Delilah Ward. "I'll have to put the number for FEMA on my contact list if she destroys anything else," I say after I've described the scene I encountered at the house. "Though the weird thing was, I liked her. She seemed . . . I don't know, like a real person."

"As opposed to what—a raving bitch?"

"Or a bereaved widow."

"People have different ways of showing grief."

"True. Also, it's been a while." She lost her husband a year ago in August.

Ivy fetches the TV tray that she decoupaged with vintage photos from the flea market, and I set out our lunch: hummus and avocado sandwiches, a large bag of Terra Chips, and bottled iced teas.

"What bothers me most is that she was doing coke. Or one of her guests was. Either way, it doesn't bode well for someone fresh out of rehab." I add, in a subdued voice, "It brought back memories."

"You were never that bad." Ivy tears open the bag of chips and crams a handful into her mouth.

"True, I never did coke."

"And you got sober."

"Only after I burned all my bridges." That was when I was a real-estate broker and wore nice clothes to work. I fooled myself into thinking no one could see through my disguise. I ignored the funny looks I used to get, the conversations that broke off when I entered a room, the buyers who were all smiles one day and not returning my calls the next. I hit bottom when a seller pulled her listing due to my "erratic behavior," and I went ballistic. I showed up at her house that night, stinking drunk, and proceeded to tell her exactly what I thought of her, a tirade that culminated in my hurling her keys, along with the remote control device to her gated community, into her koi pond. In front of her little girl no less. I was so ashamed the next morning when I realized what I'd done, I attended my first AA meeting. I've been going ever since.

"Not all. I stuck by you," Ivy reminds me.

"Yeah, so you could kick my butt."

We exchange a grin. I uncap my peach-flavored iced tea and take a swig. Ivy brushes chip crumbs from the bib of her overalls and unwraps her sandwich. I think about the night I showed up drunk at her house for a dinner party and she sent me packing. I was mad at the time, but a year later, when I was making my AA amends, I thanked her for being a hard-ass. *That's what friends are for*, she'd said.

"Talked to Bradley lately?" she asks before she bites into her sandwich.

I groan. My boyfriend is another sore subject. Bradley, a cameraman for CNN, is currently on assignment in Afghanistan. Last night while we were Skyping, I decided to surprise him with a striptease. We haven't had sex in a while, and I was feeling frisky. It wasn't until after I'd bared my boobs that I noticed the blurred figure in the background. To my mortification, I saw that it was Bradley's Afghani driver, Yusef, when his bearded face swam into view.

"Bet you made his day," Ivy comments with a laugh, after I've relayed the incident.

"Who, Bradley or his driver? If you're referring to Yusef, I very much doubt it. He looked pretty shocked. In fact, I may have set back peace in the Middle East another hundred years."

"Sure, if it had been Hillary Clinton doing the striptease."

"Over there women are stoned to death for less."

I make light of it, but I can't speak of death without a chill going through me, recalling my close call, the previous summer, at the hands of a gun-wielding psycho while I was investigating my mom's murder case. I vowed to stick to my day job from then on. I started my own business, Rest Easy Property Management, after I got sober. I tend to other people's homes as I do my own. I see to repairs and ensure that my clients aren't getting ripped off by their pool or gardening service and that any domestics in their employ possess green cards. For the vacation rentals, I screen potential renters. I'm also the soul of discretion. Recently, after I'd noticed several tampons missing from a previously sealed box of Tampax at the Millers' house while the wife was out of town, I replaced it with an unopened box so she wouldn't find out her husband was cheating on her.

"What did Bradley have to say?" Ivy brings me back into the moment.

"He wanted to know what I was doing for an encore."

She chuckles. "My kind of guy."

"He'd feel differently if a *fatwa* was issued against me. On the other hand, we're talking about a guy who isn't bothered by the fact that his parents hate me." I take a swig of my iced tea, washing away the bitter taste in my mouth at the mention of Joan and Douglas Trousdale.

"There are worse things." Ivy's tone is light, but I can see something is troubling her. Hers is the kind of face that shows emotion like a barometer shows changes in atmospheric pressure. "I had dinner with Rajeev's parents last night," she explains in response to the questioning look I give her. "Remember I told you they were coming for a visit?" Her boyfriend's parents live in Mumbai.

"Right. So how'd it go?"

"Good," she reports in a flat voice. "They were nice."

"You don't sound very happy about it," I comment before remembering who I'm talking to. "Let me guess. They don't have their hearts set on their son marrying a suitable bride of their choosing."

She makes a wry face that tells me I guessed correctly. "They were totally modern, not at all what I expected. They *adored* me, to quote Rajeev." She looks panicked all of a sudden. "Oh, God, what am I going to do if he asks me to marry him?" Which to my mind isn't a matter of *if* but *when*.

Rajeev is crazy about her. He's also a catch. He could be a Bollywood star with his looks. More importantly, he's sweet natured, funny, smart, and successful—he earns a six-figure income as a software designer. None of which I point out because Ivy has no desire to marry. She's turned down two marriage proposals already. One from the fellow artist she dated a couple years ago, and another before that from her boyfriend in college. I temper my response. "I think you should be open to the possibility that it's not the worst thing that could happen."

She groans. "It's not as if we haven't talked about it. He knows how I feel."

"Exactly. You're in love with him."

She doesn't dispute this, though you'd never guess to look at her she was a woman in love. She lapses into silence, winding a stray curl around her finger as she stares out the window. When she brings her gaze back to me, her expression is weighted with the doubts and fears I know she's feeling. "You think I should marry him." It's an accusation rather than a statement.

"I didn't say that. But I think you should keep an open mind."

It all goes back to her mother, in my opinion. Dr. Ladeaux sold her medical practice in Seattle and ended her marriage to Ivy's father to move to Malawi, where she runs a free clinic in a remote village. Ivy, who was twelve at the time, was left in the care of her dad and grandmother. She's always acted like she was totally fine with her mom's decision. *She's doing important work saving lives*, Ivy would always say in her defense. But I know from having lost my own mom at an early age how a thing like that can shape you. Or warp you.

She nods slowly, saying, "I'll try."

"Just promise not to pick a bridesmaid's dress that makes me look fat."

She growls in response and tosses her wadded napkin at me.

CHAPTER THREE

After I leave Ivy's, I drive across town to meet with Shondra Perkins, director of the Trousdale Senior Center, with whom I have a 3:30 appointment. Shondra didn't say why she wants to see me, but I assume it has to do with my brother, Arthur, who volunteers at the center. What did he do this time? Argue out loud with the voices in his head? Share one of his crackpot conspiracy theories? Inform one of the old people at the center, where he teaches computer skills, that his or her pacemaker was picking up alien transmissions from outer space?

Arthur has been doing much better since his most recent stay at the puff—insider-speak for psychiatric facility—and although I would like to believe he's turned a corner, that his current meds are the magic cocktail, or that his mental illness has lessened with age as can sometimes happen, I know better. Arthur is schizoaffective. A cross between schizophrenia and bipolar disorder, it has him subject to both delusions and manic phases, which come and go, usually without warning. He can be fine one day and obsessing over something that exists only in his mind the next: listening devices planted in his walls by the CIA or top-secret government missions for which he's been recruited to create a software program. But like I said, he's been on an even keel lately, so maybe I'm worrying needlessly. Maybe there's a benign reason Shondra wants to see me. I'll know soon enough.

The Trousdale Senior Center is located to the south of town, in an area far removed from the quaint charms of the historic district and dominated by office buildings and medical complexes. I take the old coast highway, which is slower than the freeway but more scenic. The road curves past cliffs, from which cypress trees lean leeward like grizzled mariners braced against storm winds, and ocean vistas that are indeed worthy of a film location. Of the properties that front the ocean, no two are alike, funky older cottages stand beside beautifully restored Victorians and contemporary homes like the ones you see in *Architectural Digest*. I used to love showing those properties when I was a broker, not only because of the wow factor, but because there was something for everyone—a reflection of the community itself. Driving past Paradise Point, I see the seal-like figures of surfers in wetsuits dotting the waves. A man carrying a ratty backpack ambles alongside the road. At the beach shuttle stop, several teenage girls in cutoffs and bikini tops loiter by the snack bar, purposely ignoring the boys who appear to be checking them out.

I round the bend at Dolan State Park, and I'm treated to views of the ocean to the west and the wetlands to the east. Sailboats cut graceful swaths out at sea, and ducks paddle amid the tall reeds of the saltwater marsh. The weather is unseasonably warm for the beginning of June. I'm tempted to join the beachgoers splashing in the surf. I keep a gym bag in the back of the Explorer, packed with a towel and swimsuit, for just such impulses. But duty calls. Like it or not, I am my brother's keeper.

Fifteen minutes later, I pull into the parking lot of a two-story clapboard structure, white with green trim, that has a vaguely Ethan Allenish feel, like a midprice chain hotel masquerading as a bed-and-breakfast. Conveniently situated between a medical complex and a Rite Aid, the senior center is named after the late Leon Trousdale, Bradley's grandfather and my mother's former employer. Leon donated the money to have it built. It galls me whenever I see the sign with his name, because we all know now he wasn't the man he pretended to be. But I also know good can come of evil, and this place has been good for Arthur since he started volunteering here. He's more like the confident, quick-witted brother I remember from when we were growing up.

Inside, the door to Shondra's office stands open. She rises from behind her desk to greet me as I enter. "Tish, it's good to see you. Thanks for making the time. I know it's the middle of your workday."

Shondra is in her fifties and on the heavy side, but she carries her weight well. She always dresses as though she is the keynote speaker at a convention. Today she's wearing a gold-and-black houndstooth blazer paired with a black pencil skirt, an outfit that complements her ebony skin. I feel frumpy next to her in my jeans and sweatshirt. "Everything all right?" I ask as we shake hands.

"See for yourself." She motions toward the interior window opposite her desk that looks out on the large, airy common room. My gaze travels past a pair of elderly men playing chess and three ladies practicing some sort of dance routine to where my brother sits at the computer station, as erect as Captain Kirk at the helm of *Starship Enterprise*, instructing his current students, eight women and one man. I watch them lean in as he demonstrates something on his computer. I'd expected to find him behaving strangely or sitting alone staring into space, and it comes as a profound relief to see him holding his own, commanding the respect of people twice his age.

"My brother, the rock star," I remark, smiling.

The director chuckles. "He's especially popular with the ladies. Have you met Mrs. Sedgwick?" She points out a petite, henna-haired woman who's pressed in more closely than the others. From this distance, she doesn't look like a senior citizen. In contrast to the other ladies, who are dressed in leisurewear and sweats, she wears four-inch black patent-leather heels and a chevron-pattern wrap dress that shows off her figure. I bet she still turns heads even at her age. *My brother's for one*, I think when they exchange a private smile, after she's whispered something in his ear.

"Arthur's made a real contribution around here," Shondra goes on. "We're lucky to have him."

I whip my head around to stare at her. "You mean you . . . you don't want him to leave?"

Shondra looks surprised before she seems to realize where I'm coming from. She hastens to set me straight. "Leave? God, no. I wish I had four more like him. Some of those folks don't get out much." She gestures toward the cluster of mostly gray heads bent toward Arthur. "Now they can Skype with loved ones and surf the Web, and they don't feel as isolated. All because of Arthur."

I blink back tears. "Wow. I'm . . . I'm glad it's going so well."

"I confess I had my doubts at first, given his . . . challenges. But it's worked out better than I had hoped. And I know from talking to Arthur, he feels the same way."

It occurs to me that one reason my brother has flourished here is because he's not always the craziest person in the room. Some of regulars at the center are in the early stages of dementia; others have cognitive impairment. I watch him come to the aid of a tiny, white-haired woman who's staring at her screen in confusion, cupping the mouse as gingerly as if it were an explosive device. He speaks calmly to her and puts his hand over hers to guide the mouse until she gets the hang of it.

"He's certainly in his element," I agree.

"I'd like to offer him a paid position. That's why I asked you here, Tish. I thought I should discuss it with you first."

"You're offering him a *job*?" It's all I can do not to shriek with joy.

She nods and smiles. "If you don't think it'd be too much for him. He'd be working five afternoons a week, instead of three, to accommodate all the people who've signed up for his classes."

"I'll have to run it by his psychiatrist, but I don't imagine he'll have a problem with it." In fact, it was Dr. Sandefur who'd suggested Arthur might benefit from volunteer work. "Personally, I'm all for it."

"I'm afraid we couldn't offer much in the way of salary."

"Not a problem." I explain about Arthur's SSDI benefits, which restrict how much he can earn in supplementary income. We chat a few minutes more before I take my leave. I promise to get back to her as soon as I've gotten the green light from Arthur's psychiatrist.

On my way out, I stop to say hello to Arthur. He peels away from a heavyset, platinum-haired woman in a purple pantsuit who's complaining in a loud voice that she can't find the cursor and hurries to meet me as I walk toward him. "Tish, what are you doing here?" he asks, frowning.

I'm struck by how handsome he looks. He wears a blue-striped Oxford shirt and pressed khakis instead of the baggy sweats he slops around in at home. His shaggy brown hair is styled with product except where it curls over his ears. You'd never guess this was the same Arthur who once assaulted a Greenpeace volunteer whom he'd mistaken for a CIA operative. "I was in the neighborhood," I lie.

He eyes me suspiciously behind his black-framed Clark Kent glasses. "I'm fine. Everything under control." He speaks in a low voice as if to a social worker doing an assessment.

"So I see. I'm not here to check up on you," I assure him. "And I'm not staying. I have to get back to work."

"Okay. . . . Good-bye, then." He catches himself and says in a nicer voice, "Can we talk later?"

"I'll stop by after work to pick up your laundry." Arthur doesn't own a car and the nearest Laundromat is some distance, so I do his laundry whenever the coin-operated machines at his apartment complex are on the fritz. "We can grab a bite to eat, if you'd like. I thought we'd try that new pizza place."

"Could we make it another night?" He's suddenly having trouble making eye contact. "I, um, have this . . . thing."

I can barely contain my surprise. Arthur rarely goes out in the evenings unless it's with me, or Ivy if it's the three of us. He usually stays in playing video games or writing computer programs while consuming giant bowls of Honey Bunches of Oats. His only friend is a fellow computer geek named Ray Zimmer, whom he met in an online forum. But if he had plans with Ray, wouldn't he have said so?

Before I can press for details, I'm distracted by the sight of a petite figure hurrying toward us, the henna-haired woman who was glued to Arthur's side a minute ago. "You must be Arthur's sister," she greets me, extending her hand. "I've heard so much about you, I feel as if I know you. I'm Gladys Sedgwick," she adds belatedly when it becomes clear I'm not equally familiar with her.

"Tish," I introduce myself, wondering why Arthur hadn't mentioned her to me. I know only what I learned from Shondra, that she's a wealthy widow whose late husband, Lloyd Sedgwick of Sedgwick Savings and Loan, left an endowment to the center in his will. "Nice to meet you, Mrs. Sedgwick." The emerald on her ring finger catches my eye. It's the size of a cocktail onion.

"Gladys, please. I'm ancient enough as it is," she says in the tone of a woman who's used to being told she doesn't look her age. Her blue eyes sparkle in a fine-boned face with few wrinkles, and her porcelain complexion suggests she was a true redhead before she started dyeing her hair the color of a red-velvet cake. "Arthur talks about you all the time. I was hoping we'd have a chance to meet."

I smile. "Did he have anything nice to say?"

"He said you used to stick up for him at school."

"True. I gave this one kid who was bullying him a black eye."

"I hope he learned his lesson," she replies staunchly.

"Yeah, be nice to kids with big sisters who have mean right hooks."

Gladys chuckles, and Arthur says pointedly to me, "I thought you had to get back to work."

"You act like you're in a hurry to get rid of me. Worried I'll embarrass you in front of your new friend?" I tease. His face flushes crimson, and I realize, to my dismay, I've done just that—embarrassed him.

"We don't want to keep you. Art has told me how busy you are," Gladys says, coming to his rescue. "You must have your hands full looking after all those homes." *Art?* No one ever calls my brother Art; he hates that derivative. And why is she acting like they're more than teacher and student?

Arthur directs a look of pained appeal at me.

"Later, dude." I kiss him good-bye, putting him out of his misery, and he slips away to head back to his post.

"We'd be utterly lost without him," Gladys says, walking with me to the door. "Some of us had to be dragged kicking and screaming into the digital era. It helps to have a teacher who explains things clearly, and who never loses patience."

"He's a good guy," I agree with understated pride.

"He reminds me of my late husband. Such a dear man. Fifty years, and never a harsh word."

"Sounds like you had a good marriage."

"We did. Not a day goes by that I don't miss him." She sighs wistfully.

"Must get lonely."

"Yes, but it helps to stay active. That's what I told my granddaughter, Lexie, when she lost her husband two years ago. I urged her to hang on to their cattle ranch in Montana when she was thinking of selling it. Life doesn't end when you bury your husband, I told her. You're only thirty-five. She took my advice, though I'm sure there are days she wishes she hadn't. Cattle ranching isn't for wimps!"

"You don't look old enough to have a grandchild who owns a ranch," I remark.

She beams at the compliment, twinkling up at me like a shiny ornament from a low branch of a Christmas tree. "You're only as old as you feel. In my mind, I can still turn somersaults."

I wonder if she sees herself as someone in whom Arthur could be romantically interested. *Is* he? It occurs to me he must get lonely from time to time. He hasn't had a girlfriend since Amanda, his college sweetheart who broke up with him when he first started acting crazy. Was it so hard to believe he could be attracted to the well-preserved and young-at-heart Gladys?

"We go power walking in the mornings," she says as we're saying our good-byes at the door. "You should join us some weekend. Once around the park, and breakfast afterward at the Bluejay Café." I'm about to beg off, imagining it to be some senior-group activity, when she adds, "Arthur and I would enjoy the company, and you and I could get to know each other better."

I'm speechless. *Power walking?* Since when does my brother, who avoids all forms of exercise and who smokes cigarettes, go power walking? And why is this the first I'm hearing of it? I recall how evasive he was when I'd asked about his plans for this evening. Did he have a date with Gladys?

"I'd like that," I reply when I've found my voice. I would sooner walk over hot coals than go power walking in my free time—it's less strenuous, and blistered soles would give me an excuse to put my feet up—but I'm taking her up on the invitation, because I need to find out what the deal is with Arthur and his henna-haired hottie.

CHAPTER FOUR

I do the math as I drive north on Highway One to my next stop. Gladys Sedgwick has a granddaughter who's thirty-five, a year older than my brother, which means Gladys has to be at least twice Arthur's age. My head swims thinking about it. Maybe I'm making too much of an innocent friendship, but my brother has a way of getting into situations that fall under the heading of Weird Shit That Doesn't Happen to Normal People. And it always ends the same way: a call to Dr. Sandefur, a packed bag, and a stay at the puff. I can only pray this isn't one of those situations.

Fifteen minutes later, I arrive at the Chens' Asian-themed split-level, in the residential country club of Paso Verde. It's the primary residence of the owners, but they're frequently out of town, which is why they need a property manager. Currently they're in Beijing where their export firm is headquartered. I do my walk-through and feed the koi, which are the size of puppies and snap greedily at my fingers as I sprinkle pellets into the pond. By the time I lock up, it's dark out. I swing by my brother's place on my way home and find his bag of dirty laundry inside the door but no Arthur. I catch a faint whiff of an expensive scent that I recognize as Chanel No. 5.

A perfume a wealthy older lady would wear.

* * * *

Sleep is slow to come that night; the eventful day has my mind churning. The following morning when my alarm goes off at the usual ungodly hour, I have to pry myself out of bed. Yawning, I make my way down the hall to the kitchen, drawn by the aroma of coffee. A fresh pot greets me each morning when I get up, thanks to the programming feature on my coffeemaker. I'm pouring some steaming brew into a mug when the thump of the cat flap on the back door signals the return of my tomcat, Hercules, from his nocturnal prowls. He pads over to sit at my feet, meowing.

"What, you think you're the only one with problems?" I say, looking down at him.

I named him Hercules because he's a badass, all brawn and slinky stripes. I bet he thinks he's all that with the ladies, but I had him neutered when I took him in as a stray several years ago, so there's only so much trouble he can get into. (Though judging from his torn ear, he's fought his share of battles.) He continues to meow as I mix a bowl of cat food. Leaving him to it, I sit down at my 1940s red Formica dinette to savor my coffee and one peaceful moment of the day. The kitchen of my Craftsman bungalow, with its period details, is a reminder of an era before the invention of the handheld devices that make me accessible whenever a toilet overflows or a coffeemaker goes kaput or some genius has the bright idea of taking a bubble bath in a Jacuzzi.

Fifteen minutes later, after I've finished my coffee and showered, I'm headed out the door. The sky is lightening above the rooftops of the older homes that line my street. The air is cool with the fog that rolls in most mornings in summer. It's too early for any of my neighbors to be out and about; the only sound I hear is that of breaking waves. I live two blocks from the ocean, which is the other reason I bought my bungalow. So I can fall asleep each night to the lullaby of the sea.

I drive to the Voakses', and I'm relieved to find the ants haven't retaken Hamburger Hill. Next, I head over to the Mastersons' condo, by the yacht harbor, where I replace their old broken toaster with the new one I picked up at the Sears in Harborview Plaza, and make sure the stash of porn magazines belonging to their nineteen-year-old son, who's home from college for the summer, is tucked away where Esmeralda won't come across it while she's cleaning—she spends enough time praying for lost souls as it is. At the Willets' Cape Cod, I see that the gophers have been at the tubers again. I replenish the supply at the garden center, then it's on to my next stop, the Belknaps' shingled cottage on Cliff Drive, where the lady who lives next door comes over to complain about the renters who were sunbathing in the nude. I wonder what she'd say about my having bared my boobs to a perfect stranger, a devout Muslim at that, in the Middle East.

I'm tempted to stop at Casa Blanca, if only to make sure the house is still standing, but I don't normally drop in at my vacation rentals when they're occupied, and what if Delilah's home? She might think I'm some creepy fan who wants to be her new BFF. Besides, if anything really bad had happened, like the house burning down or a flood from a burst pipe, I would have been informed by now. I leave a message on her voicemail instead.

Two days later, when she still hasn't returned my call, I give in to the gnawing feeling in my gut and head over to Casa Linda Estates to see what's what. Driving south on Highway One, I consider the many faces of Delilah Ward. There's the seemingly down-to-earth woman I met. The spoiled diva who'd driven me crazy with her long list of requirements. The grieving widow shown on the cover of *People* magazine, her head bowed in grief at her husband's memorial service. The actress who starred in the teen slasher pic that rocketed her to stardom and who was later nominated for an Emmy for her role in the HBO original series *Hard Rain*.

The movie Delilah is filming in Cypress Bay is a remake of *Suspicion*, the 1941 picture starring Cary Grant and Joan Fontaine about a wife who suspects her new husband is out to kill her. It's titled *Devil's Slide* after the famously treacherous stretch of Highway One south of San Francisco. Delilah was signed, for the role played by Joan Fontaine, after she blew the competition out of the water with her screen test. I'm sure she'll rock the part. I'd seen her in enough roles to know how talented she is. She's that rarest of creatures: the hot blonde from central casting who can act. What remains to be seen is whether or not she was putting on an act with me.

It's 11:00 a.m. when I pull up to the gates at Casa Linda Estates. I wave my key fob to activate the gate at the entrance, and as it swings open, another vehicle, a black Escalade, glides past me in the opposite lane and through the gate at the exit. I take notice only because it has tinted windows; you don't see many of those around here. I imagine it belongs to one of the movie people who's been to visit Delilah Ward, but I give it no further thought as I wind my way through quiet streets lined with Spanish colonials and Mediterranean-style villas, driving at a crawl due to all the speed bumps, which I'm convinced outnumber the children, dogs, or ducks in the gated community. Ten minutes later, I arrive at Casa Blanca. Easily the most impressive property on the cul-de-sac, the four-thousand-square-foot villa boasts a barrel-tile clay roof, a columned arcade that forms a dramatic entry to the house, and decks that look out on the ocean in back.

The massive front door is made of Brazilian hardwood with raised panels carved in a Mayan design and fitted with a wrought-iron pull. I ring the doorbell, and after I've waited long enough to conclude that no one is home, I use my key to let myself in. I see no sign of either Delilah or her dog, but I'm relieved to find the house spotless. Floors mopped and carpets vacuumed, furniture polished, the granite countertops in the kitchen gleaming. Clothes tumble in the dryer, and I'm reminded that I still have my brother's laundry, which is washed and folded in my SUV except for the red Stanford hoodie that I'm wearing. It must have fallen out of Arthur's overstuffed laundry bag before I took his clothes in to launder them. I discovered it this morning while I was on my rounds and put it on after my own sweatshirt got soaked as I was changing a water filter.

I step through the French doors that open onto the patio. The early morning fog has burned off, and the sky is blue with fluffy clouds skimming overhead. The swimming pool glitters with reflected sunlight. I notice the side gate is open. Delilah must have taken her dog for a walk and neglected to lock up. I'm walking over to secure it when I notice a blond, bikini-clad woman lying face-down on one of the chaises by the pool. Delilah Ward, as I suspected, I see when I draw closer. She appears to have dozed off. I'm thinking I should wake her before she gets any more sunburned but I'm hesitant to do so. I know from the confidentiality agreement her assistant had me sign how fiercely she guards her privacy. She might get angry that I let myself in.

Finally, I decide I have a moral obligation, if only to prevent her from looking like a lobster when filming starts. I come to an abrupt halt as I'm crossing the patio when I notice her backside isn't the only thing that's red. There's a pool of blood beneath the chaise and her hair is bloodied. Had she fallen and hurt herself? That happened to me once before I got sober. I woke one morning to find my pillow bloody and a bump on my forehead from a fall I'd taken the night before that I had no memory of. Delilah's injury, however, looks more serious than mine was.

My heart is pounding as I rush to her aid. *Please, God, let her be okay.*

That's when I see the bullet hole in the back of her head.

CHAPTER FIVE

I stand frozen, my mind refusing to believe what my eyes are seeing. Then, in my panicked state, I do the one thing I would ordinarily know not to do: I mess with a crime scene. Thinking she might still be alive, I flip her over—actually, wrestle her onto her back is more like it; there's no flipping a hundred and ten pounds of dead weight unless you're Arnold Schwarzenegger. But she's not breathing, and I can't find a pulse. That's when I notice her eyes are staring sightlessly up at the sky.

I back away on rubber legs, gulping in air to combat the nausea that threatens to further contaminate the crime scene. As I stare at the corpse, I see in my mind's eye the one I discovered rotting in a footlocker the previous summer, which turned out to be the remains of my long-lost mother. A horror show never to be repeated, I had thought. Now it's happening again. What makes it even more shocking, apart from the fact that Delilah was famous, is that she was someone I met and liked her. She was so full of life. How can she be dead? Not just dead, murdered.

When my head stops spinning, I go back inside to dial 911. It will mean having to deal with Detective Spence Breedlove, my high school crush and present-day nemesis, but that can't be helped. After I've made the call, I sit down at the distressed pine table in the breakfast nook and wait for the cops to arrive. I recognize

Esmeralda's touch in the vase of pink 'Cécile Brünner' roses from the garden that stands at the center of the table, but it makes me think of flowers for a funeral. My eyes fill with tears. Poor Delilah. So young, so beautiful. She was America's sweetheart. *People* magazine's favorite cover girl. Who could have killed her? And why?

I spy her phone lying next to the vase. Unthinkingly, I pick it up and swipe the screen. An image appears of Delilah's Yorkie wearing a doggie tux and looking embarrassed. I scroll through the text messages, thinking they might hold a clue—evidence of a disgruntled employee, a jilted lover, a crazed stalker that would shed light on Delilah's murder. The most recent message is from the director Karol Bartosz saying he was on his way over. It was sent forty minutes ago, around the time I spotted the black Escalade on my way here. There's also a ridiculously long text exchange between Delilah and her personal assistant involving arrangements for a flower delivery.

When I hear the sound of a car engine in the driveway, I quickly find my Tumi messenger bag and pull out my iPad. By the time the first responders are at the door, I've downloaded the data from Delilah's device onto mine. Illegal? Possibly. Unethical for sure. But knowing Spence Breedlove, he'll try to pin the murder on me unless I come up with an alternate theory.

The first responders are soon joined by the ME, who is followed by the crime scene techs, a young man and an older woman wearing Tyvek jumpsuits and booties. They're still combing over the crime scene when Spence arrives. Wordlessly, he strides past me with only a glance in my direction before he steps out onto the patio. I watch him walk over to the section of patio strung with yellow crime scene tape where the techs are collecting forensic evidence and snapping photos. He's the only one in civvies, and I can't help but notice how nicely he fills out the fitted charcoal blazer and light-gray trousers he wears. He's not your stereotypical high school quarterback gone to seed. Instead, he looks like a former pro athlete who earns millions in product endorsements, the only bulge that isn't muscle the side-arm holstered underneath his blazer.

There goes the biggest mistake of my life.

Actually, the second biggest if you count my drinking, though the two are intertwined. It started with a high school crush—I worshipped him from afar throughout our freshman and sophomore years—and ended with my reputation going up in smoke along with his beloved Camaro. Long story short, I lost my virginity to Spence Breedlove in a drunken hookup at a party. I have little memory of the act itself, but the torment I suffered in the weeks that followed I recall vividly. The graffiti on the bathroom walls at school, the condoms stuffed in my locker, the nasty things said about me on MySpace, and the names I was called to my face. What hurt most was that Spence never apologized for taking advantage of me or for blabbing about it afterward. He treated me the same after we had sex as before: like I didn't exist. When I torched his car, I think it was to get him to notice me as much as to get back at him. He's had it in for me ever since.

He confers with the techs and issues orders to the uniforms who are milling around outside, then comes back inside. He pauses on the threshold, his eyes meeting mine in a moment of silent communication that seems to convey our entire history, before he crosses the sunlit kitchen to where I sit. His gaze drops to the glass of orange juice on the table in front of me that I'd been sipping earlier when I was feeling light-headed. "You always know where the best parties are."

"Can it, Spence. I'm not in the mood," I snap.

"Really. I'd have thought you'd be feeling no pain."

Heat crawls into my cheeks, since I know, as I pointedly sip my OJ, it would surely have held a slug of vodka back in the day. "I'm in AA. Not that it's any of your business."

"It is when you keep turning up at crime scenes."

"Are you suggesting I murdered Delilah Ward?"

"I don't know. Did you?"

I glare at him. "Screw you."

We lock eyes, and I see he's struggling to keep a lid on his temper. "Why don't you tell me what happened, then," he says in his formal cop's voice. He lowers his six-foot-four frame into the chair opposite me and pulls out his notebook. His face is a study in manly contours; his short hair resembles blond turf. He was always too good-looking for his own good. "Did you know the victim?"

"I was acquainted with her, yes. The house belongs to clients of mine. She's . . . she was renting it for the summer." I gulp as I remember to use the past tense, feeling my stomach start to roll again.

"I'll need their names."

I provide the contact info for the Blankenships, who live in Texas and rarely visit. After he's jotted down the information, he looks up to ask, "How long have you worked for them?"

"Over a year. I take care of rentals and any maintenance that needs to be done."

"What brings you here today?"

I hesitate before I realize the confidentiality agreement I signed no longer applies now that Delilah is dead. "Honestly? I was worried. Not about her," I'm quick to add at the probing look he gives me. "The place was a disaster zone when I stopped by the other day. Delilah explained that she'd had some people over and said it wouldn't happen again, but . . ." I shrug.

"Did she answer when you knocked?"

"No. She was dead by the time I got here. I let myself in with my key."

"Are you in the habit of snooping?"

A reference to my arrest for breaking and entering last summer. I bristle at the dig, feeling my cheeks warm. "I wasn't *snooping*. I was doing my job," I reply indignantly.

Spence nods and his eyes meet mine across the table. I'm glad he stopped wearing those tinted contact lenses that made him look as though he ought to be driving a Porsche with vanity plates—he claimed they were his wife's idea; she thought they made him look like Brad Pitt. He traded them for a pair of stylish wire-rim glasses, which show his natural eye color to be gray blue. "Was anyone else here when you arrived?" he asks in a less combative tone.

"No. Not that I know of, anyway. The killer might've slipped out back when he heard me come in. I noticed the gate was open." I look out the window. Outside, the techs are bagging the swimsuit-clad body of Delilah Ward. Reflections of clouds skim across the pool beyond. I hear the crackle of a two-way as a uniform speaks into his shoulder mike. Then I remember something else. "One other thing. . . . On my way here, I noticed a black Escalade leaving as I was coming in through the gates. Custom with tinted windows. It seems to be what everyone in Hollywood is driving these days, so I figured it was someone who'd been to see Delilah." I glance at my watch—it's noon, and I got here shortly before eleven. "That was about hour ago."

"You didn't happen to get a license plate number?"

"I didn't think of it at the time. Why would I? It wasn't until I got to the house and saw her . . ." I trail off, hugging myself to keep from shivering. I'm chilled to the bone, though it must be ninety degrees inside with the sun streaming through the French doors in the breakfast nook. "I didn't know she was dead at first. That's why I moved her. To see if . . . if she was still breathing."

"You contaminated the crime scene."

"I didn't mean to. I panicked, okay? I thought I could still save her. So sue me. Or arrest me. Whatever."

His stern expression softens. "I wasn't accusing you."

If that was an apology, I'm in no mood for it. "I'll remember for next time," I retort sarcastically.

He says no more on the subject. "When you were here before, did you notice anything unusual?"

"Other than evidence of recreational drug use, nothing criminal, no."

"She was doing drugs?" He looks up from his notebook.

"I couldn't say for a fact. Let's just say no sober person would permit drug use in her home."

"Wasn't she in rehab a while back?"

"Rehab isn't a magic bullet," I say, then wince, adding, "Pardon the expression."

"It worked for you."

"If by that you mean AA, that's no guarantee, either. Some of us have an easier time staying sober than others." I don't judge. How can I? As I sip my juice, part of me wishes it were vodka.

"If you think of anything else, let me know," he says, handing me his card as we're wrapping it up.

"You should talk to Delilah's assistant, Brianna. She'd know of any meetings that were on the calendar. Also the housekeeper. She was here earlier. She might have seen something."

Spence jots down their phone numbers. Finally, he slips his notebook back into his pocket and pushes himself to his feet. He says he'll call and arrange a time for me to give my formal statement at the station. I stand and sling my messenger bag over my shoulder, still feeling shaky. The techs have moved indoors and are combing the house for evidence. I almost bump into the woman as I'm crossing the kitchen on my way out. Then something else occurs to me. I pause and turn around. Spence is on his phone, issuing orders to whoever is at the other end.

"I've got Ellis and Hansen on the door-to-door. You get hold of Sullivan? I want him and McBride to cover the surrounding area. Beach, roadways, the bike path that runs along the cliff. Find out if anyone saw or heard anything." He notices me and holds up a finger, signaling *Be with you in a sec.*

The male tech moves past me, a ghost in his white jumpsuit. "There was a dog," I inform Spence when he hangs up.

"A dog," he repeats.

"Delilah's Yorkie. Black and tan. Rhinestone collar. He was here last time."

Spence raises an eyebrow as if waiting for me to explain why this is any concern of his.

"I'm worried he may have run off." I indicate once more the gate to the patio that stands open. "He might be lost."

Spence shrugs. "Call animal control."

"But shouldn't you—"

"Good luck finding him," he says curtly, turning his back to place another call.

CHAPTER SIX

I spend the next fifteen minutes scouring the neighborhood for Mini Me without success. After I've made the circuit of the cul-de-sac twice, I follow the footpath at the end, which leads to the private beach for the gated community. Whenever I'd had a listing in Casa Linda Estates, the beach was a major selling point. Tucked into a cove, it's sheltered from the winds that often whip the shoreline and inaccessible to the public—a steep wooden staircase provides the only access. There's no sign of the missing pooch when I scan the beach below. I descend the staircase and walk the length of the beach. None of the people I stop to speak with has seen a little dog running loose. The only dogs are a Labrador chasing a stick tossed by its owner and a golden retriever snoozing on a blanket. I hope, for my sake as well as his, that Mini Me has been taken in by one of the neighbors and not hit by a car. The last thing I need is another dead body on my watch.

I pass a pair of uniforms on their way down as I'm climbing the staircase, both wearing the intent looks of men on a mission. My thoughts return to Delilah. If she had died of natural causes, her death would seem tragically romantic—the grieving widow reunited with her husband in death. Instead, she'd come to a brutal end. The question is why. Was it an act of revenge? Or was greed the motivation? I recall the obsessed fan who used to show up at her events claiming to be her fiancé. It made headlines when he was sentenced to two years in prison for breaking into her Malibu home. He must be out by now. Did he take her life in the twisted belief that it would make her his? It's a nice theory. But it doesn't fit with what I'd seen: evidence of a cold-blooded execution, not a crime of passion.

I head back to my Explorer, figuring I'll have better luck searching for Mini Me on four wheels than on foot. As I'm nearing the house, I see neighbors gathered out front, others wandering over, their curiosity aroused by the police activity at Casa Blanca. I skirt the marked vehicles in the driveway to get to my SUV, which is parked at the curb. That's when I spot the Yorkie in the arms of a young woman who stands at the foot of the driveway, looking a little lost herself.

I walk up to her. "Brianna?" I only spoke to her over the phone, so I don't know what she looks like, but from the Bluetooth device in her ear and the fact that she's here, it's safe to assume this woman is Delilah's personal assistant.

She starts at the sound of my voice, as if I had crept up from behind and weren't standing right in front of her. "I came to drop this off," she says, extracting a manila envelope from the Coach bag slung over her shoulder. "Copies of the script changes. They told me . . ." Her voice trails off, her vacant expression giving way to a frightened look. "Did something happen to her?"

I take her gently by the elbow. "Why don't you come with me."

She stares at me uncomprehendingly. "Who are you?" She's in her mid to late twenties. Pretty in a girl-next-door sort of way with shoulder-length brown hair, hazel eyes, and lightly freckled cheeks. She wears a camel skirt paired with a tweed jacket over a pale-blue silk shell.

"Tish Ballard. We spoke on the phone." *Only about eight hundred times.*

"Oh. Right. The property manager."

I reach over to pet Mini Me. "Where did you find him?"

"He was wandering in the street. Thank God I spotted him. He could have been—" She swallows the rest of the sentence, the color draining from her face. I wonder how much the cops told her.

"I know. I was looking for him. I'm glad he's okay." I haven't relinquished my grip on her arm, and now I give it a gentle tug. "Come. You look like you could use some coffee. I know I could."

"She's dead, isn't she?" she says when we're en route to the nearest coffee shop, in the upscale shopping center that lies at the heart of the nearby village of La Mar. Her voice is eerily calm.

I grimace in sympathy. "I'm sorry."

"How did it happen?"

"They didn't tell you?"

She shakes her head, absently stroking Mini Me, who's curled asleep on her lap. "When I came to the door, they told me to wait outside, that someone would be with me in a minute."

"That would be Detective Breedlove. He's in charge of homicide."

Her eyes widen and her face grows even paler. "So it was . . . ?"

"I'm afraid so. She was shot in the head."

"Oh, God." Brianna makes a moaning sound, then lapses once more into a trancelike state. I try not to think about the fact that I more or less absconded with a person wanted for questioning in a murder investigation. Spence will have a fit. He won't see it as a compassionate gesture.

When we arrive at the shopping center, which is built in the style of a Tuscan village with lots of stucco and terra-cotta and a fountain splashing in the courtyard, it's bustling with shoppers as it always is at this time of day. I park in front of Java Junction and leave Brianna to go inside. I return a short while later with two coffees and hand her one. "I got you a large. Milk and sugar."

"I take mine black," she informs me in a dull voice.

"Think of it as medicinal."

She smiles wanly and sets her coffee in the cup holder next to her seat.

I glance down at the dog. "He seems none the worse."

"Prince is a trouper." She strokes his gold-brown fur, gazing down at him with affection.

"Prince, huh?" I prefer the name Mini Me; it suits him better. "I thought that was only for big dogs."

"It's short for Prince Harry."

"Cute."

"Not *hairy* with an *I*," she says, correcting my misassumption that the name was a play on words. "He was named after His Royal Highness. He and Delilah met at the London premiere of her last picture."

"He must've made quite an impression."

"Actually, it was the other way around. He was so taken with Delilah he invited her and the others to spend the weekend with him at his country house. When it was over, he gave her the dog so she'd have something to remember him by. Prince comes from a long line of show dogs."

"An affair to remember," I comment.

She gives me a sharp look. "It's not what you think. Delilah was in mourning. It was right after Eric died."

I don't buy her explanation. The thought crosses my mind that His Royal Highness might have arranged to have Delilah bumped off. Maybe she'd had some dirt on him stemming from their fling and was threatening to go public. Though come to think of it, there isn't much about the royal bad boy that isn't already well documented.

"Did she have any enemies? Anyone who'd threatened her?" I get back to the subject at hand: the fact that her employer has been murdered. "You know, like an obsessed fan."

"She had lots of those. Most were harmless."

"What about that guy who went to prison? Isn't he out?"

"Yes, but he's in a wheelchair."

"What? When did that happen?" In the news photos of him at his trial, he'd been able-bodied.

"He was attacked by a fellow prisoner while he was serving his sentence. It left him paralyzed from the waist down. Delilah has fans in prison, too," she explains, smiling bleakly.

"What about a jilted boyfriend? Or a jealous ex?"

"I don't think I should be talking to you about this." She darts me an uneasy look.

We're interrupted by the chirping of her phone's ringtone— Beyoncé's "Single Ladies (Put a Ring on It)." Brianna answers, activating the Bluetooth device in her ear. "Hello? Uh-huh. Certainly, Detective. Of course, anything I can do to help. I'll be right over. Are you still at the house or should I meet you at the station?" Gone is the shell-shocked woman of a minute ago. In her place is the buttoned-down personal assistant I recall from our business dealings.

The transformation is so sudden it has me wondering if she was putting on an act before. It occurs to me she's a likely suspect. Maybe she secretly hated her boss and had been pushed over the edge of sanity by her diva ways. Delilah's drinking would have made it that much worse. Though I can't think why Brianna wouldn't have just quit her job if it had become intolerable.

"Do me a favor. When you see him, don't mention you were with me," I say when she gets off the phone with Spence.

"Why not?" she asks, eyeing me curiously.

"I'm in enough trouble as it is."

"Are you a suspect?" She says this as if it's a perfectly normal question.

"Me? No, of course not," I answer, too hastily. "You see, me and Spence—Detective Breedlove, that is—we go way back." I sigh and sit back, prying the lid from my coffee. "It's complicated."

Brianna nods in understanding. "I get it. I grew up in a small town myself. Woodstock, Vermont, where the summer tourists outnumber the year-round population. Everybody knows everybody else's business, and you can't turn a corner without running into an old boyfriend."

"He wasn't my . . . never mind." I sip my coffee. "What brought you to L.A.?"

"I moved there when I got the job working for Delilah. My dream job," she says with irony. I wonder again what, if anything, she's not telling me and the dark horror of what I saw earlier falls over me like a shadow while outside, the sun is shining and suburbanites in expensive threads stroll by carrying glossy shopping bags. "To answer your question, no, she didn't have any enemies. None that I'm aware of, anyway. She wasn't a saint by any means, but she wasn't a bad person. Not . . . not bad enough for someone to want to kill her," she adds in a shaky voice.

"Usually people are murdered for one of two reasons: love or money."

"We can rule out money." Brianna explains that Delilah had bequeathed everything she owned to the charitable organization Full Bucket, which she had established in the memory of her late husband, Eric Nyland. The mission of which, I know from having looked it up online, is to provide impoverished villages in third-world countries with a source of clean water.

"Insurance payout?"

"She was only insured for the movie. Standard practice," she explains. "So the studio is covered in case one of the leads gets killed or injured in the middle of filming. It happens. A few years ago, a stunt went wrong on the set of a movie my uncle was directing, and one of the actors was killed."

"Your uncle is a director?"

She nods. "That's how I ended up working for Delilah. They're good friends. *Were*," she corrects herself, her face resuming its somber cast. "He was so excited to be making a picture with her."

"Don't tell me you're related to—"

"Karol Bartosz." She finishes the sentence for me. The famous director, a contemporary and compatriot of Roman Polanski, is best known for his outsize personality. He must go to all the A-list parties, because it seems there's a photo of him, looking impresario-like with his flourish of snow-white hair and the cravats he seems to favor, on the Caught in the Act page in every issue of *People*. At the Oscars each year, he shows up with a different blonde, and they all look like they're half his age, twice his height, with boobs that could act as flotation devices.

"You came by it honestly at least," I comment.

She gives a short laugh. "So much for my Princeton degree. I majored in English lit, which doesn't exactly make me a hot commodity on the job market. When Uncle Karol told me Delilah was looking for a personal assistant, I was on a plane to L.A. the next day. I had a student loan to pay off, and I was getting desperate. When I met with Delilah, she seemed nice and the salary was generous. I didn't bother to find out why her last assistant quit," she adds on a dry note.

"How long were you with her?"

"Two years, but it seems longer." Her face goes blank again, and she stares out the window. She doesn't seem to notice that she's tightened her grasp on Prince, enough to have him squirming on her lap.

"Brianna. Let go. You're hurting him."

She snaps out of her trance and releases the dog with a cry of dismay. "Oh! I didn't mean—" Prince leaps from her lap onto mine, narrowly missing the coffee she placed in the cup holder and bumping the one in my hand, causing me to spill some of it down the front of my brother's red Stanford hoodie. The excited Yorkie plants his paws on my chest and starts to lick my face. Brianna bursts into tears. "I-I spoke to her not more than an hour ago. S-she was in a good mood. Excited about the movie. She thought this could be the one. You know, that it might get her an Oscar nomination. And now she's . . . Oh, God. I never thought it would happen like this."

"As opposed to drunk driving or a drug overdose, you mean?" Brianna gives a small, sorrowful nod. I hand her a napkin to wipe her eyes with, and I use another one to dab at the coffee stain on Arthur's sweatshirt, turning my head to keep from being French kissed by Prince as he licks my face. "Yeah, I know a little something about that." Brianna gives me a questioning look, at which I add, "Four years clean. I was luckier than most. I got sober and stayed sober."

"I wish . . ." She trails off, biting her lip.

I pry the lid from her coffee and hand it to her with a wry smile. "Bottoms up."

"I should get back," she says when we've finished our coffees. "I don't want to keep the detective waiting."

I start the engine. Ten minutes later, we pull up in front of Casa Blanca in my Explorer. She climbs out and starts toward the house. "Hold on. Aren't you forgetting something?" I call after her.

"What?" She turns to look at me.

I gesture toward Prince, standing on his back legs in the backseat, peering out the window.

"Oh, no. I couldn't possibly," she says and starts to back away. As if I'd asked a favor of her. Any sympathy I had toward her fades and I remember why I'd found her so irritating to begin with. She seems to have forgotten that her boss is dead and that I'm no longer at her disposal.

"What the hell am I supposed to do with him, then?" I reply irritably.

"Um, could you take him?" She has the decency, at least, to look sheepish. "I'm staying at a bed-and-breakfast, and they don't allow pets. Besides, I have a million things to do. Calls to make. Greta will need my help with the funeral arrangements. And my uncle! He'll be beside himself. It's only temporary. I'll make other arrangements." With that, she goes flying up the driveway, Bluetooth device glowing in her ear, calling over her shoulder, "Thanks! I'll be in touch!"

CHAPTER SEVEN

'm still feeling shaky, and it seems I have a dog to look after, so I decide to take the rest of the day off. I stop at the pet store in Harborview Plaza and buy dog food and a leash on my way home. I'm barely in the door before Hercules appears out of nowhere, morphing from tame pussycat into a flesh-eating zombie. With his back arched and fangs bared, hissing, he advances on the Yorkie. I bend to scoop up Prince, who's cowering at my feet, and scold my cat, "Is that any way to treat our guest? Honestly, where are your manners?" Hercules lets out another hiss.

It's been a long day, and it's not over yet.

The plan was to let my furry friends get acquainted, but Hercules has made it clear that's not going to happen anytime soon. I deposit Prince in the guest room that doubles as my office. "Trust me, it's for your own good," I tell him when he starts to whine. I head for the kitchen and pour myself a glass of milk. I'm stirring in a generous slug of Hershey's syrup—chocolate milk is my drug of choice these days—when the phone rings.

"Ballard." A gruff voice greets me at the other end. "What the fuck."

Tom McGee. My erstwhile sidekick and self-appointed bodyguard.

"I see you've been listening in on your police scanner." A former NYPD detective, he likes to stay abreast of police activity in

Cypress Bay. There's no such thing as retired law enforcement, I've learned from him, only police officers who are no longer on active duty. His current job is as manager in residence of a self-storage facility, but he still keeps a finger on the pulse.

"Imagine my surprise when I found out you were involved in another homicide." One of his sources at the station must have given him the fill. The brotherhood of the men in blue knows no jurisdiction. That's another thing I've learned from McGee. "Seems wherever you go, a dead body is sure to follow."

"You make it sound as if I'm cursed. It's just bad luck is all."

"Tell that to the press. Jesus, a movie star no less. Only you, Ballard." I picture him shaking his ponytailed head.

"Are you suggesting I had something to do with Delilah Ward's murder?"

"Wouldn't dream of it. Or I might be the next corpse to turn up on your watch." He speaks with a Bronx accent, which is as thick as mustard on a hot dog at Yankee Stadium when he's being a wiseass.

McGee and I were thrown together by a curious set of circumstances. We met the day I discovered my mother's remains at the self-storage facility he manages. When I learned he was a retired NYPD homicide detective, I enlisted his help in cracking the case, which had the local authorities seemingly stumped. He's stuck to me like glue ever since. I'm grateful to him because he saved my life at one point during the course of our investigation, but mostly he rubs me the wrong way. He's also frequently intoxicated, although he doesn't appear to be at the moment.

"Don't tempt me," I growl.

He chuckles. "You have a soft spot for me. Admit it, Ballard."

"Right. Because you're so lovable." Like my cat.

"Detective Hard-on take you in for questioning?" he asks. I cringe at his crude nickname for Spence Breedlove. McGee seems to think Spence has a thing for me. Either that, or he finds it amusing that we hate each other's guts. Fortunately, he knows nothing of my history with Spence.

"I'm not a suspect. I'm just the person who found the body, purely by coincidence I might add."

"Cops don't believe in coincidences. Once is a coincidence, twice is a pattern."

"So what does that make me?"

"A person of interest."

"Thanks," I reply, taking a swig of my chocolate milk. "I knew I could count on you to reassure me."

"You want someone to hold your hand, you got the wrong number."

"You called me," I remind him.

"To warn you. The cops'll have the press crawling up their asses, and until they name a suspect, you've got a bull's-eye on your back. You were first on the scene, you own a gun, and it ain't your first rodeo."

"Circumstantial. There's no evidence against me, and ballistics will show the bullet wasn't fired from my gun." Even as I say this, I remain fearful. How far would Spence go to get back at me for destroying his most prized possession? There's no statute of limitations when it comes to guys and their cars.

McGee echoes my fears by reminding me, "They don't need a warrant to bring you in for questioning. They can make your life extremely unpleasant. But luckily you have me, so I wouldn't worry too much."

"Worry?" I cry. "Now I'm totally freaking out." McGee may be a former detective, but he's also a loose cannon. Make that an alcoholic loose cannon. I need him like a hole in the head.

This conjures an image of the actual hole in Delilah's head, and I feel the chocolate milk I just drank curdle in my stomach.

"Relax, Ballard, I got this." McGee's voice sounds far away. "Just give me the facts."

I take him through it, and he asks all the right questions. Was there any sign of a forced entry? Any evidence of a person or persons other than the victim having been at the house prior to my arrival on the scene? Did there appear to have been a struggle? I answer no to all of the above. "This may sound weird, but she looked . . . peaceful," I say in response to the last question. "Which suggests the killer was either someone she knew and trusted, or she didn't see him coming."

"What makes you think it was a he?"

"She was shot execution style. That's not something I see a woman doing."

"A good cop never jumps to conclusions. You follow procedure—collect evidence, interview witnesses, do your door-to-door—then if the gods are smiling, the pieces of the puzzle start to come together. *Blue Bloods* it ain't. If you watched investigative work in real time, it'd put you to sleep."

"Yet curiously you seem to miss the action," I observe.

McGee has never told me the reason for his early retirement from the NYPD—though I imagine his drinking played a part—and he doesn't satisfy my curiosity on this occasion. He only grunts in response.

"Will I see you on Thursday?" I ask before we hang up. I go to the AA meeting held on Thursday evenings at St. Anthony's, the Catholic church where I used to attend Mass as a child. I never miss a meeting if I can help it. McGee's attendance is sporadic, usually determined by how much he's had to drink.

"Do I look like I need saving?" His standard response.

"Do I need to answer that?"

"Anyone needs saving, it's you, Ballard," he says with a rasp, and I know he isn't referring to AA.

"Seriously, how worried should I be?" I ask nervously.

"Trust no one." His words echo in my ears after the line goes dead.

I'd phoned Ivy on my way home with the news of the murder, and she's at my door within minutes of my hanging up on McGee. She throws her arms around me. "You poor thing. What a nightmare!" Later, when I pull out my iPad to show her what I downloaded from Delilah's phone, her eyes light up even as she cries, "Are you insane, woman? You are so dead if Spence finds out."

"What he doesn't know won't hurt him."

We scroll through Delilah's photos as we sit side by side on the green Morris sofa in my living room. "I wouldn't kick him out of bed," Ivy comments as we study an image of Delilah's late husband, Eric Nyland, posing next to his twin-engine Cessna. The plane he went down in, I realize.

"Fine talk for a woman who's practically engaged." I give her a mock scolding look, at which she grimaces, before I go back to studying the image of Eric Nyland. He was the quintessential man's man, at once ruggedly handsome and sensuous with bedroom eyes and a mouth that seemed designed for kissing . . . and not just on the lips. In another age, he'd be a dashing World War I aviator or a Great White Hunter. His lean, muscular physique looked to have been shaped by athletic feats, not pumping iron. Dark hair and almond eyes hint at a mixed-race heritage.

Hell, I wouldn't have kicked him out of bed either.

There are other photos of Eric: at the beach, carrying a surfboard under his arm; in the swimming pool at their house in Malibu; bare chested, holding a chainsaw and standing next to a sawed-off tree limb bigger around than he was. In the photos of him and Delilah together, they appear very much in love. I linger over a candid shot of them lounging aboard a yacht, wearing swimsuits, their faces flushed and their hair tousled as though they'd just surfaced from a tumble belowdecks. The look they're exchanging is so steamy, I can almost feel the heat.

Now they're both dead.

"It doesn't seem possible," Ivy says, echoing my thoughts. "One

minute you're welcoming her to Cypress Bay, the next she's floating facedown in the pool."

"She wasn't in the pool. She was lying next to it," I remind her.

"Right. I was thinking *Sunset Boulevard*."

I shake my head slowly. "I can't believe she's gone. She was
so . . . She just glowed, you know. She was sweet, too, for all my
bitching about her diva ways. Who could have wanted her dead?"

"A rival actress who was jealous? Someone like the evil stepmother in *Snow White*. 'Mirror, mirror on the wall, who's the fair-
est of them all,'" Ivy intones in a spooky voice.

"Evil is the word for it. You'd have to be a monster to shoot a
defenseless person in the head while she was asleep." I shudder at
the imagery.

"I wonder how long she'd been lying there before . . . you
know." Ivy's face is somber beneath her curls, which are gathered
in a loose knot atop her head. She wears holey jeans and a T-shirt
that says "Praise the Lard" with a picture of a pig on the front.

"The clothes dryer was still running, so it was between the time
Esmeralda left and when I got there. Half an hour maybe? Enough
time for the killer to slip in and out."

"Just think, if you'd shown up sooner . . ."

"Let's not go there." I start to tremble, and Ivy puts her arm
around me until I stop shaking.

We go through Delilah's text messages. Most are exchanges
between Delilah and her "people": her agent, Sarah Fineman,
regarding various projects that Delilah was either considering or
that Sarah thought would be perfect for her; her manager, Chuck
Newcomb, about a personal appearance she'd been booked to do
in Denver; her publicist, Lisa Devour, about the wording of a
press packet bio. There's also a text exchange between Delilah
and a woman named Greta Nyland, who had to be related to
Delilah's late husband, regarding a charity event she and Delilah
were organizing, and between Delilah and her personal assistant,

Brianna, confirming this or that appointment—with the stylist, manicurist, massage therapist, personal trainer, dog groomer, you name it. One text from Brianna reads, *Your usual suite at Hotel du Cap for Cannes?*

I consider the message from director Karol Bartosz saying he was en route. He could have gone to the house, shot Delilah, and been making his getaway, assuming it was him in the black Escalade I spotted.

There's a text from Brent Harding, the former TV actor with whom she made one picture, a thriller set in London, and was slated to do *Devil's Slide*. It was sent the day before yesterday. *When can I see u? We need to talk,* he texted. *Talk about what?* I wonder. Had his and Delilah's relationship been more than professional?

"It could have been any one of them. . . . Or none of them." Ivy echoes my thoughts.

"We won't know until the cops make an arrest. Unless it's me they arrest."

Ivy's eyes widen. "You're not serious!"

"McGee seems to think I'm a person of interest. And I wouldn't put anything past Spence Breedlove."

"You really think he still has it in for you?"

"Apparently, not all of us have moved on." I recall his hostility toward me at the crime scene. "Which is why I'm covering my ass. I need an alternate theory in case he tries to pin the murder on me."

Ivy motions toward my iPad. "I don't see anything here that looks suspicious. Not counting creepy pet photos." She refers to the image of Prince in a doggie tux.

"Her assistant must know where all the bodies are buried. So to speak," I'm quick to add. "We can enlist her."

"We?" Ivy brightens. "So we're really doing this?" Typical of her, she's excited about the prospect, apparently not having had her fill of murder and mayhem—which included at least one brush the law, a close call at the wrong end of a shotgun, and my near death at the hands of a psycho—when we were investigating my mother's case. "But why would she want to help us?"

Just then, I hear a scratching noise from the hallway and the muffled sound of Prince whining. My cat is pacing back and forth outside the closed door to my office, tail twitching. Ivy gives me a questioning look, and I sigh as I get up to lock Hercules in my bedroom so I can let Prince out.

"Brianna owes me."

CHAPTER EIGHT

"God grant me the serenity to accept the things I cannot change, the courage to change the things I can, and the wisdom to know the difference." I recite the Serenity Prayer along with the others in attendance at the AA meeting on Thursday evening of the following week. The basement social hall at St. Anthony's, with its chipped paint and scuffed linoleum, fluorescent lighting and metal folding chairs, is hardly conducive to serenity, but I'm surrounded by my brethren, and there's strength and hope in that.

After the reciting of the prayer, there are various announcements and the distributing of chips—for thirty days, ninety days, ten years—the latter being a ceremony that takes place monthly, and which I always look forward to, even when it's not my turn to receive a chip. I look around me and see mostly familiar faces. People who have come to seem like family . . . if family is the disparate, quarrelsome bunch seated around the table at Thanksgiving that makes you wonder how you could possibly be related to them. There's the woman called Mustang Sally, who was in and out of homeless shelters and state-run drug rehab clinics before she got sober; Junior R., a former gang member, with his shaved head and Latin Kings tat; Sue Ann G., a blond-bobbed soccer mom, looking sporty in Lululemon yoga pants; Matt L., who did time at San Quentin, where he found Jesus . . . I watch the speaker for tonight's meeting, Jim O., shuffle to the podium. Jim had thirty years of sobriety before he got hooked on painkillers while recovering from hip surgery. If he can go out, it can happen to any of us. That's why we're here. To be reminded.

McGee and I head for the refreshment table after the meeting. He had decided to grace us with his presence after all. Better yet, he doesn't smell of alcohol. He's his usual charming self, however. "You look like shit, Ballard," he observes as I pour myself a cup of coffee.

"You would too if you hadn't slept in a week." Between the nightmare images that keep me awake at night and the press calling at all hours, I haven't had more than four hours of continuous sleep in the eight days since I discovered Delilah Ward's dead body. I stir a spoonful of sugar into my coffee and help myself to a chocolate-chip cookie, homemade, naturally—Sue Ann was in charge of refreshments for this week's meeting. "Last night, I was woken at three a.m. by a reporter calling from L.A. I don't remember what I said to him, but I'm pretty sure it wasn't fit for print."

He flashes me a snaggletooth grin. "Next time, try shutting off your phone."

"What if it was one of my renters calling to say the house was on fire?"

"That's what the fire department is for." In his Levis and desert-camo jacket with his brown hair scraped back in a ponytail that looks like something fished from a drain, McGee would appear to be just another lost soul at an AA meeting if not for his eyes. *Cop's eyes*, I think as I watch them survey the room, lighting briefly on a group of people chatting animatedly over by the bookcase that holds the prayer books for Sunday services (nothing like talk of a celebrity death to liven up a meeting). "Your detective friend making any progress?" He helps himself to coffee and a cookie.

"With me or the case?" I quip.

McGee studies me as he noisily slurps his coffee. "You don't look like you're getting any."

I sigh. "You're right about that, sadly." Not only have I not had sex in a while, Bradley and I haven't Skyped in over a week, not since I told him about my gruesome discovery. He's currently incommunicado while the infantry unit with which he's embedded is on the move.

I step aside to make way for Brenda T., a middle-aged woman with cropped gray hair. She's a professor at the university who teaches a women's studies course, and she's what's known in AA as a "high bottom," meaning she got sober before she hit rock bottom—in her case, after she'd had too much to drink at a faculty party. As opposed to "low bottom," which would be me.

"As for the case . . ." I move out of eavesdropping range. "Spence won't tell me squat. All he does is ask questions. He keeps having me go over and over it, like he thinks I'm lying or something."

"I know a good lawyer if you need one."

I narrow my eyes at him. "Don't even."

His expression turns serious. He takes a bite out of his cookie and chews thoughtfully. "He's gotta be getting pressure from the top. In a high-profile case, each day that goes by without an arrest the DA sees his career go up in smoke. Which means putting the screws to the chief investigator."

"Then Spence is getting it from both ends. He said the movie people were impossible." It's the one bit of information I gleaned from him. "For everyone he questions, he has to wade through six layers of *their* people." I have some sympathy, from my dealings with Brianna. "What, do they think they exist on some exalted plane and can't breathe the same air as us regular folk?"

"I wouldn't know, but he seems to be breathing just fine." McGee points toward a tall man conversing with a group of people across the room. He looks to be around my age, midthirties, and is wearing wraparound shades and a Giants ball cap, pulled low over his forehead, a common disguise at AA meetings, worn by those seeking to hide the fact that they're hungover. As if that ever fooled anyone. Before I can ask McGee what he means, I gasp in recognition.

"Oh, my God, is that—?"

"Laserman. In the flesh."

I thought the guy looked familiar when I noticed him slipping in the door shortly after the meeting started. Now I know why. He's Liam Brady. Star of the mega blockbuster *Laserman*, about a middle-school science teacher who develops superpowers, in the form of laser beams with the strength of military-grade weaponry, as a result of an accident involving a linear accelerator. It made Liam a household name and spawned two sequels. The picture he's currently making is *Devil's Slide*, which is why he's here in town. "I didn't know he was one of us," I remark.

McGee gives me a look that seems to say *Speak for yourself.*

"It's a miracle he's managed to keep it under wraps," I continue. These days, it seems a celebrity only has to stumble walking out of a nightclub in order for rumors that he or she was under the influence to go viral.

I watch Liam Brady back away from his groupies—there's no other word to describe the women who are pressed in around him, their faces aglow—and slip through the doorway to the floor above. On impulse, I follow him. As I step from the passageway at the top of the stairs, the familiar scents of the sanctuary, a mixture of beeswax candles and incense and furniture polish, bring back memories of when I used to come here on Sundays with my family. The sanctuary is dimly lit, except the spot where the exterior lights shining through the stained-glass windows illuminate the lone figure seated in a front-row pew. Liam took off his cap, I notice, but he still wears his sunglasses.

"Not now. Sorry, love," he says wearily when I slide in next to him, without so much as a glance in my direction. He speaks with an Irish brogue, not the midwestern accent he uses when playing Laserman, a.k.a. Danny Miller from Fort Wayne, Indiana. Liam is from Dublin. On a late-night talk show, I once heard him talk about the rough neighborhood he grew up in. "*Angela's Ashes* it was." Delivered in a light tone and not elaborated on, the remark explained the rough edges that are part of his appeal. He's the Bradley Cooper of the working class.

"I don't mean to bother you. I just wanted . . ."

"What? My feckin' autograph? A quote for your bloody rag?" He turns to face me, pulling off his sunglasses. His cobalt eyes flash with an intensity that causes me to pull back like I've been burned. "Or have you come to share your tale of woe? If you have, I can't help you."

"I just wanted to say I'm sorry for your loss." He and Delilah had been friends, I learned when he made a public statement after her death—his words sounded heartfelt, unlike those of other celebrities who seemed to be using the tragedy to showcase their latest projects—and were possibly romantically linked as well. Their chemistry onscreen was undeniable. Liam and Delilah had made a movie together, *Return of Laserman*, in which she played his female sidekick-slash-love interest, Phantasmagora, and they were to have shared top billing in *Devil's Slide*.

"Why? Did you know her?" he asks in a mocking tone.

"I'm the one who found her."

"Jesus." He stares at me as if seeing me for the first time. His Black Irish features, curly, dark brown hair and blue eyes in a face saved from bland handsomeness by a hawk nose and cheeks faintly pitted with old acne scars, are prominent. "For the love of . . . Why didn't you say so?"

"You didn't give me a chance. Tish Ballard." I extend my hand.

His face relaxes in a smile as he shakes my hand. "Pleased to make your acquaintance, Tish Ballard."

"How long have you been in the program?" The standard question for newcomers.

"Coming up on six months. Two and a half years before that," he answers.

I nod in understanding. Relapse is more common among AAers than not. We all struggle, and many of us fail. "Either it was the best kept secret in Hollywood, or you liked to drink alone."

He chuckles as though I've said something amusing. The force of his magnetism—akin to the superpowers possessed by Laserman—is such that I have to concentrate in order to keep from becoming a simpering groupie like the ladies who cornered him earlier. "With me it was drinks all around, and I was always the last to leave a party. What saved me from public disgrace was that I was too big to fail. Too much money riding on my sorry arse. Whenever one of my drunken antics was leaked to the press, the suits did what they do best: They paid to have it buried."

"I'm guessing you don't have a lot of enemies either." I'd heard of stars having their careers ruined through a combination of their own misbehavior and their being universally loathed by their peers.

He shrugs. "We'd murder our own mother in her bed for a percentage of the gross, but we look out for our own. Glass houses and all." I must appear taken aback by his casual mention of murder, because he says, in a mild voice, "I didn't kill Delilah if that's what you're wondering."

"I wasn't." Liam doesn't seem the homicidal type, although I've been fooled in the past.

"We were in rehab together. We'd known each other for years before that, but I didn't get to really know her until then. That's when you get the true measure of another, is it not? When you stand naked and shivering, stripped of all your lies and excuses." I smile at his theatrics, and also in understanding: The first time I shared at an AA meeting, I felt as if I'd been stripped, not just of my clothes, but of my skin. "We used to stay up nights talking. We'd both known the mean streets growing up, so we had that in common, too. After rehab, we went to meetings together. For a while."

"Until she stopped going." He confirms my guess with a nod, wearing a sorrowful expression.

"We argued about it. She told me to fuck off. I told her she was a feckin' idiot, that she was throwing her life away, and I wasn't going to stick around to watch. Fateful words as it turned out."

"She didn't die of the disease," I remind him.

"True." He turns his gaze to the teak crucifix that hangs over the altar. "May the bastard burn in hell. The killer," he clarifies when I look startled. We sit in silence for a minute, then he collects himself with an audible exhalation and stands. "Well, it was nice chatting with you, Tish Ballard."

I stand to shake his hand. "Likewise." On impulse, I ask, "Listen, do you want to grab a bite to eat?" Lest he mistake my intention, I add with a wry smile, "I promise no selfies." It's not bragging rights I'm after but to learn more about Delilah. Maybe he knows of someone who had a motive for murdering her. With Liam, a fellow drunk in recovery, I have an in that Spence doesn't.

"Alas, I have to be on set first thing in the morning, so it's early to bed for me." He places his hand over his heart, theatrically, though he seems genuinely regretful. In the old days, we'd have made good drinking buddies.

I look at him in surprise. "Oh. I thought . . . So soon?"

"What did you expect? Black armbands? Flags flown at half mast?"

"No. A hiatus maybe."

Liam gives a hollow laugh. "Any crying that's done won't be on the studio's dime. We make all the right noises, sure, but even Karol, who claims to have loved Delilah like a daughter, won't let sentiment get in the way of financial considerations."

"It seems so . . . cold."

"Make no mistake. We're all alike and a bad lot at that. We differ only in our ability to disguise it." He dons his cap and slips on his sunglasses, and with that he takes his leave. I watch him make his way down the aisle before he disappears into the shadows at the back of the church.

CHAPTER NINE

I phone Arthur on the way home and the call goes straight to voicemail. What's up with that? He always answers when he sees my name on his caller ID because he knows I'll hit redial as many times as it takes until he does. Or at least he did until recently. Lately, he's been ducking my calls. And whenever I ask about his plans for the evening, he's either evasive or downright untruthful. Twice this week I stopped by his place to find no one home on a night when he'd claimed he was staying in. I wonder if he's out tonight with his new lady friend, Gladys Sedgwick.

The thought of my brother burning up the sheets with a woman who's old enough to give new meaning to *Fifty Shades of Grey* is enough to give me heartburn. It seems ludicrous, but then Arthur isn't your typical thirty-four-year-old guy. We're talking about someone who once gave himself up to a cop on the street for an unspecified crime he didn't recall having committed. I need to find out what, exactly, is going on between him and Gladys—and if it means he's headed for another crackup—before a situation that's manageable becomes *Houston, we have a problem.* . . .

I stop at my brother's place to see if he's home. Arthur lives in one of those open-air sixties-era apartment complexes that are popular nowadays only as the settings for drunken swan dives into the swimming pool from upper floors on TV dramas. His building is composed of four terraced floors that overlook a pool and patio. It's badly in need of an upgrade, and I wouldn't swim in the pool if you paid me, but the tenants don't seem to care, and rents are cheap. I climb the concrete steps to the second level and knock on the door to Arthur's apartment. No answer. I'm inserting my key into the lock when a voice cuts through the muttering of TV sets and other night-time noises from behind closed doors, startling me.

"Hold it right there, young fella!"

I look up to see a skinny, bald man in a plaid robe standing in the doorway to the apartment one down from Arthur's, brandishing a phone in one hand and a lit cigarette in the other. "Evening, Mr. Fossum," I greet him. He squints at me through the gloom of the poorly lit walkway.

"Tish?" He steps outside, peering as he draws closer as if to make sure it really is me. "I thought you was one of them ghetto boys looking to rob the place in that getup." He gestures toward the dark-gray, hooded sweatshirt I have on, its hood pulled up against the chill of the evening.

"Sorry, I didn't mean to scare you." Mr. Fossum is a bigoted old goat, but he's been a good neighbor to Arthur. "I'm looking for my brother. Have you seen him by any chance?"

"He stopped by earlier. Said he was going out of town and asked me to look after his hamster while he was away."

The news that Arthur has left town delivers a jolt, and my heart starts to race. I take a deep breath to calm my anxiety. "Did he say where he was going or when he'd be back?"

"Nope, and I didn't ask." His expression shifts to one of concern. "Say, he's not in any kind of trouble, is he?"

"No, nothing like that. It's just . . . I worry, you know?" The old man nods in understanding and takes another drag off his cigarette, his plaid robe fluttering around his white stick legs in the breeze. He always phones to let me know whenever my brother is behaving strangely, which makes us allies of sorts. "Do me a favor. Let me know if you hear from him." Arthur might call to check up on Mr. Chips, though I consider it unlikely. Who worries about a hamster?

"Will do." The old man is turning to go back inside when something occurs to me.

"You wouldn't happen to know if he was traveling alone?"

"Couldn't say, but that redheaded gal was with him. I seen her waiting down by the pool."

"Mrs. Sedgwick?" I squeak in alarm.

"Don't know her name, we weren't introduced. But she's been by before. A real looker, that one." Mr. Fossum smacks his lips appreciatively as my panic mounts. Oh, God. This is worse than I'd feared. Where could they have gone? Best-case scenario they went on a sightseeing trip or a weekend retreat. Worst-case, they're headed for Vegas, and not to play the slots.

I let myself into Arthur's apartment, hoping I'll find some clue about where he and Gladys went. It's a one-bedroom unit, and the furnishings consist of a futon sofa and seventies-era coffee table, a recliner that sits opposite the forty-six-inch flat-screen TV, and a particleboard computer desk. It looks as it always does, except the suitcase that's normally in the hall closet is gone, as is the toothbrush from the medicine cabinet. There are no travel brochures lying around, and when I check the search history on the computer, I don't see any links to travel-related sites.

I try my brother's number one more time, and the call goes straight to voicemail. I leave another message, this one more pointed than the last. "Arthur. Where the hell are you? Call me, dammit."

Next, I dial the home number for Shondra Perkins, the director at the senior center. She picks up after three rings. "Arthur asked for some time off. He didn't mention anything about a trip," she says after I've explained why I'm calling. "But I can give you Mrs. Sedgwick's number. I also have a number for her son. He might know something." She puts me on hold for a minute.

After she's given me the numbers, I broach a more delicate topic. "You mentioned she and Arthur had become close. Did you get the impression they were . . . you know."

"Romantically involved?" Shondra doesn't sound shocked. In her years of dealing with senior issues, I'm sure she's seen it all. "No, the thought never crossed my mind. But I don't see the harm. It would be . . . unusual, yes, but Mrs. Sedgwick is young for her age, and they're both adults."

"As long as Arthur remembers to take his meds," I mutter.

"Good luck," she says. "Let me know when they turn up."

I dial Gladys's number and leave a message asking her to call me back, then try her son. The voicemail message on his cell provides me with his home number. "Sedgwick residence. Howard speaking," answers a deep male voice when I finally reach him. He sounds like the butler in *Downton Abbey*. I explain why I'm calling, but from the way he acts, you'd think I dialed the wrong number. "I don't know anyone named Arthur. You say he's a friend of Mother's?"

"He gives computer lessons at the senior center. That's how they met."

"I know about the computer course. She even bought herself a laptop of all things. My mother!" He says this as though she were a ninety-year-old who was missing some marbles and not a spry septuagenarian. "But she never mentioned anything about a new friend. You say she and your brother went away together? I'm sorry, Miss Ballard, but that's absurd. Mother wouldn't go on a trip without letting me or my sister know."

"When was the last time you spoke with her?"

"Just yesterday, and she didn't mention any travel plans. She doesn't even own a car." He explains that she'd gifted her Pontiac to his youngest son when she'd sold her former home and moved to Oak Knoll.

"Why don't you see if you can reach her?" I suggest. "I didn't have any luck."

"She's probably out with friends. I'll check with her, of course, but I'm sure this is all a misunderstanding."

"Believe me, nothing would make me happier."

He mutters something and hangs up.

Fifteen minutes later, I'm talking to an irate Howard Sedgwick. When he was unable to reach his mother, he called a neighbor of hers, who reported that she'd seen Gladys leaving with her suitcase earlier in the day. "This is totally unacceptable!" Howard thunders as though my brother were entirely to blame. "We're talking about a seventy-four-year-old woman with a heart condition! If anything should happen to Mother . . ."

"She wasn't forced at gunpoint."

"We don't know that," he replies darkly.

"Please. They're friends."

"It would seem they're more than that."

"It kind of looks that way, doesn't it?" I'm forced to admit. "I didn't think so at first, on account of the age difference, but . . ." I trail off, wishing I had withheld that piece of information.

"Just how old is your brother, anyway?" he asks, and when I tell him Arthur's age, there's a pregnant pause at the other end before he utters, "Dear God."

"He's a very nice person," I supply weakly.

"I'm sure he is. A nice man who's after her money." Howard's voice takes on a nasty edge.

"That's ridiculous. He's not—"

"Why else would a thirty-four-year-old man be interested in a woman her age?"

"You're making him out to be some sort of a gigolo." This asshole is starting to piss me off. "He's nothing at all like that. Believe me, if they went on a trip together, it was her idea, not his."

"Are you suggesting my mother was the instigator?" Howard cries in outrage.

I take a deep breath, struggling to keep from losing my temper. Casting blame isn't going to help. "The point is they're both adults, and no one was forced into anything. Anyway, what's the worst that could happen? Because I think we can rule out unwanted pregnancy."

Howard is not amused. "Why did you call me, if you weren't concerned?"

He has me there. "Arthur is . . . I just wanted to make sure he's okay."

"Is there any reason he wouldn't be?"

I hesitate before deciding I have an obligation to provide all the facts. "My brother is . . . He's schizoaffective. He's on medication, and most of the time he's fine, but—"

"Are you telling me Mother's run off to God knows where with a possibly dangerous psychotic?" Howard blurts before I can finish.

"Arthur is perfectly harmless! And it's been months since he's had one of his . . . episodes." I do my best to defuse the situation, but my reassuring words have the opposite effect.

"*Episodes?* You mean like the nutcase who shot those Amish kids? That's it. I'm calling the police."

"There's no need for that." I speak in a crisp, authoritative tone to mask my rising panic. I can't have the cops involved. I have enough troubles as it is. "I'm sure they're fine, so let's not blow this out of proportion. We need to stay calm and see if we can figure out where they might have gone."

Howard exhales audibly and says in a less hostile tone, "My sister might have some idea."

"Call her. In the meantime, I'll see what I can find out."

"Wait. I just thought of something." He informs me that, as his mother's banker and legal proxy, he has the pin number for her account at Sedgwick Savings and Loan. He puts me on speakerphone, and I hear the sound of him tapping on a keyboard at the other end. Then, he stops tapping and says, "Oh." And somehow that one word is more ominous than all his bluster.

"What is it?" My heart starts to pound.

"Mother made a substantial cash withdrawal this morning. Twenty thousand dollars to be exact."

CHAPTER TEN

By the following Monday, I'm at my wit's end. It appears the lovebirds haven't just flown the coop, they've vanished into thin air. There's been no word from Arthur, and none of Gladys's friends or family seem to know where she's gone. Nor did she leave a paper trail. Howard Sedgwick has been monitoring her accounts and there have been no ATM withdrawals or recent charges on her credit cards, which doesn't surprise me given the sizable chunk she took out of her savings account. Twenty grand will take you pretty far.

I'm worried about Arthur. Any change in his routine tends to make him squirrelly, which was why I was nervous about his volunteering at the senior center at first. I tried explaining all that to Howard Sedgwick when I went to see him, but he was as unpleasant in person as he'd been over the phone. A large man in his fifties whose bald crown makes his head look like a battering ram, he lives in a McMansion the size of his ego, which I only saw from the outside because I didn't get past the entryway. We talked briefly— or rather I listened while he talked at me—after which I came away feeling grateful that I didn't work for him. His employees at the bank must wish his father, their former boss, who'd been a kind man by Gladys's description, were still alive.

"Where could they have gone?" I fret aloud to Ivy as we sit in her front parlor that evening, she drinking tea while I pluck pills from the cable-knit throw pillow on my lap. "No, don't answer. I have a sinking suspicion, and it's too horrible to contemplate."

"Does it involve Elvis impersonators?" she says in an attempt to lighten the mood.

I groan.

"For all we know, it's perfectly innocent," she goes on. "Maybe the Grand Canyon was on her bucket list, and he went along for the ride." Nestled in the overstuffed armchair opposite the sofa where I sit, Ivy looks like Goldilocks trying out Papa Bear's chair. She wears a pair of drawstring cotton pants and a colorful tie-dye tunic. Her curly black hair cascades over her shoulders.

"Then why the secrecy?"

Ivy calmly sips her tea from one of the Haviland teacups she inherited along with the house. "Isn't she, like, a hundred years old? Can you really see him having sex with some wrinkly old lady?"

"She's not that old, and I think I have more wrinkles than she does."

"In that case, he's totally doing her." Ivy grins, and when I don't respond in kind, she abandons her effort to cheer me. "We can't always choose who we fall in love with," she says gently.

"Says the girl who's praying her boyfriend won't propose."

"This isn't about me and Rajeev." She picks up the teapot that sits on the antique piecrust table between us and pours more tea into our cups. "Besides, what makes you think the odds of us making it are any better? Maybe they're soul mates."

"What about when she becomes decrepit?"

"She can afford live-in help, from what you've told me. She also has grown kids."

"I want him to be happy," I say into the de-pilled pillow on my lap. "I just wish I knew where the hell he *is*."

Ivy considers this, then sets her teacup in its saucer with a decisive clink and springs to her feet, catlike. She pads over to the oak rolltop desk that stands against one wall. When Grandmother Ladeaux had owned the house, it had looked pretty much as I imagine it had when it was built around the turn of the century. The parlor had William Morris wallpaper, oriental rugs, and porcelain figurines scattered throughout it. Now it has neutral walls hung with bright canvases and contemporary furniture mixed in with the antiques. Ivy pulls a yellow legal pad and pencil from a desk drawer and joins me on the sofa. "Let's make a list," she says.

"A list?"

"Of possible destinations. Places Arthur's always wanted to go to. Or that they'd have reason to visit." She writes down *Vegas* and cries, "You said it, not me!" when I level an accusing look at her.

Half an hour later, we have a list of possible destinations that include all the national parks west of the Rockies; Vegas, for obvious reasons; and Bozeman, Montana, where Gladys's granddaughter, Lexie MacAllister, owns a ranch. I'd spoken with Lexie over the phone. She told me her grandmother hadn't said anything about coming to visit, the last time they'd talked, and she promised to call me if she had any news. She sounded nice. Unlike her uncle Howard, she seemed as concerned for Arthur's welfare as for Gladys's.

"There's just one problem," Ivy says, frowning as she chews on the eraser end of the pencil.

"More than one actually, but what were you thinking?"

"Where would we begin? We could call motels along those routes to see if anyone remembers a couple that looked like they could be mother and son, but who has the time? We'd need an army."

"Or one crack assistant."

"Do you know of any who are looking for temp work?"

Delilah's personal assistant instantly comes to mind. "Brianna would be perfect. And I could kill two birds with one stone. Put her on my brother's trail and pick her brain about Delilah."

"Why is she looking for temp work? She could have any job she wanted with her résumé."

"She's stuck in town while the investigation is ongoing. She sounded desperate when I last spoke with her." I'd called yesterday to see if she'd found a home for Prince and to feel her out about Delilah.

Ivy perks up, like my cat at the scent of raw chicken liver. "Is she a suspect?"

"Everyone's a suspect until an arrest is made." Including me, I suppose. "Also, I imagine she knew Delilah better than anyone else. She managed her affairs and knows all the players."

"Sounds like she's made to order."

"Except for one thing: I can't afford to pay her more than minimum wage."

"You could sweeten the offer by including free room and board." Before I can object—because I'm thinking if Brianna were to move in with me, I'd have to move out or there'd be another dead body after I was done strangling her—Ivy says, "She's welcome to stay with me. I have more than enough room."

Warmed by Ivy's generosity, I'm reminded of why we're best friends. "I couldn't let you do that. You don't know what you'd be getting in to." I recall the Bluetooth Brianna who'd coolly presented me with the list of her employer's demands, and then acted as though *I* was the one being unreasonable when I drew the line at procuring the white coffee beans harvested only in the highlands of Peru and not available from any vendor in the States.

"Consider it my contribution to the cause. Besides, it would only be temporary. How bad could it be?"

"It's your funeral," I warn.

An hour later, Brianna is at the door with her suitcase and laptop. I'd expected her to sleep on my offer, but she'd leaped at it instead. I got the feeling she would've worked for free room and board alone, if only because she was going stir-crazy. She'd expected to help with the funeral arrangements and with wrapping up her late employer's affairs, she explained, but her services weren't required as it turned out. Delilah's sister-in-law, Greta Nyland, has her own people, and in lieu of a funeral (Delilah's remains had been cremated following the autopsy) there is to be a memorial service at a future date that has yet to be announced. Brianna's uncle had offered her a job on the film set, but she'd turned him down. She confided that she'd had her fill of celebrity egos.

Ivy shows Brianna to her room, which we refer to as the Lincoln Bedroom because it's the only one of the three guest rooms with a four-poster bed, and leaves her to unpack. Minutes later, Brianna is back downstairs, powering up her laptop at the kitchen table, Bluetooth device—which I'm pretty sure would have to be surgically removed—glowing in her ear.

"Does your brother's phone have a locater?" she asks.

"Yes, but it only works when the phone is on." I haven't been able to pick up a signal, which means either the battery is dead or the phone is shut off.

"I know of one that works a little differently. You get pinged if the phone is switched on," she explains. "All he'd have to do is power up and you'd have his location." She starts clacking away at her keyboard, while I look up the account info for Arthur's phone, which is in a folder labeled "Arthur" on my iPad, and which also holds the contact info for his shrink and the medications he's on. Ivy puts the kettle on to make a fresh pot of tea. By the time the tea is brewed, Brianna has the app installed. Ivy and I exchange a look over her bent head as she's creating an Excel spreadsheet for her to-do list. Ivy looks impressed. She also looks like she doesn't know what hit her.

I'm thinking it was a smart move to hire Brianna—so what if she irons her jeans and the color of her lipstick matches the cashmere sweater she's wearing?—but at the same time, I have a niggling sense of unease, wondering *Is she too good to be true?* Did Spence tell her to stick around because of her intimate knowledge of the victim . . . or so he could keep an eye on her?

The three of us are sitting around the kitchen table, drinking tea and strategizing, when Rajeev shows up. Brianna appears dazzled by him as Ivy makes the introductions. Most women are when they meet Rajeev the first time. With his toffee skin and shiny blue-black hair, high cheekbones, and brown eyes with the longest eyelashes I've ever seen on a man, he's beyond gorgeous.

He's also a good sport when Ivy informs him that they'll be sharing a bathroom with her new housemate on the nights he stays over. "Two ladies and one shower, how did I get so lucky?" His lightly inflected British accent makes the joking comment seem endearing rather than sleazy.

Brianna blushes. "Thanks for being so accommodating."

"Not at all. I have three sisters, and they trained me well." He slips an arm around Ivy's shoulders. He stands more than a foot taller than her, so her head fits perfectly in the curve of his shoulder.

"I'm an early riser. You'll hardly know I'm here," Brianna says. Somehow I doubt that.

Soon she and Rajeev are immersed in talking shop, comparing the merits of various software programs. Ivy orders pizza and she and I make a salad to go with it. When we all sit down to eat, I'm surprised to find myself wolfing down my food. It's the first time in days I've had an appetite. All too soon, it's time to leave. "I have to walk the dog," I explain with a pointed look at Brianna. She annoys me by shrugging, as if to say, *We all have to make sacrifices.*

Ivy accompanies me to the door while Brianna and Rajeev finish cleaning up in the kitchen. "You weren't kidding," she says, lowering her voice. "She's like a heat-seeking missile."

"If anyone can zero in on the target, she can," I agree. "The question is: Will there be a ring on it?"

* * * *

Meanwhile, back at the ranch, it seems my cat, Hercules, has decided to let Prince live. I find him reposing on the back of the Morris sofa, like a feudal lord on his throne, where he watches through slitted yellow eyes while I clip the leash to the Yorkie's collar.

"You guys hungry?" I ask when we return from our walk. Prince gives an excited yip. Hercules stares at me with reproach. Seems he's not ready to forgive me for sharing my affections.

"Fine, go ahead and sulk," I tell him. "You're only punishing yourself."

My cat's hunger strike proves short-lived. At the whirring of the electric can opener, Hercules is at my feet, rubbing against my ankles, meowing piteously, while Prince watches from a safe distance. Leaving them to their food, which I've placed at opposite ends of the kitchen, I head for the shower.

Later on, I have a Skype date with Bradley, who's currently in an undisclosed location somewhere along the Afghanistan-Pakistan border. I bring him up to date, starting with the murder investigation and ending with my brother. "Just when I thought it couldn't get any worse."

"Worse than finding a dead body?" I detect a smile behind the sympathetic expression he wears, as if he's thinking it's about time Arthur got some, even if the lady in question is past her prime.

"Okay, so not as bad as that. But if he marries her, I may revise my opinion."

"Would that be so terrible?"

"Ask me that when he's spending his honeymoon in the puff."

"Aren't you being overly dramatic? You were also worried about a possible *fatwa*," he reminds me.

"That could still happen."

He laughs. "I think Yusef has recovered from the shock of seeing you topless."

"Did he say anything to you?"

"He wanted to know if all American women were like you. I told him you were special."

"Special over there can get you beheaded."

"Don't worry about Yusef. He's a good guy."

"Like someone else I know," I purr.

"Does this mean what I think it means?"

His eyes light up, and he leans in close. I want to jump his bones even though it's Virtual Bradley, not Bradley in the flesh. He's not handsome in the way that Rajeev is—his features are uneven and his face bears the faded scars from shrapnel he caught in an explosion years ago—but he's sexy as hell. Tanned with deep-blue eyes and curly dark-brown hair bleached a dusky gold by the Middle Eastern sun. In the army flak jacket he wears open over a maroon Hard Rock T-shirt, he reminds me of Indiana Jones. "Not a chance, buster," I tell him. I learned my lesson after the last time.

He sighs. "Can't blame a guy for trying."

"You can feast your eyes on me in all my glory when you get back. Only a few more weeks."

His smile fades and his face recedes on my screen as he sits back. He's in an army tent, and I can hear the muffled sounds of men and vehicles on the move outside. "Listen, about that . . ."

"Don't tell me." I groan, anticipating what he's going to say. "I can't believe I ever thought you were actually getting some time off." This is the third time he's had his vacation deferred.

"We're seeing some action up north, and Fettie wants me to stick around a while longer." "Fettie" is Brian McFettridge, the Middle East bureau chief for CNN. "Sorry, babe. I know it's a disappointment."

For you or for me? It's been four months. How much longer does he expect me to wait? Then the voice in my head reminds me, *You knew what you were getting into.* My boyfriend made no promises and never pretended to be someone he wasn't. So I swallow my disappointment and say lightly, "Well, at least I don't lack for male companionship."

Bradley's eyebrows go up. "Should I be jealous?"

"Oh, definitely. He's cute, has all his hair, and he doesn't snore or hog the bed." I pull the Yorkie from the afghan at the foot of my bed where he was curled asleep and hold him up for Bradley to see. "Meet the competition. His name is Prince." Bradley laughs.

We talk a little longer before we say our good-byes around midnight my time. Normally, I'm asleep by the time my heads hits the pillow, but tonight I lie awake, the wheels in mind turning. When sleep finally comes, I dream of an Elvis impersonator singing Gladys and Arthur down the aisle.

CHAPTER ELEVEN

The following morning, I wake to all hell breaking loose.

I look out my living room window as I'm making my way to the kitchen to pour myself some coffee, and find news crews on the sidewalk in front of my house and satellite trucks parked two deep along the curb. It's barely light out, but the glare of handheld lights makes it look like high noon. The hum of voices is punctuated by the trilling of ringtones. I watch a shapely, coiffed blonde in a powder-blue dress whom I recognize as Kendall Benson, the morning anchorwoman for the local CBS station, perform the gravity-defying feat of balancing on my lawn in five-inch heels while doing her standup. I wish now I'd installed that automated sprinkler system.

What in God's name is going on? I've had reporters calling, wanting to interview me, because I have the dubious distinction of having discovered Delilah Ward's body, but this is a whole other level of media attention. I throw on a pair of jeans and a sweatshirt, and step outside. Questions are fired at me as the pack of reporters moves in.

"Tish, can you confirm that your brother is wanted for questioning in connection with the murder of Delilah Ward?" A deep baritone cuts through the other voices. Improbably, it belongs to a scrawny little guy, who thrusts a mike flagged with his station's call letters in my face.

"What kind of dumb-ass question is that?" I shoot back, forgetting, for the moment, that I'm surrounded by video cams.

"So you're denying that your brother is wanted for questioning?" Little Guy homes in.

"Damn right. I don't know who your source was, but they're full of—" I catch myself before I can say something that will get bleeped. "They don't know what they're talking about."

"I heard your brother left town," Little Guy persists. "Can you confirm that?"

Blond, bubble-headed Kendall Benson asks, "Is he in hiding?"

"He's not *in hiding*," I blast back. "He went on a trip."

Have you spoken to him?

Where is he?

Is he a suspect?

Can you confirm he has a history of mental illness?

The barrage of questions continues, swamping me. I duck back inside to call Spence. "Is my brother wanted for questioning?" I demand when he picks up, sounding groggy as if I'd woken him.

"Where'd you hear that?"

"From the reporters outside my house." He mutters an expletive. "So it *is* true. What in the hell is going on?"

Spence sighs. "I can explain, but I'd rather do it in person. Can you meet me in an hour?"

Forty minutes later, I'm sitting down opposite Spence in a booth at a diner on Freedom Boulevard, which seems to be patronized mainly by truckers. He wears jeans and a tan windbreaker over a navy Lacoste polo. If he looks unhappy, it doesn't appear to be directed at me for a change. He signals to a plump brunette waitress, who hurries over to take our orders.

"I know this place doesn't look like much," he says, after she's left, "but the food's good."

"I didn't come for the eggs and hash browns," I reply grumpily.

"I want to know why a bunch of reporters seem to think my brother is a wanted man. Let me guess. Howard Sedgwick. He's behind this, isn't he?"

Spence lets out a frustrated breath, which tells me I'm right and also expresses how he feels about Howard Sedgwick, who's been pestering the cops to issue an APB for his missing mother. "He seems to think we've been remiss in not questioning Arthur in connection with the murder."

"He'd say anything to get what he wants."

"Which is what, exactly?"

"For his mother's fun and games to be over. He wants her to be a doddering old lady who he can control, not a geriatric cougar."

"Whatever the reason, Arthur's on the DA's radar now."

I feel a trickle of cold fear in the pit of my stomach, followed by a rush of heat to my face. "That son of a bitch. I'll kill him. I swear." Belatedly, I remember I'm talking to a cop, who may see me as a person of interest in Delilah's murder. "This is bullshit. You know that, don't you?"

I'm surprised when Spence says, "Between you and me? Yeah. Guys like Sedgwick, they throw their weight around to compensate for not having been the big man on campus. Unfortunately, we can't just ignore him."

"Because he's a prominent citizen?"

"Also because he and his wife hosted a fund-raiser when the DA was up for election."

I feel sick all of a sudden. "So the DA owes him."

Spence nods. "It's not just that. He's under pressure to make an arrest. All the media attention is making him look bad." And Spence is taking the brunt of it, if what McGee said is true.

"You're wasting time chasing after Arthur when you could be looking for a *real* suspect."

"Believe me, I'm trying." I see the frustration on his face. "The reason I asked you here was so you'd know where I stand.

Personally, I don't think your brother had anything to do with either the murder of Delilah Ward or the abduction of Mrs. Sedgwick." He makes air quotes with his fingers around the word *abduction*. Sedgwick hadn't gone so far as to accuse Arthur of it, but he'd implied as much.

"So what now?" I pick up the coffee in front of me that our waitress must have poured, though I don't recall her doing so. I notice my hand is trembling as I lift it to my lips to take a sip. A trucker in a gimme cap and plaid shirt who's eating at the counter flirts with our waitress, who seems to know him. The bell over the door jingles, and I see a young woman with bottle-blond hair enter, looking frazzled and pulling a whiny little boy by the arm.

"I can only stall for so long." He leans in, saying urgently, "Tish, you need to tell your brother it would be in his best interests to come in on his own."

"I would if I knew where he was. I don't, and he's not returning my calls."

He stares at me with a flat expression. Clearly he doesn't believe me. "If you know and you just aren't telling me, you're not doing him any favors," he says in a stern voice. "I don't want to see him railroaded any more than you do. But I can't prevent it if we're working at cross-purposes."

"This isn't you playing good cop, is it?" Spence isn't the only one with trust issues.

"No, but I know there's nothing I can say to convince you, so I'm asking you to take a leap of faith. Can you do that?" I hesitate before giving a small nod. What choice do I have? Deep down, I also wonder if maybe, just maybe, I misjudged him.

"I swear to you I don't know where he is."

He holds my gaze and seems to debate with himself before he decides to take me at my word. "But you'll let me know as soon as you hear from him?" I nod again. He looks past me out the window, remarking, "Well, what do you know. We agreed on something and the world didn't come to an end."

"Yet."

He smiles and I smile, too, because I know what he means. It seems strange to be on the same side for once. Our food arrives, and Spence dives in like there's no tomorrow, while I nibble on the toast I ordered. "First decent meal I've had in a week," he says around a mouthful of bacon and eggs.

"Looks like you're making up for lost time," I observe.

He chews and swallows, while chasing another mouthful from his plate with his fork. "This is what comes of living alone. You open the fridge expecting it to be magically stocked and end up dining on canned soup and Saltines."

"What, did your wife leave you?" I say in jest, thinking she must be out of town.

He stops eating and stares down at his plate for a second. His expression is pained when he lifts his head to look at me. "Other way around actually. It was me who moved out, though it wasn't my idea."

I'm surprised. I've never met his wife, but I assumed he was happily married. I glance down at his hand. "You're still wearing your ring."

"I'm hoping we can work it out. We're in counseling."

"How's that going?"

His weary expression says it all, and my heart goes out to him unexpectedly. Maybe because he seems human, whereas before he only seemed like a jerk. "I don't blame Barb. All the years I was working crazy hours, I wasn't much of a husband or father. To be honest, I wasn't always in a hurry to get home. There's a reason the divorce rate is high among cops. If you don't decompress, you end up taking it out it on your family, so you have a beer with your buddies after work, and one beer becomes two. Most wives, they don't get it. And why would they?"

"How are your kids taking it?"

"Katie keeps asking when I'm coming home, and Ryan's decided he wants to live with me."

"I imagine that wouldn't go over too well with your wife."

His mouth stretches in a cheerless smile. "She'd serve me my balls on a platter."

Silence falls. The sun glares through the window behind him, highlighting his blond hair, which I notice is starting to thin on top, another thing that makes him seem disturbingly human. "Sorry," he says after he's chewed and swallowed another bite. "I didn't mean to lay all that on you."

"We've all been there," I reply with a shrug, though my own breakups, most recently with my ex-boyfriend Daniel, hardly compare with the ending of a marriage. "I hope it works out for you." I spread jam on the uneaten portion of my toast to keep from making eye contact. We're like dance partners made clumsy by a change in tempo; we don't know the steps to this number.

"Get you folks anything else?" the waitress asks when she returns to clear away our plates.

"Just the check," Spence says with a glance at his watch.

"I'll let you know when I hear from my brother," I promise when we're saying our good-byes in the parking lot, then I call after him as he's walking toward his car, "Don't let it go too long!" When he turns to look back at me, I explain, "The fridge. Man cannot live on hash browns alone."

I phone Ivy on my way to work. She shares my outrage at Howard Sedgwick, but she's glad to hear that Spence and I are working to-gether. "It's about time you two buried the hatchet."

"I prefer to think of it as a temporary alliance."

"Call it what you like. I've always suspected he had a heart under all that muscle."

I'm cruising through the historic district in my Explorer. I drive past stucco storefronts painted in pastel shades and curlicued in decorative wrought iron. Most of them date back to the twenties, excluding the ones that were destroyed in 1989 by the Loma Prieta earthquake and were rebuilt in the same style. At the Bluejay Café, where Ivy and I often eat lunch on days when she's pulling a shift at the Gilded Lily, the line of customers waiting for tables stretches out the door. A busker strums his guitar outside the new-and-used bookstore, the Dog-Eared Page, collecting spare change and dollar bills in his velvet-lined guitar case.

"Did you know he and his wife split up?" I ask Ivy.

"Wow," she expresses surprise at the news. "I wonder what brought that on. I saw them in the shop a few months ago, and they seemed fine. I didn't get the impression their marriage was headed for the rocks."

"He seems sad about it."

"He won't be for long. The women will be lining up."

The less I think about Spence's romantic prospects, the better. "How's it going with Brianna?" I inquire, changing the subject. "If she's driving you nuts, you have only yourself to blame."

"You warned me she was annoying, but you didn't mention she was anal."

"Why, what did she do?"

"She was up at dawn cleaning the house. Believe it or not, she says she finds it relaxing."

"Why soak in a hot tub when you can scrub toilets?" I brake at the crosswalk opposite the old art deco courthouse, which was converted into a mall with boutique shops and eateries, to allow pedestrians to cross—a gay couple holding hands and what appears to be an Elder Hostel tour group who are walking at a pace far more sprightly than the dreadlocked stoner trailing behind.

"I'm getting free maid service at least."

We say a quick goodbye and my next call is to Brianna, who texted me while I was on the phone with Ivy. "I got a ping!" she says excitedly. The signal from my brother's phone came out of Paso Robles, she reports, which is on the route to Vegas, and which seems to confirm my worst fear. I pray I'm not too late.

"With any luck, the next sound we hear won't be wedding bells," I say.

Brianna informs me she made up a flyer to fax to the motels along US 101 between Paso Robles and Vegas with a photo of the couple that she'd found on Gladys's Facebook page and a number to call. I praise her for the progress she's made so far and ask how she's settling in at Ivy's. She replies cautiously, "Maybe you should ask her."

"I did. She said you were up early cleaning house."

"She's not mad, is she?" An anxious note creeps into Brianna's voice. "I didn't realize she was still asleep when I vacuumed the hallway. I saw Rajeev leave, and I thought . . ." She trails off.

"Do you have any hobbies that don't involve a vacuum cleaner?"

She's quiet for a moment, then she bursts out, "I know what you're thinking. You think I'm some kind of freak. I know I can be a bit . . . obsessive. My college roommate requested a room change after the first semester. I don't know what Courtney told them, but I was assigned a single every semester after that. 'Psycho singles' they were called." She sounds bitter about it, even after all this time.

I'm not unsympathetic. As difficult as she can be, it must be even more difficult to *be* her. "Well, when you see her at your next class reunion, she'll probably weigh three hundred pounds, and you can have the last laugh."

Another silence falls, then, "I won't. See her again, that is. She died."

"Seriously?"

"Hit-and-run. Senior year."

A chill runs through me. "Did they ever catch the driver?"

"No, they never did."

The feeling of unease intensifies, and I quickly change the

subject. "Listen, I was wondering if you could ask a favor of your uncle." I explain what I have in mind, and she agrees to put a call in to Uncle Karol. Ten minutes later, she calls me back. "He says we're more than welcome to visit the set. Oh, and he also invited us to a get-together at his house tomorrow evening."

"Tell him I accept."

When I learned that Arthur was wanted for questioning in Delilah Ward's murder, I realized I had to find another suspect and fast. The DA will stop at nothing to get reelected, from what Spence told me, even if it means railroading my brother, who, in many ways, is a prosecutor's dream.

He has a history of mental illness.

He's been in trouble with the law. He was twice taken into custody, though never booked, the first time for assaulting a Greenpeace volunteer who he'd mistaken for a CIA operative.

He arguably had access to Casa Blanca through me.

His alibi is flimsy. He said he was home alone on the morning in question.

He has a connection to the victim besides me. His buddy Ray reminded me of it when I called him looking for Arthur. He and Arthur designed a computer game featuring Phantasmagora, the female superhero played by Delilah in *Return of Laserman*. Which could make it appear as though Arthur had been obsessed with her.

His current whereabouts are unknown. And a prominent citizen is claiming that Arthur coerced his elderly mother to flee town with him.

And to think my biggest worry was that Arthur would crack up if he didn't have his Honey Bunches of Oats or he woke up in a strange bed. What's a stay at the puff compared to prison?

CHAPTER TWELVE

When I arrive at the Cummings family's California Tudor on Windlass Lane, the first stop on my rounds the following morning, I'm greeted by the sight of trash from an overturned garbage receptacle. The masked bandits have struck again. As I pick up the trash strewn across the yard, I discover a number of empties, and figure the raccoons weren't the only ones who were up to no good. The current guests are a pair of attorneys, and their two teenage sons, from New York. Mr. Powers and Mrs. Smith-Powers don't seem the type to guzzle beer and Bartles & Jaymes wine coolers, so the culprits must be their sons. Normally, I wouldn't object, but this neighborhood is subject to a zoning ordinance that prohibits loud parties among other things. If the neighbors were to complain, the owners could lose their vacation rental permit.

I march inside to have a word with the boys' parents. But no one's home except the housekeeper, Esmeralda. The Powerses had arranged for her to clean for them. I find her in the sun-filled kitchen, emptying the dishwasher. "The raccoons have been at it again," I grumble as I head over to the sink to wash up. "And they weren't the only ones. Do you know what those boys were up to?"

"They're nice boys," she says, darting me a nervous look. She doesn't want any trouble.

"Nice boys who seem to have made a lot of new friends." The

power of social media. "They'll wish they'd played Monopoly instead, after I'm done talking with their parents."

"They are sorry. I explain to them already." Esmeralda beseeches me with her big brown eyes.

"If it was *your* boys, they wouldn't be sitting down for a week."

"My sons know better," Esmeralda says firmly, not seeming to realize she's contradicting herself. But she has every reason to be proud. Both her boys are honor students at the Catholic school they attend, and the eldest, Eduardo, will be the first in Esmeralda's family to go to college.

"How'd Eduardo do on his SAT prep?" I ask, changing the subject.

"Best in his class!" she reports, beaming as I high-five her. With her smooth caramel skin and dark hair pulled back in a ponytail, she looks way too young to be the mother of three. She had her first child, Alicia, when she was sixteen, and she still has the figure of a teenager. Esmeralda is also the best-dressed woman I know, though she buys her clothes at discount stores. Today she wears an above-the-knee pencil skirt in a jazzy zebra stripe and a white cotton-knit top shot with gold threads. I notice she's also gotten a manicure. Her sister, Flor, owns a nail salon.

I compliment her on her outfit. "What's the occasion?"

I'm hoping she'll say she has a date with the gardener, Manuel, who has his eye on her, though she claims she has no time for men. Instead, she claps her hands and squeals, "I'm going to be on TV!"

Esmeralda is a huge fan of *Survivor*—she's watched every episode of the reality show—so my first thought is that she auditioned and was picked, and now her dream of being on an island with Jeff Probst is finally being realized. "Wow. That's great. Congratulations. I didn't realize you—"

"Telemundo!" My heart sinks when she names the premier network of the Spanish-speaking world.

"Esmeralda, is this about Delilah? Did you agree to an interview?"

She nods excitedly. "Everyone in my family will be watching."

"Esmeralda, you can't do this. You'd be making a huge mistake."

Her smiles fades. "I don't understand. Why do you say this?"

"You don't know what these people are like. They'll make you look bad."

She shakes her head vigorously. "No, these are *my* people."

"Just because they speak the same language as you doesn't mean they have good intentions. They only care about ratings." Esmeralda has little to offer, having worked for Delilah only a short time, but the public appetite is such that they'll seize on any crumb about Delilah's last days. Also, Esmeralda was the last person to see her alive—other than the killer. "If you say anything that makes her look bad—like that she'd been drinking—her fans will call you a liar."

Esmeralda gasps. "I am not a liar! I only say what is true. I tell about the lady."

I frown in confusion. "What lady?"

"She call. I say, 'Miss Ward is not home and can I take a message?' And the lady say . . .'" Esmeralda hesitates, her cheeks coloring. "'Tell the bitch to call me.'"

I feel my pulse quicken. "Did you get her name?" Whoever the mystery caller was, she had the number for the landline, which would have been given out to only a select handful of people.

"The lady say, 'She will know.'" Esmeralda wrings her hands, looking distressed.

"Did you tell this to the police?" Esmeralda nods unhappily.

"Well, I'm sure they're looking into it. But they won't want you talking to the press."

"Then I will say nothing about the lady."

I hate to be the one to burst Esmeralda's bubble, but . . . "You won't mean to. But things you never meant to say have a way of coming out on camera." I recall my outburst on my front stoop; I cringed when I watched it on TV. "And then it will haunt you forever. Trust me, I know."

"I would never say anything bad," Esmeralda insists. "She was nice to me. I feel bad for her. To lose her husband so young. The baby, too." She sighs and places a hand over her heart, the way I'd seen her do when engrossed in the *telenovelas* she sometimes watches when she's cleaning.

"Um. I don't think she was ever actually pregnant."

"*Sí*. It was in *¡Mira!*"

Not just the Spanish-language tabloid, the story ran in all the rags: It was said that Delilah had been eight weeks pregnant when her husband perished, and that she'd lost the baby in the throes of her grief. *Don't believe everything you read*, I want to say. But I don't. Bad enough that I'm robbing Esmeralda of her fifteen minutes of fame. "So will you tell them you changed your mind?"

Esmeralda sighs again and nods. She looks like a child who had a new toy snatched away from her. After she's made the call, she looks so glum, I try to think of something that will cheer her up. "You know, it'd be a shame to let that outfit go to waste," I say as she's dragging the sponge mop from the broom closet as if it were a lead weight. "What do you say we make an audition tape for *Survivor*? I bet when they see it, they'll fly you to New York for an interview." Esmeralda has survived far worse than the jungles of *Survivor*. She emigrated to this country from Mexico with her husband, who then left her with three small children to raise on her own.

Esmeralda brightens. "Really? Oh, Tish, that is my dream!"

I head home to fetch my video camera. This will put me behind schedule, but it's worth it to see Esmeralda smile.

Two hours later, I arrive at my next stop, the Russos' midcentury modern, where I notice an older-model blue panel truck parked at the curb. Its front end is dented and its rear tire wells are speckled with rust, which tells me it doesn't belong to a resident of the exclusive neighborhood. Likely a service person . . . or possibly a burglar who's casing the joint. As I'm walking over to investigate, the window on the driver's side rolls down to reveal a familiar face, scruffy and unshaven.

"Got her off Craigslist. Ain't she a beaut?" McGee calls out.

"What are you doing here?" I demand.

He shrugs, his expression inscrutable. He wears wraparound shades and his desert camouflage jacket over a rumpled shirt. He jerks his stubbly chin toward the house. "You know this guy?"

"I should hope so. I work for him."

"You know he has suspected mob ties?"

"It's just a rumor. It's never been proven."

"Russo was the target of a RICO investigation in 1989. Him and his associates. Then whaddya know, just as the feds are closing in, their chief informant is found floating facedown in the East River. My cousin Johnny was on the task force. He says Russo's as dirty as they come."

"Then why was he never charged?"

"They couldn't make it stick."

"All I know is he's a nice man who pays me on time."

"A real gent," McGee says, sneering.

"Are you suggesting that I'm in some sort of danger? Because that's ridiculous. I've never had a problem with the Russos. I rarely see them." Besides this home, they own one in Vegas.

"You're involved in a murder investigation. Which is going nowhere. No witnesses, and no one heard the shot. The thinking is that it could've been a professional hit on account of the vic's being shot execution-style." McGee's source at the station has been keeping him up to date. "On top of which, you work for a guy with suspected mob ties. What, I gotta spell it out?"

I frown at him. "The only thing I see that's *suspicious* is a *suspicious*-looking vehicle, belonging to an even more *suspicious*-looking character, parked where it shouldn't be."

McGee flashes me a grin and hops out. "Anyone asks, I'm your associate."

I'll never admit it to him, but the truth is I kind of like having him around, so I don't object when he falls into step with me as I head up the front walk.

The home, which was designed by Neutra, is composed of three cubes of varying sizes sided in quarry-cut stone with the tallest at the center and looks out on a lush garden in front and a pool and a patio in back. As we approach, I can see through the sidelights on either side of the door into the slate-floored atrium. "Tell me, does this look to you like the home of a mobster?" I ask when we're inside. The decor is tasteful, no gilded furniture or mirrored walls.

McGee shrugs. "I wouldn't know. Unlike you, Ballard, I don't keep company with wiseguys."

We move deeper into the house. "Sorry, but I can't picture Russo in a rubout suit," I say. I'd never seen my seventy-five-year-old client dressed in anything but casual slacks and golf sweaters.

"Appearances can be deceiving," McGee comments.

We enter the living room, which has a double-sided fireplace at one end and a glass wall through which the swimming pool shimmers in the morning light at the other. The Calder mobile above the Heywood Wakefield coffee table revolves lazily in a current of air. The Eames chair by the fireplace has me coveting it as usual; I'd love to have one of my own, but my house is the wrong era.

McGee makes himself at home, peering into rooms and closets until he's satisfied there are no suspicious characters lurking about, nor any evidence of criminal activity. He stops at the closed door to Russo's study. "He always keep this locked?" he asks, after he's tried the doorknob.

"When he's not in residence." I've never been inside. Which didn't strike me as odd until now.

Before I can stop him, McGee has the door open. Among his many hidden talents is picking locks, which he learned growing up in a sketchy part of the Bronx (the less I know about his activities prior to becoming a cop, the better). We walk into a room with a picture window at one end and a built-in bookcase at the other. A leather sofa and a matching club chair stand opposite a desk from the same era, above which hangs a collection of framed eight-by-tens. Russo's ego wall. I move in for a closer look. There are photos of a younger, trimmer Russo before he went gray, with his black hair slicked back in a fifties do, posing with individual members of the Rat Pack—Sammy Davis Junior, Dean Martin, Frank Sinatra—and other entertainers of the day. The more recent ones show a portly, silver-haired Russo grinning alongside present-day Vegas headliners such as Barry Manilow, Neil Diamond, Celine Dion, and Elton John.

McGee gives a low whistle. "Get a load of this."

My blood turns cold when I see what's got his attention: an eight-by-ten of Russo with his arm around Delilah Ward, who is shining like the evening star before the other stars come out at night.

CHAPTER THIRTEEN

I wonder what the photo means, or if it means anything at all. Is there a connection between Russo and the dead woman besides her having visited his casino? As I drive to my next property, I consider the theory that Delilah's murder was a professional hit. Ordered by Russo? I find it hard to believe that my client, who, as far as I know, only hits golf balls at the country club, could be so coldhearted. Besides, what possible motive could he have?

I'm hoping other suspects will reveal themselves at this evening's get-together, where I'll be introduced to the main players who are involved in the making of *Devil's Slide*. I'm nervous about it. And not just because the killer could be among them—I can't figure out what to wear.

It's 6:30 by the time I arrive home, leaving me with an hour to shower and dress. Brianna and Ivy come over as I'm combing through my wardrobe, becoming increasingly discouraged with each wrong outfit I try on. Brianna is carrying a garment bag. She unzips it to reveal a slinky cocktail dress. "Perfect," she pronounces as she holds it up to me. "It's a little big on me so I figured it would fit you."

I finger the shiny fabric. "Didn't your uncle say not to dress up?"

"They always say that, then they show up looking like they're at an awards ceremony."

"I don't know . . ."

"Trust me," she says. I wonder if I can, and not just about the dress, before I dismiss the thought. Brianna's been a godsend. She spent the day calling and faxing motels. One of the motel managers called back to say he'd seen a couple who looked like the one in the photo on the flyer. They'd been breakfasting together at a nearby diner, but they hadn't checked into his motel, so he couldn't tell us their current location. But it meant we were on the right track.

Five minutes later, I'm standing in front of the full-length mirror in my bedroom, smoothing the borrowed dress over my hips. Made of brushed satin in a greenish bronze with a flirty hem and spaghetti straps, it clings to my body and shows more cleavage than I'm comfortable with. "You don't think it's too . . . ?"

"No, I don't," says Brianna firmly. I notice the outfit she's wearing, a plum-color taffeta skirt paired with a black velvet jacket over a pale-pink silk cami, is far more modest than what I have on.

"I don't want to send the wrong message." I bite my lip as I study my reflection.

"Think of it as a disguise," Ivy says, reminding me that I'm going undercover.

"About that," Brianna says, frowning. "If my uncle knew you were conducting your own investigation . . ."

"He wants Delilah's killer brought to justice, doesn't he?" I reason.

"Of course. But that's what the cops are for. It seems sneaky to show up at his party with an ulterior motive. Also, he's between blondes at the moment, and when he sees you in that dress . . ." She lets the implications hang in the air.

Ugh. But I can't think about that right now. "I need to know if any of those people had a motive for killing Delilah."

"I already told you—"

"That she didn't have any enemies, I know. But *somebody* wanted her dead, and all I know is that it wasn't my brother."

"Still. I'm not sure I should be helping you with this."

I turn to face her. She's sitting on the end of my queen bed with her pantyhosed legs crossed, jiggling her foot—a nervous habit of hers. "I don't want us to find Arthur just so he can end up in jail."

"Well, when you put it that way . . ." she relents.

"You look beautiful," pronounces Ivy, after I've donned heels and my gold-and-pearl teardrop earrings.

"Hold still." Brianna bends to pluck a loose thread from the hem of my dress.

The ninety-mile stretch of coastline between Cypress Bay and San Francisco is fogged in more often than not this time of year, but on a clear day like today, the view is awe inspiring. I can see the ocean stretching to the horizon, over which the setting sun has cast a glittery net, the sky above streaked with orange and crimson. Close to shore, whitecaps roll in and batter the cliffs.

On the drive, Brianna briefs me. "You already know Liam. The other cast members will be there, too. And some of the crew. The executive producer and his second in command, the director of photography, and the assistant director."

"Liam's quite the charmer. I've heard he has a reputation as a ladies' man."

Brianna shrugs. "He never hit on Delilah."

"At least we know it's not because he's gay." He's reportedly dated some of the world's most glamorous women.

"You wouldn't know if he were. It's why they all have wives or girlfriends. Coming out would be career suicide."

"It doesn't seem to have hurt Ellen Degeneres's career."

"People don't pay to see Ellen kissing someone of the opposite sex."

"Did Liam and Delilah have a falling-out?" I ask, changing tack. We pass the old lighthouse, which is the tallest man-made structure for miles, its beacon shining at the tip of Lighthouse Point.

"They had a huge argument a few days before she left to come here. I could hear them, it was so loud. When Delilah was drinking, she could be a real . . ." Brianna trails off, biting her lip. "Anyway, I heard Liam say she was digging her own grave, and he wasn't going to stick around to watch."

"Good for him."

"The others . . ." She makes a disgusted noise. "They were either pouring her a drink or turning a blind eye. Her manager only cared about his percentage, and time off to get sober meant no money was coming in." I wonder what role Brianna had played other than that of dutiful assistant. "Liam was the only one who stood up to her. And it bit him in the ass."

"How so?"

"I heard him say something about how you're only as sick as your secrets." I'm familiar with the quote. It's from the Big Book of Alcoholics Anonymous. "And Delilah—like I said, normally she wasn't mean, only when she was drinking—she says in this nasty voice, 'I'm not the only one with secrets.'"

I feel my little gray cells, in the words of the fictional sleuth, Hercule Poirot, start to stir. "I wonder what secrets Liam is keeping." Maybe he really is gay. He didn't seem so, but he's an actor. His adoring public doesn't know he's an alcoholic, either.

Half an hour later, we turn inland toward Salema, a former fishing village that's now populated mainly by artists and other off-the-grid types. The movie people leased ten acres of farmland several miles east of town where they constructed an elaborate film set, and where the crew outnumbers the locals, I'm told. We drive through artichoke fields and past farmhouses before we reach the main drag, which is composed of a post office, grocery/hardware store, coffee shop, a store that sells bait and tackle, an eatery where the menus are laminated and the pies are homemade, and art galleries and craft shops sprinkled in between. It's been dubbed Hollywood-on-Highway-One by the press, but it's sleepy at this time of day.

Ten minutes later, we pull in behind a line of vehicles parked along the curb in front of Bartosz's rented digs in the hills above Salema, a two-story cedar A-frame that sits atop a wooded rise. I look up to see windows aglow with the last light of the setting sun and figures milling on the upper deck. Brianna and I get out and walk toward the house. One of the parked vehicles catches my eye, a silver Maybach 57 Zeppelin. It's among the priciest cars money can buy, I know from an old boyfriend of mine who was a car enthusiast, and it makes my Explorer look like a beggar among royalty.

"I know this is the right address, but I'm not sure we're on the same planet," I remark.

Brianna smiles thinly. "Welcome to my world."

We climb a set of stone steps to the front entrance, where a burly guy who's dressed in black checks our IDs against the guest list before we're waved through. It's odd to see security at an informal get-together. Bartosz must be taking extra precautions with a murderer on the loose. We walk down a short hallway before entering a wood-paneled great room with a cathedral ceiling, from which hangs a chandelier made from antlers. The stone fireplace, where a log fire crackles, is the size of a medieval castle's, and the walls are hung with western art. The guests, a dozen or so by my count, seem out of place dressed in their haute couture and bling.

An older man who's holding court by the fireplace walks over to greet us. Short and barrel chested with a snowy mane that brings to mind a cockatoo's crest, Karol Bartosz exudes an aura of power that makes up for what he lacks in stature. He wears what appears to be the regulation attire of the male guests: black jeans and a bespoke blazer, his a dove gray, over a black silk tee.

"Dearest girl!" He embraces Brianna before kissing her on both cheeks continental style. He has the sonorous, accented voice of the stage actor he was in his former life in Poland before he became a director. "Delighted you could come. And this lovely lady"—he turns toward me—"must be Tish." He got my name right. He gets points for that, even if he is checking out my cleavage. It seems Brianna was right in warning me about his predilection for blondes with big boobs.

"It's an honor, Mr. Bartosz," I say as we shake hands. "I'm a great admirer of your work. I've seen every one of your pictures. My favorite was *Trial by Fire*. The part where the bad guy is stalking his victim in that slaughterhouse? I was on the edge of my seat. It gave me goose bumps."

"You are too kind," he murmurs as his eyes travel over me, taking the scenic route. To Brianna he says, "Bree, why don't get yourself a drink while I show Tish around?" He waves his hand toward the rustic-looking trestle table against one wall that serves as a bar.

Brianna shoots me a meaningful glance before she leaves me alone with her uncle. He has one of his minions fetch us drinks, white wine for him and Perrier for me, then proceeds to take me on a tour of the house. The owner, a Silicon Valley software executive, had it built in the style of a Montana hunting lodge. One suitable for the likes of Ted Turner, I note as I look around.

"I'm sorry for your loss." I offer my condolences as he's guiding me down the hallway to the rear of the house, his hand resting lightly against the small of my back. "I understand you and Delilah were close."

Bartosz nods, his expression turning sorrowful. "Lest you think my little soirée in bad taste, it was only because we've been in a daze, not knowing what to do with ourselves. I thought we should gather together, lift our glasses to her memory," he explains. "It's what she would have wanted."

"No doubt," I murmur.

I ask if he's found an actress for Delilah's part in *Devil's Slide*.

"I have in fact. Taylor Ramsey." He names the actress best known for her series on the Disney channel, now in reruns, in which she stars as a teen math wizard who has a secret life as a CIA agent. Since she came of age, Taylor has been working to establish herself as a serious actress. "I met with her and her agent yesterday in L.A. I was lucky to get her on such short notice." Bartosz explains that another project Taylor was slated to do fell through at the last minute.

"I liked her in *Tara Times Two*." We reach the study, a large room with built-in bookcases on three sides and a fireplace that's a smaller version of the one in the great room, where a bronze statue of a cowboy on horseback sits on a pedestal under a spotlight. It looks to be a Remington.

"Lovely girl and underrated as an actress," he agrees. "You'll see when you meet her. I'll introduce you."

"She's here? Wow, she didn't waste any time," I remark in surprise.

"There is no time to waste." Bartosz pauses to study an oil painting of Custer's Last Stand that hangs on the wall. "For every day that production is delayed, you can add another zero to the cost, and if filming doesn't wrap on schedule, you lose actors who have other projects lined up." I recall Liam's words about how any tears that were shed wouldn't be on the studio's dime. No kidding.

"I saw you that day," I say when the subject turns to the murder of Delilah Ward as we're returning to the party. He cuts me a sharp glance. "At least, I think it was you. Were you driving a black Escalade?"

"Delilah and I had some business to discuss," he replies tersely.

"Brianna mentioned you'd been to see her." I'm lying—Brianna told me there were no meetings scheduled for that morning—but Bartosz doesn't seem to know this.

"Yes. I was surprised when she didn't come to the door. I waited, thinking she must have stepped out and would be back any moment, but . . ." He shakes his head mournfully. "I explained all that to the police, but it seems I'm a 'person of interest.' Of all the cruel ironies. I would have cut off my own arm before I touched a hair on her head!" His voice cracks with emotion.

I flash on an image of Delilah lying by the swimming pool, a pool of her own blood beneath her. Bartosz's emotion seems genuine, but how do I know he didn't go around in back instead of ringing the doorbell, slip in through the side gate, and put a bullet in Delilah's head? Though I don't know what he would have stood to gain. From what I can see, he only stood to lose. He's out his first choice of female costar and looking at staggering production cost overruns.

I pull one of my business cards from my silver clutch and hand it to him. "Here's my number. If there's ever anything I can do for you . . ." I'm hoping he'll call. Not because I want to get to know him better, but because I want to keep my eye on him. And because my favorite movie, unlike that of every other woman on the planet, is *The Godfather* and not *Sleepless in Seattle*.

Keep your friends close and your enemies closer.

He examines my card. "Rest Easy Property Management. Clever. Though it does strike a rather macabre note under the present circumstances."

I smile thinly. "The same thought occurred to me."

Drinking has begun in earnest, I see from the flushed faces all around me and the overloud laughter I hear when we rejoin the other guests. A buffet supper has been laid out in the dining room that's adjacent to the great room. One of the other guests, a dark-haired man wearing a turtleneck, is playing a tune on the baby grand piano. I spy Liam Brady and walk over to him.

"If it isn't Tish Ballard herself." Liam kisses my hand. "And looking quite fetching I might add." His blue eyes travel over me in a way that has me thinking he couldn't possibly be gay unless he's the best actor on the planet. "To what do we owe the pleasure?"

"Brianna scored me an invitation." I remind him that our host is her uncle.

"Ah, yes, I heard she was working for you now. So she's gone to the dark side, has she?"

"I only worship the devil on weekends. And it's just temp work while she's in town."

Liam's smile falls away, and he replies in a bitter voice, "We're all caught like flies in a web, are we not? Wriggling while the spider decides which of us to feed on next." I can guess who the "spider" is, but it doesn't parse with Spence's take on the investigation. "And if they don't find their man before it's time for us to move on? Will they detain me? Confiscate my passport?"

I'm thinking of my brother as I reply, "None of us can breathe easy until the killer's caught."

"*If* he's caught."

I eye Liam speculatively, wondering what, exactly, he means by that. If he's the killer, he could be hinting that he's too clever to be caught. "The spider always gets the fly in the end."

"I'll drink to that." He raises his glass, his eyes crinkling in a wry smile when my gaze lingers on it. "Ginger ale," he says, adding with a rueful shake of his head, "More's the pity." He doesn't appear to have gotten the memo on the men's dress code. He wears faded blue jeans and a buffed black leather motorcycle jacket over a plain white T-shirt. James Dean in *Rebel Without a Cause*.

Liam introduces me to his fellow cast members. It's weird because although I'm meeting them for the first time, they seem as familiar as people I've known all my life. I know Jillian Lassiter from the movies in which she plays the redheaded sexpot, a role she was born to play with her curvy figure and fire-red hair. Jolly fat man Rick McVittie used to crack me up when he was a regular on *Saturday Night Live*, before he started making lame comedies for the beer-funnel-and-bong set. Mandy Drexler, a Halle Berry look-alike, is familiar from her breakout role as a stripper who turns her life around in the movie *Fan Dance*, which gained her an Oscar nomination. Delilah's replacement, Taylor Ramsey, who currently stars in the HBO series *Jungle Red* as the lesbian CEO of a cosmetics company, is the grown-up version of the cute, bespectacled blonde in *Tara Times Two*, while mustachioed Brent Harding still looks the same as he did when he starred in *Steele Case*, the hit nineties TV show about a Pittsburgh PI, due to the wonders of cosmetic surgery—you could bounce a quarter off his cheeks.

Brent shares the happy news that his wife is pregnant with twins as a group of us stand chatting. They had been trying for over a year before artificial insemination did the trick, he says. "All it took was pointing my swimmers in the right direction." He seems prouder of his sperm count than he does about becoming a dad. The young woman standing next to him, a spiky-haired platinum blonde wearing black velvet hip-hugger jeans and a clingy top made of shiny gold fabric, smiles in a way that seems forced. I assume she is his wife, because of the possessive way she keeps touching his arm, until I learn that Mrs. Harding is home in L.A.

Inevitably, talk turns to Delilah. I mention that I was the one who found the body, wanting to see how the others will react. It's a showstopper. There are gasps and exclamations all around. Jillian Lassiter recalls seeing me on the news. She thought I looked familiar when I first walked in, she says. Rick McVittie jokingly remarks that I could sell the movie rights. Taylor Ramsey takes the opportunity to gush about what a "huge honor" it is for her to have taken over Delilah's role in the movie. "I idolized her as a kid. I wanted to be just like her when I grew up." Never mind she and Delilah couldn't have been more than six years apart in age.

Brent Harding is the only one who seems interested in hearing the details. A little too interested. "Did you find anything besides the body? A bullet casing . . . a name scrawled in blood?"

"She was shot in the head," I remind him. "I imagine she died instantly. Besides, I never heard of a homicide where the victim wrote the killer's name in blood. I think that's only in movies."

"Maybe you saw someone fleeing the scene, then. Don't hold out on us." Brent's tone is playful, but I notice the avid gleam in his eyes behind the mask that cosmetic surgery has made of his face. He's trying to provoke a reaction. He's had too much to drink, and this is what drunks do.

"It's an ongoing investigation. I'm not at liberty to discuss what I may or may not have seen," I say to mess with his head. I hate how he reminds me of what I was like before I got sober.

After I've drifted away from others, I notice a woman around my age, slim and attractive with chestnut hair cut in a layered bob, wearing a simple black dress, sitting alone on the padded bench by the fireplace. Greta Nyland, Delilah's sister-in-law and the director of the charitable foundation, Full Bucket, established in the memory of her late brother. I recognize her from the photos on the foundation's Web site. She's in several of the pictures from Delilah's phone as well. The resemblance to her brother is striking: the same pronounced cheekbones, Roman nose, and gray-green eyes. I'm walking over to her when I run into Liam, who's headed in the same direction.

He introduces me to Greta. "As grand a girl as you'll ever meet," he says to me, draping an arm over her shoulders. "Not like our lot. Her soul hasn't withered and her heart hasn't turned black."

"And you're still full of blarney, I see." Greta smiles fondly at him.

I offer my condolences after Liam has wandered off to talk to some other people. "It still hasn't sunk in," she says, her eyes pooling with tears. "I'll go to call her, and as I'm picking up the phone . . ." She trails off, dabbing at her eyes with the handkerchief she pulls from her Coach handbag. "We were planning our next fund-raiser. Now I'm planning her memorial service."

"Have you set a date?" I ask.

"Not yet. I want to accommodate as many people as I can—they'll be coming from all over the world—and the arrangements . . . well, you can imagine. My feet have barely touched the ground since I arrived!" I recall that she flew in from New York when she got the news about Delilah.

"Let me know if there's anything I can do to help."

"Thank you. You're very kind. Will you excuse me?" she murmurs in a choked voice before hurrying off to step outside.

I follow her onto the deck, where we're alone for the moment. "I'm sorry," I say, placing a hand on her shoulder. "This must be so hard for you."

She nods, seemingly overcome with emotion. It's a moment before she regains her composure. "She was like a sister to me. We each were the only family either of us had after Eric died."

"It's like that with me and my brother. We lost both my parents."

She dabs at her eyes. "I'm afraid I handled it badly with Brianna." She looks past me through the glass slider to where Brianna stands chatting with the assistant director, David Abramowitz, a good-looking guy in his thirties, medium height with a shaved head and a diamond stud in one ear. "She's just so . . ." Greta makes a vague gesture. "I couldn't cope with it on top of everything else."

"She can be kind of . . . intense," I agree.

Greta goes on some more about Delilah, about how she couldn't have gotten through the dark days following her brother's death without her sister-in-law to lean on. They talked on the phone every day, sometimes for hours at a stretch. They kept each other from falling apart, she says. Listening to her speak of a Delilah, who'd been kind and caring, I find it hard to believe she's describing the same person who turned on Liam. It's more in keeping with the sweet, down-to-earth woman I met. Greta says her one prayer is that the murderer will be brought to justice. "Justice is cold comfort," she adds with a bleak smile, "but cold comfort is better than none."

"I just hope it's not my brother they arrest," I blurt out. She looks startled, and I explain about Howard Sedgwick's allegations, which dovetail with the DA's eagerness to name a suspect. "People can be so ignorant. Just because someone's mentally ill doesn't necessarily mean he's a threat to society!"

Greta appears sympathetic. "Detective Breedlove said they were questioning everyone who knew Delilah or who had any connection to her."

"Except none of the others left town in a hurry without telling anyone where they were going."

"That *does* put him in a bad light," she agrees.

"Believe me, I'm doing everything I can to clear his name."

She smiles. "I saw the article about you in *The Huffington Post*. 'Badass' was how the writer described you, I believe." My fifteen minutes of fame in the local news the previous summer, following the arrest of my would-be murderer who is currently awaiting trial, led to a few human-interest stories in national newspapers and magazines.

"I don't know about 'badass,' but I've been known to kick ass," I reply modestly.

"If I could have saved Eric, I would have moved heaven and earth," Greta says with quiet intensity.

Just then, I hear a low moan from the dark recesses at the other end of the deck. When I peer into the shadows, I see a couple going at it. They have their hands up each other's shirts, and their tongues down each other's throats from the looks of it. They draw apart briefly, and the light from inside falls over them. I see that it's Brent Harding and the spiky-haired blonde who is not his wife.

"Get a room," I mutter under my breath.

"I pity his poor wife," Greta says in a low voice.

After I've gone back inside, I chat with some other people and join in a chorus of 'Stardust'—Delilah's favorite oldie, I'm told—at the piano, then it's time to call it a night. I get a Coke from the bar to fuel me for the drive back to town and visit the powder room. I find Liam standing outside waiting to use it when I emerge. "I'm glad I caught you." I retrieve my Coke from the hall table where I left it and take a sip. "I didn't want to leave without saying good-bye."

"Good-bye is it?" He makes a disappointed face. "Ah, but the night is young, Tish Ballard."

I glance at my watch. "If I stay any longer, my coach will turn into a pumpkin."

"Can't let that happen." He kisses me on the cheek. He smells of expensive aftershave with a note of curry from the samosas that had been among the buffet options. "Till we meet again, love."

I find Brianna, and we go to say our good-byes. Bartosz won't hear of us leaving so soon. I explain that I have to be up early for work tomorrow. Brianna, however, is persuaded to stay the night when David, the assistant director, comes over and slips his arm around her waist. "One for the road?" Bartosz eyes me expectantly.

"I'm driving," I remind him, saying nothing of the fact that I don't drink, which I don't generally share with new acquaintances unless they're a "friend of Bill" as we say in the program.

"Let me refresh that for you, then." He relieves me of my Coke and returns with a full glass, after a trip to the bar. I don't want to be rude, so I stick around long enough to finish my drink. Then he walks me to the door, promising to have his niece back in time for work tomorrow. I can feel his thumb lightly stroking me through my dress where his hand rests against the small of my back. "Drive safely!" he calls after me. I glance back to see him standing in the doorway, his white mane making him look like a cockatoo on its perch, eyeing a tasty morsel.

CHAPTER FOURTEEN

Halfway home, I find myself becoming drowsy. I fight to remain alert as I navigate the hairpin turns of Highway One, but my eyelids only grow heavier and my movements more sluggish. At one point, I see I've strayed over the center line. I yank on the wheel, only to come close to driving off the road when I overcorrect. I slow to a near crawl, breaking into a cold sweat. Each year, this perilous stretch of highway claims more than one life. If I don't watch out, I could become another fatality.

It's weird because this is how I used to feel after a night of barhopping, and I haven't touched a drop in over four years. I know I should pull over, but where? There's only the sheer rock face on one side and the steep drop to the ocean on the other, separated from the road by a narrow shoulder, which I can barely make out in the fog that's rolled in. A thick white mist obscures the landscape and the road ahead except where the glare from my headlights forms a tunnel. Vehicles whiz past unseen in the oncoming lane, their lights blooming briefly amid the fog. This is crazy. *I have to pull over before I get killed. . . . Or kill someone.* A hysterical laugh claws its way up my throat. A head-on collision or plunge to my death—those are my two options.

The one time I had surgery, when my tonsils were taken out at the age of twelve, the anesthesiologist had me count to ten as I was going under. I'm currently at the count of five. *What's wrong with me? Am I having a stroke?* I slap my face to stay awake, and in lifting my hand from the wheel, I almost veer off the road again. I do a quick course correction, and once again miscalculate. I hear the blare of a car horn, but the sound is muffled as though I had cotton balls in my ears.

Somehow, I manage to keep all four wheels on the road as I make the next hairpin turn. I'm moving at a speed of fifteen miles per hour—any slower and I'd have to worry about someone plowing into me from behind—and I'm so scared, I'm shaking. But even with adrenaline coursing through my bloodstream, I have a hard time keeping my eyes open. When I hear the *whoop whoop* of a siren and see a lightbar flashing atop a black-and-white in my rearview mirror, I could cry with relief, which is ironic because in my drinking days I would have been freaking out.

Miraculously, the fog thins as I round the bend and I spot a turnout up ahead. I pull over and brake to a stop. I'm drenched in sweat, my dress plastered to my body beneath my coat. I hear the sound of tires crunching over the gravel behind me, followed by the slamming of a car door. Moments later when I lower my window, I'm confronted by the stern face of a CHP patrolman. He doesn't show concern or ask if I require medical attention. He doesn't request a driver's license and registration. Instead, he speaks the words that I once lived in fear of.

"Ma'am, please step out of your vehicle."

"Party's over."

Hours later, I'm woken by a different male voice as I lie dozing on a cot in the holding cell at the police station. I open my eyes to see Spence looking in through the bars wearing a stony face. He produces a set of keys and unlocks the door while I struggle into an upright position. I don't know what time it is, or whether it's day or night. My head is pounding, and my eyelids seem to have lead sinkers attached to them. I have only a fuzzy memory of what occurred after I got pulled over. I only know I flunked the field sobriety test, or I wouldn't be here. I muster my remaining faculties in a show of bravado. "Gee, and just when they were playing our song."

Spence is not amused. "Keep talking, and I might decide to book you."

"On what charge?" I say as I wobble my way into the corridor.

"Driving under the influence. Reckless endangerment. Failure to comply. Should I keep going, or is it coming back to you now?"

"I'm not drunk. I need to see a doctor."

"I was going to drive you home, but I can take you to the hospital if you'd prefer." His voice is flat.

"No, that's okay. I . . . I want to go home." I'm suddenly on the verge of tears.

Spence shrugs, unmoved. "Suit yourself." He takes hold of my arm, half supporting and half pulling me down the hallway that leads from the secure area to the bullpen. I notice the collared shirt he wears isn't tucked into his jeans all the way, as if he threw his clothes on in a hurry.

"This is what I get for sticking my neck out," he mutters.

"I told you, I wasn't drinking!"

"I thought we had an understanding," Spence says as if I hadn't spoken. "I was even starting to think I could trust you. Christ, what an idiot!" He shakes his head. "I should have known."

"Aren't you going to at least give me the benefit of the doubt?"

He comes to an abrupt halt and faces me. "The only reason you're not under arrest," he says in a tight voice, "is because I need this like a hole in the head and because the officer who brought you in is a friend of mine. Seems you were muttering my name." He regards me with disgust. "What the hell happened to you, Tish?"

I'm flooded with shame, a kneejerk response. How many times have I heard those words spoken by other people? Friends, coworkers, employers. "I-I don't know. I swear I'm not on anything."

"You expect me to believe that?"

"It's the truth! You'll see when you get the results from my blood test."

"The suspense is killing me."

We're buzzed through the door at the end of the hallway. He returns my personal items, then we're outside, where the night air is cool and clear. "All right, take me through it," he says in a calmer voice when we're in his car, turning out of the parking lot. I glance at the clock on the dashboard. It's one a.m. The buildings of the municipal complex are closed up tight, windows dark except for those of the police station.

I give him an account of my evening, not mentioning my ulterior motive for being at Bartosz's party or that I wrangled an invitation. I remind him that the director is Brianna's uncle.

"I heard you'd hired her," he remarks. "Why Brianna?"

"She was the most qualified person for the job."

"She's also a person of interest."

"Because she worked for Delilah? Please. She's no more a murderer than my brother is." Or so I keep telling myself. I can't stop thinking about the story she told me about her college roommate.

"Speaking of whom . . ."

"I have an idea of where he might be headed. I'll let you know as soon as I can confirm it."

"You do that." He cuts me a mistrustful glance.

I know I'm on thin ice, but I venture nonetheless, "In the meantime, it would help if I had my driver's license." Spence didn't return it along with my other personal items.

He gives a harsh laugh. "Nice try. You'll get it back if and when your story checks out."

"How am I supposed to get to work?"

"Not my problem."

I mutter, "You're all heart." When he doesn't respond, I try a different approach. "Listen, I know how it looks, but I swear I haven't touched a drop. And no, I didn't pick up somebody else's drink by mistake. I didn't start to feel funny until I was driving home. I was looking for a spot to pull over when your friend came along."

"You on any kind of medication?"

"No, and I got a clean bill of health at my last physical."

Spence grunts. It's obvious he still doesn't believe me.

I open my window a crack, and the cool air blowing in has a restorative effect. My head starts to clear. The car he's driving, a black Mazda sedan with a child seat in back and a pack of Wet Ones in the side pocket of the passenger door, clearly isn't an unmarked, and I'm reminded that he's a family man who is currently without a family, or at least one in which everyone is living together under one roof. I study his face in the dim glow of the dash. He looks tired. The kind of tired that doesn't come just from being pulled from bed by a phone call in the middle of the night.

"From the look of you, I'm not the only one having a rough night," I observe.

He exhales audibly. "I had the kids over earlier."

"I'm guessing it didn't go so well."

"They were fine until it was time for them to go, then Ryan threw a fit, and that set Katie off. They wouldn't get in the car, and I couldn't get them to calm down, so I had to get Barb to come over. She wasn't too happy about it. She thinks I'm using them to get back together with her."

"Was that what you were doing?"

"No."

He says no more. For a while there's just the hum of the engine. Outside, darkened streets lined with houses stream past. The night air grows cooler, and I roll up my window. "I've been sober four years," I say quietly. "That includes recreational drug use, which was never my thing. So unless someone slipped something in my Coke—" Suddenly it hits me. "That's it!" I recall setting my drink down before I went into the powder room. I ran into Liam on my way out, so that makes at least one person who had the opportunity; Bartosz was another—he handed me a fresh glass of Coke as I was leaving the party. "I was drugged. It's the only explanation."

"You seriously expect me to believe that?" Spence speaks in the same tone I do with my brother whenever he tries to convince me he's being followed by CIA spooks or that he picked up alien transmissions from outer space.

"Don't you see? It makes sense," I insist.

"Why would anyone want to drug you?"

"I don't know. Date rape? Bartosz was hitting on me. He could have roofied me."

Spence shakes his head. "You'd be out cold. Also, you'd be with him and not me."

"Okay, so I wasn't roofied. But someone did *something*, unless I'm suffering the effects of a stroke."

"You wouldn't still be talking if you'd had a stroke," he notes drily.

When we arrive at my house, my nerves are shot. The homes on Seabright Avenue were built in an era when people didn't always lock their doors and a dog was the only security that was needed, and even in this day and age, it's a safe neighborhood for the most part, but I'm on edge nonetheless. I'm thinking that the murderer might have broken into my house if it's the same person who drugged me. Did I remember to set the alarm? I muster my courage to leave the safety of the car. I have one foot out the door when I feel Spence's hand close over my wrist.

"Wait. I don't want you going in alone."

I nod wordlessly, grateful. He's not such a bad guy, I'm realizing. He only let me out of jail because it suited his purposes, but at least he doesn't want me to be murdered in my own bed.

It turns out I remembered to set the alarm. But Spence has a look around anyway, as I imagine he does when he has to reassure his children that there are no bogeymen in the closets or under the beds. "All clear," he calls from the back of the house while I stand in the kitchen with my heart racing.

"Do you want some coffee?" I ask when he rejoins me. I'm surprised when he accepts. He's not one to consort with the criminal element, so he must have decided to give me the benefit of the doubt.

"I didn't know you had a dog," he says when we're seated at the kitchen table with our coffees, Prince at my feet, looking up at me expectantly. If he thinks I'm walking him at this hour with a murderer on the loose, he's got another think coming. He'll have to make do with the backyard.

"He's not mine. Remember when I told you that Delilah's dog was lost?"

"Yeah. Now that you mention it."

"Well, he was found and now he's with me. At least until Brianna can find him another home."

Spence reaches down to scratch the Yorkie behind his ears. "Cute little guy. What's his name?"

"Prince. After Prince Harry. Seems he was a gift from His Royal Highness."

Spence smiles. "Every girl deserves a prince."

"Yeah, except I want one who's taller and doesn't slobber when he kisses." Spence smiles, and I feel my cheeks warm, remembering when I was in ninth grade and thought I'd die of happiness if he were to kiss me.

"My kids are after me to get a dog. Their mom is allergic, and they're hoping Dad will come through."

"If only to show there are some benefits to divorce."

He chuckles knowingly. I toy with the idea of asking him if he'd like to take Prince off my hands, but for some reason I'm reluctant to do so.

It's weird to have Spence seated opposite me at my red dinette, his large frame—his very maleness—seeming to fill the space I think of as mine alone. Even weirder, it doesn't feel wrong. It feels . . .

companionable. He doesn't seem as stressed as he was earlier, and I'm feeling more relaxed as well, sleepy as opposed to whacked out. Coffee and conversation—sometimes it's the little things that make all the difference. He finishes his coffee and rises to his feet.

"I should get going," he says. "And you should get some sleep." I walk him out, and he pauses to nod toward the alarm console by the door. "Do you always set that before you go to bed?"

"I will from now on," I vow.

CHAPTER FIFTEEN

I wake to daylight peeking through the blinds the next morning. Odder still, Hercules and Prince are both curled asleep on the crocheted afghan that's folded across the foot of the bed. I must be dreaming if I'm still in bed at this hour and my cat is sleeping with the enemy. Then I remember about last night. I let out a groan, at which my cat cracks his eyes open and slinks over to curl up next to me, purring. We're soon joined by Prince, tail wagging as he noses under my other armpit. "What is it with you guys? Were you watching the Disney channel while I was out? Is this group-hug time?" Hercules looks at me with his inscrutable yellow eyes, while Prince licks my cheek.

I get out of bed and head for the bathroom, where I fill a glass with water and down four Tylenol before shuffling down the hall to the kitchen to pour myself some coffee. I carry my mug to the table, where I sit down to phone Ivy. "You'll never guess what happened last night. . . ."

"Thank God you're all right. You could've been killed!" she cries after I've described my close call.

"I don't know who drugged me, but I'm pretty sure that was his or her intention." I pull my bathrobe around me, feeling chilled even with my coffee mug warming my hands. "Unless it was to warn me."

"Warn you against what?"

"That if I don't mind my own business, he won't stop at drugging me next time."

"Why would they see you as a threat?"

"I don't know. But I know one thing: Whoever murdered Delilah was at last night's party."

"Sure seems that way. Any idea who it could have been?"

"Liam Brady for one."

"I thought you liked him." Ivy sounds surprised.

"I do. But he had the opportunity. I put my drink down to use the bathroom before I left, and guess who was standing there when I came out? Also, Brianna says she overheard him and Delilah arguing a few days before she was murdered. Apparently, Delilah was threatening to expose him."

"Expose him for what?"

"That I don't know." I sip my coffee, staring thoughtfully out the window that looks out on my backyard, where my cat is currently on the prowl, searching for mice or moles to slaughter.

"Anyone else strike you as suspicious?"

"Brent Harding." I recount my conversation with him, in which he pressed for details about what I'd seen. Like a murderer would if he thought I might know something that could place him at the crime scene. "Bartosz was another one." I recall the director's parting words. *Drive safely.* His idea of a private joke? "I told him I'd seen him at Casa Linda Estates the day of the murder. I didn't say where exactly. If he killed Delilah, he might think I was driving past the house when he was coming out. In which case, I would know he was lying when he told me he left without seeing Delilah."

"Yes, and so would the police."

"Not if I had withheld the information from the police. Like, say, if I was planning to blackmail Bartosz. Or I was looking to crack the case so I could hog all the glory." My words are met with silence at the other end. "Please tell me you *know* I would never do either of those things!"

"I know you wouldn't stoop to blackmail."

"Nor would I withhold information that would keep a murderer from being locked up."

"I know that, too," Ivy says belatedly. "You've done some sneaky, low-down things, but that would be a new low even for you." I hear the sound of the teakettle whistling at her end. "Okay, so we have a motive. Did Bartosz have the opportunity? You know. To slip you a Mickey."

"'*Slip me a Mickey?*' You watch too many old movies. Roofied is more like it." I tell her about Bartosz getting me a refill of my Coke. "Though I'd have been out cold if I'd been roofied, according to Spence."

"What does he think happened?"

"What it looked like," I reply glumly. "But he's giving me the benefit of the doubt."

"That's big of him." I hear the smile in Ivy's voice.

"He's not such a bad guy," I'm forced to admit. "Who knew?"

"Does this mean you're starting to like him?"

"I'm not answering that until he decides to give me back my driver's license."

"No driver's license?" Ivy groans in sympathy. "This is bad."

"You're telling me. I have no way to get to work."

"No, but you have Brianna."

I brighten at the reminder. "Is she there?"

"She just walked in."

An hour later, the three of us are headed up the coast in Ivy's orange VW bug to retrieve my Explorer. It's a beautiful day, clear and breezy. Seals bask on the rocks at Año Nuevo, and glassy swells heave out at sea, gulls wheeling lazily in the sky above.

"It's a blessing in disguise," Brianna pronounces. She's riding in the backseat, while I sit up front with Ivy. "If that cop hadn't pulled you over, you could have gotten into an accident, or driven over a cliff."

"Don't remind me." I suppress a shudder.

"What I don't get is *why*. I mean, it's not as if you'd been drinking." My temp assistant looks remarkably chipper for someone who has been up half the night partying. She wears khakis and a navy-and-white cotton sweater with a nautical motif. I, on the other hand, look like the wreck of *Hesperus* in the jeans and wrinkled purple Henley that I'd pulled from my laundry basket.

"I guess I was more tired than I realized." Ivy and I exchange look. I didn't tell Brianna the whole story. I don't know if I can trust her not to blab, and my celebrity access would dry up in an instant if her uncle knew I suspected him of having drugged me. I need answers, which means further digging is required. There's plenty of dirt under the red carpet, from what I've seen so far.

"What was it like meeting all those famous people?" Ivy comes to my rescue.

"Surreal," I answer. "It's the land where no one ever gets old and no woman is larger than a size two. They don't even sound like us. It was like being in a play and I was the only who didn't know my lines."

"I warned you they weren't like other people," Brianna says.

"No, but most of them were nice. They didn't treat me like I was a nobody. And I enjoyed meeting your uncle. He's quite the character." *Even if he's a murderer.*

"Well, you certainly made an impression on him." Brianna's tone is one of dry amusement. Because she knows it wasn't my sparkling wit that won him over as much as my blond hair and bra size. "I arranged for us to visit the set tomorrow morning if that's okay with you."

"Sounds like a plan." It will mean putting in a long workday tomorrow, but I have more pressing concerns than my

livelihood right now. Such as staying alive. And keeping my
brother out of jail.

When we arrive at the spot where I was pulled over last night,
near Bean Hollow state park, I'm relieved to see my Explorer still
parked where I left it. Abandoned alongside the highway, it's the
vehicular equivalent of the walk of shame, but at least it wasn't
towed (another favor for which I'll owe Spence?). I get in the passenger side while Brianna climbs in behind the wheel, and we
wave good-bye to Ivy. "Did you have a good time last night?" I ask
as we head back to town.

"Better than I expected." Brianna hadn't been keen on going to
the party. She said she'd had her fill of "Hollyweird" working for
Delilah and hanging around her uncle as a kid.

"Would that be because of a certain assistant director?" I hint.

"David?" She laughs. "He's nice, but he's also gay."

"Really. I wouldn't have guessed." I'm reminded of our conversation yesterday about gay actors who'd be ruined if their
private lives were to become public knowledge. I wonder again
about Liam, recalling the comment he made about how actors
disguise their true selves. Did he have a secret life? One that
could turn beefcake into box-office poison and cost him millions
in lost income if TMZ were to get wind? The threat of exposure
would provide a powerful motive for murder.

Conversation turns to my brother. Brianna received a call from
another motel manager earlier that morning. He reported that a
couple who fit the descriptions of Arthur and Gladys had stayed
the night at his motel in Pocatello, Idaho, which is on the route
to Bozeman, Montana. It would seem the lovebirds are headed
for Gladys's granddaughter's ranch, in Bozeman, and not honey-
mooning in Vegas. I can only pray they didn't get hitched along the
way and that I won't have to spend Thanksgivings with Howard
Sedgwick in the future. I call Lexie on the drive back to town and

give her the heads-up. She seems relieved and promises to let me know if and when they turn up.

The first stop when Brianna and I arrive back in town is the Voakses' Spanish colonial. I picked up a fresh supply of ant traps, but I'm more worried about Brianna than I am about whether the ants had retaken Hamburger Hill. This sort of work isn't in her job description and she might see it as beneath her. By the time I've climbed from my SUV, however, she's already halfway up the front walk, rolling up her sleeves as she goes. I hurry to catch up and hand her the bag of supplies.

"How are you with ants?"

She grins. "Death."

It seems no job is too dirty or disgusting for Brianna. She pulls clumps of hair from shower drains, empties mousetraps, and scrapes crud from filters as we go from one property to the next. She sprays Raid like it's air freshener and fearlessly knocks a black widow spider's nest from an eave with a broom handle. The only time she wrinkles her nose is when she finds a used condom under a bed at the Millers' place. "Too much information," she mutters as she deposits it in the trash can.

I notice a change in her demeanor as soon as we arrive at Casa Linda Estates. As we pass through the gates, where offerings from Delilah's fans—bouquets of flowers, candles, stuffed animals—form a small avalanche, Brianna falls silent. When we get to the house, she doesn't get out; she grips the steering wheel as if we were moving at a high speed and not parked in a driveway. Her face is pale. Officially, Casa Blanca is no longer a crime scene, but to her it always will be.

"Do the owners plan to sell?" I detect a slight tremor in her voice when she speaks.

"They might have to if bookings don't pick up." The Blanken-ships were horrified when they learned of the murder, and though they seemed more concerned about the victim and the trauma I'd suffered than any losses they sustained, the fact remains that this is an income property.

"What about all those people who emailed you?" Brianna refers to the recent flood of inquiries that have come in through VRBO and FlipKey, the two online sites on which the house is listed.

"Ghouls." I got the impression they were more interested in seeing the place where Delilah Ward had died than enjoying the ocean views. One person asked which room the body was found in.

Brianna shudders visibly.

"Why don't you wait here," I say gently. "I won't be long." She nods without speaking, and I go in alone. I'm pretty creeped out myself, and I don't linger once I'm inside. I stay only long enough to see that Esmeralda has been in to clean and to make sure there are no leaks, ants, or mice droppings.

We head over to the Russos next, where I'm relieved to see no evidence of dubious activities. No guns or dead bodies lying around. I mention the photo of Russo and Delilah that I saw on the wall in Russo's den, but Brianna only shrugs and says, "They all wanted their picture taken with her."

Our last stop is the Chens' split-level, where I give Brianna the job of watering the houseplants while I feed the koi in the pond. Afterward, I do my walk-through, pausing on my way out to rub the belly of the marble Buddha that sits on the carved rosewood console in the entryway for luck. By 5:30, we're headed back to my place. Normally, my workday doesn't end until after dark, but despite the late start we got, we finished early. For which I have Brianna to thank.

"And I thought *I* was a hard worker," I comment.

"Sometimes it pays to be a clean freak," she replies, blushing at the praise.

"Most women would freak out at finding a half-dead mouse in a trap."

"Believe me, it was nothing compared to some of the stuff Delilah had me do."

"Like what?" I'm curious.

"Well, for one thing, she'd have me book interviews with journalists and then not show, and the person would scream at me like it was my fault. It wasn't just once in a while, either. It was constant."

"That's pretty bad," I agree.

"Also, to say she was high maintenance is putting it mildly. This one time? She had me standing on the tarmac at LAX for an hour while her manager tried to coax her onto the private jet that was waiting to take her to Cannes. She'd decided at the last minute she couldn't possibly go. Why? Because she'd gained a few pounds and the gown she'd planned to wear was a little snug."

"Did she end up going?"

"Of course. Like I knew she would."

"Why didn't you quit if she was so impossible?"

"I came close. But in the end, I couldn't. She needed me."

"More than you needed her from what you're telling me."

"There were compensations. The gown, for instance. A Valentino. She gave it to me after she got back from Cannes."

"Sweet."

"She could be extremely generous. You never knew which Delilah you were going to get from one day to the next. It used to drive me crazy, but I can't say my job was ever boring."

"Kind of like this one?"

She grins. "Minus the bug spray."

After she drops me off at my house, taking the Explorer with her to Ivy's so I won't be tempted to drive without a license (she thinks of everything, that girl), I walk the dog, then shower and change into my sweats. Supper is canned tomato soup and a grilled cheese sandwich. I watch TV, my cat curled on one side of me and the dog on the other, until it's time for my Skype date with Bradley. I'm struggling to stay awake when I log on at midnight.

Bradley looks even more ragged than I do, and it's only 8:30 in the morning where he is. Disheveled, with smudges under his eyes that aren't dirt. He explains that he's in a yellow zone near the Pakistan border where IEDs and sniper fire have everyone on edge. I'm worried for his safety, but I'm also worried about my own. After I tell him about what happened last night, he shakes his head in disbelief. "Tish, only you could make a combat zone seem like a walk in the park."

My nerves frayed, I find myself snapping at him. "It's not like I asked for it. If it weren't for my crazy brother, I would have been home instead of getting drugged at a party. I wouldn't have a killer after me!" In the military there's a term for it: FUBAR—Fucked Up Beyond All Recognition.

Bradley's face creases in sympathy and he reaches out as if to touch me. It's moments like this I feel every mile that separates us. "I'm sorry, babe. I wish you didn't have to go through this alone."

"I'm not alone. I have Ivy and McGee and—" I stop myself before I can say Spence's name. "Never mind. What's that noise?" I can hear muffled explosions in the background.

"Mortar shells," he informs me, grim faced, then turns to speak briefly to another man who entered the room just then. "Babe, I'm sorry, but I'm going to have to cut this short. We're being evacuated."

"Be safe," I tell him as I always do.

"You too," he says, and the screen goes dark.

You know how you know that a situation is fucked up beyond all recognition? When you're thinking you might not have a future with your boyfriend because one of you will soon be dead.

CHAPTER SIXTEEN

Brianna arrives early the next morning, just as I'm returning from walking the dog. I unclip his leash and he dashes to greet her, jumping up and down, doing his bouncy-castle thing. "Looks like he's found himself a home," she says as she bends down to pet him.

"He's not staying," I reply gruffly.

"They seem to be getting along." She watches as my cat emerges from the living room to pad toward us.

"Stockholm syndrome."

"Well, if you decide to keep him . . ."

"I won't."

The truth is I've grown fond of the little guy. I scratch behind his ears before giving him a rawhide bone to chew. I've taught him to use the cat door for when he needs to go out, and he and my cat seem to have arrived at an understanding. As long as Prince steers clear of Hercules, he's permitted to roam freely. "Be good," I call to my cat nonetheless as I'm headed out the door.

I climb into my Explorer, ready to visit the movie set, and am pleased to see Ivy sitting in the backseat. I'd asked her to join us— Brianna's uncle said she could bring as many guests as she liked— but Ivy hadn't been sure she could get the time off work. "Parker practically pushed me out the door," she reports. "He wants me to text him from the set." Parker Lane, her boss and the owner of the

Gilded Lily, is celebrity obsessed. For him, the Holy Trinity is Barbra, Bette, and Cher.

"Text him photos, you mean."

"But of course," she replies in a phony French accent.

Brianna starts the engine. She's dressed in a fitted herringbone blazer over a striped blouse, a camel A-line skirt belted in faux alligator the same tobacco shade as her calf-length boots. I wonder if I should have worn something nicer than the jeans and ribbed turtleneck I have on. I'm reassured when I see Ivy's Dr. Martens peeking from under the long skirt that covers her ankles.

After stopping at the Bluejay Café for coffee and muffins, we head into the hills northeast of town to pick up McGee, who will act as my eyes and ears. When we arrive at the self-storage facility where he's resident manager, we find him smoking a cigarette outside the office below his living quarters. He's been trying to quit and claims he's down to two a day. He drops the cigarette he's smoking and grinds it out with his shoe before climbing in back. "I didn't inhale," he says with a grin when I raise my eyebrows at him.

"What's with the *Miami Vice* look?" I pass him a coffee and the bag with the last of the muffins. Instead of his uniform, he wears off-white chinos and a cream linen blazer over a Hawaiian shirt.

"When in Rome." He pries the lid from his coffee. "And no, I'm not packing." Forewarned about the tight security on the set, I told him to leave his gun at home. "What you have here, Ballard, is a lean, mean fighting machine. Anyone fucks with you girls, he'll be on the ground before he sees me coming."

"Who are you calling 'girl'?" Ivy lightly punches his arm.

He smirks at her. "Would you prefer 'little lady'?"

"You're disgusting."

"Kids, behave yourselves," I call back from the front seat.

On the drive up the coast, Brianna instructs us in the manners and mores of La-La Land. "Don't expect them to remember you from the party," she tells me. "They won't. Even if you had a deep and meaningful conversation with them. Even if they had their tongues down your throat."

Even if they drugged me? I don't voice the thought. I haven't decided whether I can trust Brianna not to blab to her uncle. Instead, I groan and say, "Please. I just ate."

"There are exceptions, of course," she goes on. "But as a rule, unless you're making them money or you can offer them a part, or you're one of them, they have no use for you." I flash on Brent Harding making out with the spiky-haired blonde who is not his wife. If he forgets he had his tongue down her throat, he'd be doing her a favor. "My friend Anna? She hooked up with this guy at a party, one of the actors on the TV show where she works. When she ran into him on the set the next day, he acted like he didn't know her. Anna thought he was just blowing her off, but it turned out he really didn't remember her. Why should he? She's just a lowly production assistant."

"That's harsh," comments Ivy.

"Was he drunk when they hooked up?" I ask.

"Is your friend hot?" asks McGee.

Brianna replies, "No, he wasn't drunk. And as for my friend, that's totally beside the point."

"Not if you're a guy," says McGee, unrepentant.

Brianna picks up speed to pass a VW Bug plastered with political bumper stickers, then doesn't slow down. I find myself stepping on the invisible brake at my feet, still on edge after my close call the other night. It's a foggy morning and visibility is poor, the lighthouse up ahead a sketchy outline amid the fog. I ask about Brent Harding. "Does his wife know he's cheating on her?"

Brianna shrugs. "Probably, if she's like most Hollywood wives. They turn a blind eye as long as it's not too blatant because they know what it would mean if they got divorced."

"What?"

"They'd lose the perks that come with being Mrs. So-and-So—the invitations to A-list parties, the red carpet events, the prime tables in hot restaurants, and the courtside seats at Lakers games."

"I would think she'd be more worried about being a single mom," I say.

"With what she'd be getting in child support, she could hire a nanny, but that's not what matters. In La-La Land, it's all about status. If she's like the others, she's scared of becoming a nobody."

"She wouldn't be a nobody. She'd just be who she was before she became Mrs. Harding."

"Olivia Harding was a cocktail waitress when she and Brent met."

"Something wrong with that?" Ivy pipes up from the backseat, sounding defensive. Occasionally, she gets customers at the Gilded Lily who don't know that she is an artist and treat her as a mere shopgirl.

"Not at all," says Brianna. "Except it was a gentlemen's club. Need I say more?"

We turn off the highway fifteen minutes later, heading east toward Salema. The fog thins as we travel inland, and I see the morning sun peeking above the hilltops in the distance. Day laborers toil in the artichoke fields, but when we get to the village, the storefronts along the main drag are shuttered except for the coffee shop. Soon, we're in deep countryside, where we see more cows than people. We turn onto an unpaved road, where we're stopped at a checkpoint half a mile or so down. I recognize the guy who asks for our IDs as the bull-necked security guard from the other night. We're waved through after he sees that we're on his list. There's another checkpoint when we arrive at the set, where a security guard waves a metal-detector wand over us while another guard circles my SUV with his bomb-sniffing dog. Finally we're free to enter the parking area.

The set is spread over roughly three acres, a minimetropolis plunked down in the middle of nowhere in which monster trailers serve as offices and the landscape is composed of cameras and equipment, banks of computers, standing lights, and props. Thick electrical cords snake over the ground. Crew members are either rushing around or busy at some task. A three-sided log house ringed with lights and cameras stands at the center. As we walk alongside a row of trailers, I quickly notice a pecking order. Each is assigned to a different actor, I see from the names taped to the doors, with the largest belonging to the biggest names. Liam Brady's, not surprisingly, is the granddaddy of them all. By chance, he emerges, bare chested and wearing jeans, as we're passing by.

"Tish Ballard, as I live and breathe," he greets me, slathering on the Irish brogue. His cobalt eyes crinkle with good humor. "If I didn't know better, I might think you were stalking me."

I smile. "That would be a first—stalking by invitation." As he stands before me in all his glory, his ugly-handsome face gilded by the morning light, it doesn't seem possible that he could be a killer.

"My uncle's invitation," Brianna chimes in.

After Brianna has made the introductions, Liam invites us in for coffee. "You won't want to be drinking that swill." He nods toward the catering truck where coffee urns and steam trays sit on the long tables that have been set up outside. McGee and Brianna decline the invitation and head off in different directions, Brianna to look for her uncle, McGee to visit with his brethren, in this case the men in black, most of whom are retired cops. Ivy and I follow Liam into the trailer.

I step into a seating area that's more spacious than my living room. It opens onto a small but well-appointed kitchen at one end that has a fancy espresso maker like the one I bought for Delilah's use. The aroma of fresh-brewed coffee permeates the air. Liam motions for us to have a seat, then goes in back, returning a minute later wearing a chambray shirt. Except he's left it unbuttoned, so I'm still finding it hard not to stare—you could tenderize a steak with those abs.

"Black as the devil's heart," he says as he serves us espresso in dainty porcelain cups with slivers of orange rind.

"And you had me at hello." I bat my eyes at him. But my attempt to flirt with him fails to get a reaction. Either I'm not his type, or he's playing for the other team. He seems charmed by Ivy, however.

"You remind me of a girl I knew in Ireland," he says, sitting down next to her. "Megan O'Reilly was her name. Raven curls and blue eyes like yours. Had all the boys eating out of her hand."

Ivy looks more amused than flattered. She's used to having men flirt with her. "That must be why Irishmen have silver tongues," she says, and he throws his head back with a roar of laughter.

Talk turns to Delilah, after Ivy has expressed her sympathies. "She was a complicated creature," Liam says. "Smart with money and a fool with men. She could be hard at times, and gentle as a mother's touch at others. If she loved you, you got all of her. But you didn't want to be on her bad side."

"I wonder if she was killed by a friend who felt betrayed . . . or who she'd threatened to betray." I hint at the fight Liam allegedly had with Delilah. "Do you know if she had a falling out with anyone?"

Liam gives me a sharp look. "What makes you think it was one of us?"

Someone tried to kill me the night before last. "Usually it's someone the victim knew." I keep it vague.

We're interrupted by a knock on the door. A bearded young man pokes his head in to announce, "They're ready for you in makeup, Mr. Brady."

We follow Liam outside. "Stick around and you can watch them film my scene," he says as he's leaving us. "Try not to get too excited, though. Can't have you passing out from the sheer thrill of it."

I don't understand what he means by that until Brianna explains, when we catch up to her over by the catering truck where she's eating scrambled eggs and bacon from a paper plate, "They do a million takes, and there's usually a long wait in between. Seriously, it's like watching paint dry."

Ivy says to me, "Don't tell Parker. I don't want to burst his bubble."

"Did you find your uncle?" I ask Brianna.

She points to where Bartosz is conferring with the assistant director over by the trailer that appears to be his office. "I spoke with him already, so he knows we're here. I was just getting a bite to eat while I waited for you guys." She grabs my arm, whispering, "He said he wanted to talk to you about something. He's probably going to ask you out, so be prepared."

"Thanks for the warning," I reply, my stomach doing a flip.

As we head in that direction, we pass redheaded Jillian Lassiter, her braless boobs bouncing in the sweater she wears. Brianna murmurs, "She's slept with everything that moves and some that don't." She points out a baldheaded man, ancient but ambulatory. "He's the reason she has a career."

"Who is he?" Ivy asks.

"Werner Baumgarten. Head of the production company."

We run into Brent Harding, who appears even more bizarrely well preserved in the light of day than he had the other night at the party. His face is waxy where it's stretched taut and his eyes are tipped at the corners. I wonder if he uses Grecian Formula on his mustache as well as his hair; both are a shade of brown that I associate with mink coats. He seems to recognize me but not in a good way. As he and Brianna stand chatting, I notice he keeps glancing over at me as though I'm making him uncomfortable. Maybe he remembers seeing me on the deck at the party and he's wondering if I snapped a picture of him making out with the blonde who isn't his wife.

Bartosz greets us warmly when we finally reach him. Once again, I'm struck by the air of power he exudes. He's several inches shorter than me, but I'm scarcely aware of the difference in our heights. In the safari shirt he wears, with his snowy cockatoo's crest and thick, black eyebrows, he seems a throwback to the Golden Era of Hollywood. "Bree tells me you ran into some trouble on your way home the other night," he says to me after we've exchanged pleasantries and Brianna has dragged Ivy over to meet David. "I'm delighted to see you're still in one piece."

"It wasn't that big a deal." I figure if Bartosz was the one who drugged me, it's best he not know that he nearly succeeded in killing me. "I was pulled over, but the cop let me off with a warning." It's not the whole truth, but it's not a lie exactly. "Brianna said there was something you wanted to speak to me about. What can I do for you?"

"Ah yes." The older man's look of concern gives way to a smile. "I was hoping you could recommend a restaurant for a dinner party I'm hosting next week. One with a private dining room."

"The Shady Brook Inn," I reply without hesitation. "It's the only one in town with two Michelin stars, and it has more than one private dining room. They're usually booked pretty far in advance, but I'm friendly with the owner, so if you want, I can call and see if he can fit you in."

"Please. I'll have my assistant email you the particulars. Oh, and I insist you come as my guest."

"I'd love to. Will your wife be joining us?" I didn't even know he had a wife until Brianna told me. I'd never seen her with Bartosz in any of the photos of him at awards ceremonies and various A-list events. Apparently, she's a zoologist who studies elephants in Southeast Asia.

"Sadly no. Edith is in Thailand for the summer." His regret seems genuine.

Bartosz assigns one of his lackeys to us, and then he and his assistant director head over to the three-sided log house, where the actors have gathered and the crew is busy setting up for the shoot. We settle in our canvas chairs with the bottles of Evian the production assistant brought us, then a voice calls "Roll sound!" and seconds later "Roll cameras!" The scene we're watching is between Liam Brady and his costar, Taylor Ramsey, who play the parts of the newlyweds in *Devil's Slide*. I'm amazed by how natural they seem. Apparently oblivious to the lights and cameras that surround them, they share a passionate kiss, one that involves tongue, I can reliably report. Taylor is working hard to shed her squeaky-clean image from when she was a Disney star.

I'm less enthralled after sitting through multiple takes. Brianna wasn't exaggerating when she warned us that filming could be tedious. There's an interminable wait between each take while the director and his AD confer with the actors and each other, the set stylist takes photos that are used to ensure every detail of the set looks exactly the same from take to take, and the actors get their hair and makeup touched up. I'm standing to stretch my legs when I hear a door bang shut over by the trailers. I turn to see a tall, brunette woman exiting Brent Harding's trailer in a hurry. I'm guessing the woman is his wife because she's hugely pregnant. She appears upset.

I follow as she moves toward the parking area. "Excuse me?" I call after her. The ground over which she's waddling at a fast pace is pocked with gopher holes, and with her big belly and the high-heeled ankle boots she's wearing, I'm worried she'll fall and hurt herself. She comes to a halt at the sound of my voice and turns to face me.

"Are you fucking him, too?" she snarls.

CHAPTER SEVENTEEN

I stare at the pregnant woman in surprise while she glares back at me, sparks of sunlight shooting from the enormous sunglasses she wears. Finally, I find my voice. "Um. No? I just thought . . . I saw you leaving and you looked like you could use some help. Are you all right?"

"Do I look all right?" she chokes out.

"You look pregnant, actually."

"You noticed, huh? More than I can say for my husband."

"Hi, I'm Tish Ballard." I step forward, extending my hand, from which she recoils, as if it were a petition I had thrust at her to sign, before she finally takes it. "And you must be Mrs. Harding."

"That would be me." She laughs mirthlessly. "Brent doesn't know I'm here. I was going to surprise him. But the surprise was on me instead." With that, she bursts into tears.

I take her arm. "Let me help you to your car. Where are you parked?" She leans into me, weeping silently. When we get to the parking lot, she can't find her rental car, she's so distraught. Finally, I think to thumb the key fob, and we follow the flash of lights to a white VW Passat. I get her settled in the driver's seat, then dart around to jump in the passenger side before she can drive away.

Her weeping subsides at last and she reaches into her Louis Vuitton shoulder bag and pulls out her phone. "I found this in his trailer." She shows me a text she forwarded from Brent's phone. A selfie of the spiky-haired blonde wearing a saucy smile and little else. The message reads, *Sneak preview of what ur getting tonite.* The blonde's name is Tara.

I can't think of anything to say. The image says it all.

"I should have known," she says. "I was the other woman when he was married to his first wife. A leopard doesn't change its spots, right? Back then I was the hot babe. Now look at me."

"You're still beautiful." I'm not just saying it to make her feel better. She's gorgeous even with her face blotchy from crying. She'd taken off her sunglasses, revealing hazel eyes fringed with dark lashes. Tawny hair falls in loose curls over her shoulders, and her cheekbones could cut glass. She's also at least half her husband's age, which has to be around sixty, given that Brent was in his early thirties when he starred in *Steele Case.*

Mrs. Harding waves away the compliment. "My friends tried to warn me. They said he'd do the same to me, but I thought I was special. That he loved me too much to ever cheat on me."

"I'm sure he does." I don't know that for a fact. It's just what women say to each other.

"No. They were right. He's a dog. And I'm fat and ugly." She starts to cry again.

I do my best to comfort her. "You're not ugly, and you won't be fat much longer. And just think, pretty soon you'll be a mom. How awesome is that? Congratulations, by the way. I hear it's twins."

My words seem to have a calming effect. She gives me a watery smile as she strokes the mound of her belly. "I always wanted to be a mom." Then, as if realizing belatedly that she was baring her soul to a perfect stranger, she says, "My name's Olivia. What did you say yours was?"

"Tish Ballard. And if it means anything, I'm sorry. You're right, it sucks."

"Please tell me you're not having sex with him," she says plaintively.

"God, no." I bite my tongue before I add that I find Brent repulsive. "I don't do married men."

"You're a better person than me, then."

"No, I'm not. I've made my share of mistakes. That just didn't happen to be one of them."

"Some would say I got what I deserved."

"You can't think that way."

Olivia stares sightlessly ahead as she continues to stroke her belly. "She's not the first."

"Oh?" It comes as no shock to learn that Brent Harding was fooling around with someone else—or more than one woman—before spiky-haired Tara, but for Olivia's sake, I act surprised.

"He swore there was nothing going on between them, that they were just friends. And like an idiot, I believed him. The whole time we were trying to get pregnant, he was fucking *her*."

"Who are we talking about?"

"Delilah." She spits out the name, bringing her gaze back to me. Now I am shocked. Delilah and Brent? Ugh. "When they were filming that picture together in London? I flew in one weekend and noticed they seemed awfully chummy. He claimed he was helping her through a rough patch. It was right after Eric died when she was Jackie fucking Onassis. What could I say?"

"Maybe he was telling the truth." *What about Prince Harry? And why Brent if she could have His Royal Highness?*

"Well, she's dead now so we'll never know, will we?" Olivia slips her sunglasses back on, but not before I see the blaze of hatred in her swollen eyes. "Maybe she got what she deserved, too."

I rejoin the others after I've seen Olivia Harding off. We're given a tour of the set, followed by lunch with the cast and crew. It's 12:30 by the time we leave. I quiz Brianna on the drive back to town.

"Why didn't you say something?" I ask, annoyed that she didn't tell me about Delilah's affair with Brent.

She replies, with a shrug. "It was just a fling. It didn't mean anything."

"Hello. Your former employer was murdered! You don't think the fact that she was sleeping with a married man might've had something to do with it? His wife seemed pretty angry about it."

We pass a bicyclist, a young man in a helmet and blue Lycra bike shorts, pedaling alongside the highway. I notice that Brianna doesn't cut a wide berth like you're supposed to. The bicyclist veers onto the shoulder as we whiz by, wobbling a bit on his bike as if blown by the back draft. "I'm surprised she found out," Brianna remarks. "The affair was over by the time the film wrapped."

"Would this be when Delilah was doing Prince Harry?"

"I told you . . ."

"Right. Like I believe she spent the weekend with Britain's most eligible bachelor and they didn't have sex." Brianna's ensuing silence tells me I'm not wrong. What else has she lied about?

"Delilah was doing Prince Harry?" Ivy pipes up excitedly from the backseat.

"It would appear so," I reply.

"The thing with Brent . . ." Brianna begins. "They'd known each other forever. Eric was the stuntman for one of Brent's pictures, and he and Brent became friendly. The three of them used to pal around together. After Eric died . . . I think Brent kept his memory alive for Delilah."

"Who ended it?"

"Neither, as I recall. It simply ran its course. No hard feelings."

"Yeah, except now she's dead."

"It's not as if Brent killed her," Brianna says dismissively.

"We don't know that," rumbles McGee from the backseat.

I recall the murderous look in Olivia's eyes. "Maybe it was his wife." I tell them about the angry woman caller who left a message with Esmeralda in the days before Delilah was shot. "If it was

Olivia Harding, she could have followed up with a surprise visit."
And paid her respects with a bullet.

"Didn't you say she just got here?" Ivy asks.

"That's what she said, but for all we know, she's been in town all this time." Olivia could have traveled here by car, so her name wouldn't appear on a passenger manifest, then swapped her own vehicle for a rental car. "If she wore a disguise and stayed at a motel under an assumed name . . ."

"Please." Brianna still isn't buying it. "The affair was months ago, and from what Olivia told you, she didn't just find out about it. Why wait all this time to kill Delilah?"

"They were doing another picture together. It must have made Olivia crazy thinking of them on location together. Plus, she's hormonal. I know how I get when I'm PMSing. I could totally kill someone."

"She didn't snap in the heat of the moment. This was carefully planned and executed," Ivy points out.

"The cops are thinking it was a professional hit," McGee agrees.

"I still don't see it," Brianna says, shaking her head. "A jealous wife goes after her ex with a baseball bat or runs him over with her car. She doesn't hire a hit man."

"She would if she was a sociopath." I turn to McGee. "Could you have one of your people do a background check?" By "people" I mean his vast, extended family back east, most of whom are in law enforcement. "See if Mrs. Harding has a criminal record or a psychiatric history."

"I'm on it," he says, pulling out his phone. "I'll see what I can dig up on Casanova, too."

I smile. "Casanova, huh?"

He explains that Casanova is the code name given to Brent Harding by the security detail on the set, information he gleaned from the guard he'd chatted up, a retired cop named Jimmy O'Rourke. "Standard operating procedure with VIPs. Like with the Secret Service, only this ain't POTUS and FLOTUS. Seems Harding's got his you-know-what in more than one honey pot."

"I would have thought Brent's stud-muffin days were over," Ivy says with a sniff.

"The thinking is that he must have a big—"

I groan. "Please. Spare us."

"—supply of Viagra. Get your mind out of the gutter, Ballard." McGee gives a wicked chuckle.

I feel my cheeks warm. "What else did you learn?"

"O'Rourke says it ain't just hanky-panky. Harding is hard-core."

"Meaning . . . ?"

"He's into the kinky stuff. Keeps a set of handcuffs and a riding crop in his trailer."

In my line of work, I've seen it all, from porn mags and DVDs to sex toys that included whips and handcuffs, so I'm hardly shocked. I only comment, "Personally, I don't see the appeal."

"Not to mention he's *old*," Ivy pronounces with disgust.

"He may be old, but he's also Casey Steele." Brianna explains Brent Harding's enduring appeal. "Men who are icons never get old when it comes to scoring with women. Look at Mick Jagger."

"Mick Jagger is Mick Jagger," I say. "Besides, he still tours."

"*Steele Case* is in syndication, and don't forget his Jack Dawson movies." Brianna refers to the string of action flicks in which Brent Harding starred as a Texas Ranger named Jack Dawson before he began dyeing his hair and putting his cosmetic surgeon's kids through college. "He has a following. Why do you think my uncle cast Brent in this picture?"

Brianna's rhetorical question hangs in the air. I still don't see the appeal, but I can't dispute the fact that Brent Harding has no trouble getting laid, even at his age. The same goes for Karol Bartosz, and he's even longer in the tooth than Brent. Fame is a powerful aphrodisiac, I suppose.

Outside, the sky is clear. The fog from earlier in the day has receded and forms a thick, gray band along the horizon like a rolled-up carpet that'll be unrolled again once the party's over. We're passing the state beach at Waddell Creek, where monster waves pound the shore and surfers dot the swells beyond the breakpoint. There's just one flaw in my theory about Olivia Harding, I realize: She wasn't at Bartosz's party, so she couldn't have been the one who drugged me.

Lost in thought, I don't notice we've arrived back in town until I look out and see that we're driving along Pacific Avenue, where the sidewalks are thronged with shoppers and sightseers, and flowers bloom in the tubs that sit outside the stucco storefronts painted in sherbet shades. I spy Ivy's boss, Parker Lane, in the front window of the Gilded Lily as we drive by; he's rearranging the window display, which he does at least once a week. The sign on the surfboard that's propped outside Hang Ten Surf Shop advertises a sale of ten percent off all merchandise.

I hear the muffled sound of my ringtone from inside my Tumi bag. My heart leaps into my throat when I pull out my phone and see Spence's name on the caller ID. Is he calling with the results of my blood test? If so, the news won't be good. Because there's no test to determine whether any drugs in your system were ingested voluntarily or not.

Spence's voice is low and tense. "Where are you? We need to talk."

"I just pulled into town. What's up? Can you tell me over the phone?" My heart starts to pound at his dire tone. I wonder if it might have something to with my errant brother.

"I'd rather not. Meet me at the park across from the station."

"Okay, but—?"

"I'll be there in ten," he says before hanging up.

CHAPTER EIGHTEEN

I'm seated on a bench in the stone plaza across the street from the municipal complex five minutes later. The park is a sprawl of green around me with paths winding through it. A fountain splashes at the center of the plaza, its soothing sound mingling with the happy cries of children from the playground nearby. I watch the passersby as I wait for Spence—moms pushing babies in strollers, joggers and skateboarders, office workers headed back to work after their lunch breaks. Everyone looks relaxed, while my own stomach churns. I'm worried about my brother.

I start at the trilling of my phone and see Lexie's name on the caller ID. "Guess who just showed up?" she says when I answer.

"I'm guessing it wasn't the Ghost of Christmas Past."

She chuckles. "You'll be happy to know they arrived safely."

"Thank God." I'm flooded with relief. "How does my brother seem?"

"Fine except for being a bit travel worn. I wasn't expecting"—*A crazy person to seem so normal*, I mentally fill in the rest of the sentence, then relax when she goes on—"such a gentleman after what Uncle Howard told us."

"Your uncle seems to think he's a gigolo."

"Only because he's worried Grandma will remarry before he can get his hands on her money."

"So they didn't make it legal?"

"God no." She lowers her voice as if she doesn't want them to overhear. "Actually, their plan involved me. Seems Grandma had this crazy idea that if she showed up with an eligible bachelor in tow, I'd fall head over heels. She's been worried about me ever since I lost my husband."

"Oh, for the love of . . ." I trail off, stifling a laugh.

"Not that Arthur isn't a great guy, but I have my own life."

I wish I could say the same for myself, but between fretting over my brother and getting caught up in a murder investigation, I don't seem to have a life at the moment. "So this whole time we were worried sick, they were arranging a love match? Unbelievable."

"Blame it on Grandma. She means well, but she sometimes goes overboard. I think she does it partly to tweak Uncle Howard. He can be a bit of control freak."

"I noticed. She sure pulled one over on him this time. One thing I'm curious about, though . . . Since neither of them owns a car and they didn't rent one"—Gladys seems to have been careful not to leave a paper trail—"how did they get there? Please tell me it wasn't by way of stolen vehicle."

"Not even Grandma would go that far," says Lexie. "She bought a used car."

"Whew." I breathe a sigh of relief. "I was having visions of Bonnie and Clyde."

She laughs, and I join in. It feels good to laugh.

"Grandma's staying on a few days," Lexie informs me as we're saying our good-byes. "I told Arthur he was welcome to stay, too, but he seems eager to get home." I promise to arrange it. I'm just as eager for him to get home, mainly to clear his name so he can be eliminated as a person of interest.

I'm looking up flight information when I glance up to see a grim-faced Spence striding toward me across the plaza. He wears jeans and a tan blazer, underneath which I can make out the bulge where his sidearm is holstered. He nods in greeting as he sits down next to me. "Good news," I tell him. "I just got off with the phone with Mrs. Sedgwick's granddaughter. My brother turned up at her place along with Mrs. Sedgwick, which means you can call off the dogs. I'm booking him a flight home." Spence's expression remains grim. "What is it? Why are you looking at me like that?"

"A warrant was issued for Arthur's arrest."

"*What?* You can't do that. We had a deal. You agreed—"

"We have DNA linking him to the crime scene."

I stare at him. His words might have been the buzzing of bees for all the sense they made. Then the blood drains from my face. "That . . . that's impossible!" I sputter. "My brother was nowhere near the crime scene. Besides, he doesn't own a gun and wouldn't know how to shoot one if he did."

"We found a hair that didn't belong to the victim, but we couldn't find a match on any of our databases. It wasn't until we searched Arthur's place—" He puts his hand out, stopping me before I can object. "The DA got a judge to issue a search warrant based on Sedgwick's allegations. We took DNA samples, and they matched the DNA from the hair that was found at the crime scene."

I continue to stare at him. It still doesn't make any sense. Then it hits me. "Wait. I remember. I was wearing his sweatshirt that day. When I turned the body over . . ." I trail off, feeling sick. In contaminating the crime scene, I had unwittingly implicated my brother, I realize.

"Do you still have the sweatshirt?"

"No. I gave it back after I washed it."

"Did anyone see you wearing it?"

"I had it on when you interviewed me."

"Red Stanford hoodie, torn pocket on the right side?"

"Good memory." I pull up a photo on my phone of Arthur wearing his favorite sweatshirt at the pizzeria where I'd treated him to dinner on his birthday in March. "See. This proves he didn't do it."

"No. It only proves he owns a red sweatshirt. May I?" Spence takes the iPad from me to send the photo to his own device, but I know he's merely following protocol. My anxiety mounts as he goes on, "We found something else when we confiscated his computer—a game he appears to have made. I spoke with his friend Ray Zimmer, who confirmed that it was Arthur's concept, though he said he helped design it." He could only be referring to the game featuring Phantasmagora, the character played by Delilah in *Return of Laserman.*

It's an effort to speak in a normal voice with my breath short and my heart racing. "I know all that. But you make it sound like Arthur was obsessed with Delilah or something. He wasn't. The game had nothing to do with her. He was only interested in Phantasmagora."

"That's not how it will look in court, and together with the DNA evidence . . ." Spence shakes his head. "The prosecution will also argue that Arthur had access to the premises through you."

"Oh, my God." I bury my head in my hands. I feel the walls closing in, and this time there's nothing I can do. Not even Dr. Sandefur can help. When I look up and see compassion in Spence's eyes, I grab hold as if to a lifeline. "Do *you* think my brother murdered Delilah?"

"It doesn't matter what I think."

"It does to me."

"Then no, I don't. There's enough evidence to charge him, but not to get a conviction in my opinion."

It's not the rousing show of faith that I was looking for, but if Spence isn't fully convinced of Arthur's innocence, he's at least willing to keep an open mind. "So what now?"

"The chief will alert the local authorities in Bozeman and have them make the arrest."

I picture lawmen swarming in, guns drawn. "They'd put him in handcuffs. He'd be scared to death! Please, Spence, don't let that happen. It's not like he's some criminal!"

"It's not our jurisdiction, so technically, I can't make the arrest, but I might be able to coordinate the effort at that end if they'll agree to it. The chief will see the wisdom in handling this quietly. The local boys go in with guns blazing, it would reflect badly on us."

"Not to mention somebody could get hurt."

"I'll speak to the chief."

It's hardly a reprieve, but I'm grateful nonetheless. "Thank you." Spence nods, looking like he wished he could do more. I give him a weak smile. "Did I just thank you for arresting my brother?"

"No one's been arrested yet."

I hold his gaze. "I want to go with you. I can talk to Arthur. Get him to cooperate." When Spence doesn't answer right away, I swallow my pride and say, "Please. I'm begging you."

I'd never begged anyone in my life. I hate being at someone else's mercy, especially the man who was once my sworn enemy and who might be looking to even an old score. I wait with my heart in my throat while Spence deliberates and watch a little boy who stands by the fountain, clutching a coin with his eyes squeezed shut. I make a wish of my own, and with the plink of the coin hitting the fountain, I hear the magic words from Spence: "I think we can make that happen."

He drives me to my place, where I throw some things into an overnight bag. On the way to the airport, I phone Ivy to give her the heads-up and Brianna to instruct her on managing my properties while I'm away. Brianna offers to housesit and I gratefully accept—I still don't trust Hercules alone with Prince—although I'm worried I won't be able to find anything after she's done organizing my cupboards and drawers. Next, I call Lexie to tell her of the change in plans. I swear her to secrecy, at Spence's insistence—he's afraid Arthur will flee if he learns there is a warrant out for his arrest. I can tell she's uncomfortable with it, and who can blame her? First her grandmother tries to hook her up with a total stranger, then she finds out the stranger is a wanted man.

"I thought you were calling with the results of my blood test when I saw your name on my caller ID," I say to Spence when we're at the airport, waiting at our gate.

He looks up from scrolling through his text messages and frowns. "Yeah, about that . . ."

"Uh-oh." I feel the knot in my stomach tighten.

"Your blood alcohol level was zero, but the test results showed a high concentration of diazepam—the active ingredient in Valium."

"Jesus. No wonder I felt like I'd been shot with a tranquilizer gun. Listen, I know this looks bad, but I swear I wasn't lying before when I told you—"

He lifts his hand, stopping me. "I'm not going to arrest you, Tish. I have bigger worries at the moment."

"What about my driver's license?"

"We'll discuss that later."

Aware of the precarious position I'm in, I don't press my case. I, too, have bigger worries at the moment. I need to find out who killed Delilah Ward before I become the next victim or my brother is charged with a crime he didn't commit. On the flight to Bozeman, I float my theory about Olivia Harding.

Spence dismisses it. "So we're back to playing Nancy Drew, are we?" He sounds annoyed.

"You don't have to take that tone. I'm only trying to help."

"You aren't helping." After a minute, he says, in a less gruff voice, "Not that it's any of your concern, but we questioned Mrs. Harding, after her husband confessed to the affair. Her alibi checks out. She was home in L.A. on the day of the murder. Her housekeeper confirmed it."

"How do you know the housekeeper wasn't lying?"

"Why would she lie?"

"Maybe Olivia asked her to, and she was scared she'd lose her job if she didn't."

"Employees who lie for their bosses tend to cave under questioning or recant under oath. You'd have to be stupid not to know that, and Mrs. Harding doesn't strike me as a stupid woman."

"Still, I would do some more checking on that alibi if I were you."

"Are you telling me how to do my job?" Spence's frown deepens. We're back to sparring with each other, and in a weird way it feels more comfortable than when we were getting along.

"I wouldn't dream of it. I was merely making a suggestion."

He sighs. "There's a big hole in your theory about Mrs. Harding. She couldn't have been the one who drugged you at Bartosz's, because she wasn't at the party."

"I know, and I've been thinking about that. Brent was at the party. He could have drugged me."

"Why would he do that?"

"Let's say he found out his wife had killed Delilah, or she confessed. He wouldn't want the mother of his unborn children to go to prison, would he? Not to mention what it would do to his career."

Spence doesn't bother to disguise his incredulity.

"I know it's a stretch," I plow on. "But he was acting suspicious at the party."

"In what way?"

"When I mentioned I was the one who found the body, he kept asking questions."

"What kind of questions?"

"He wanted to know what else I'd seen. You know, like incriminating evidence or someone fleeing the scene. I'm telling you, I got a weird vibe from him. And did you see the face work on that man?"

"We don't make arrests based on 'weird vibes' or personal

appearances. Not to mention he's Casey Steele. That alone gives him indemnity," he adds with a smile tugging at his lips.

"He *was* Casey Steele. That's my point. He's hanging on to what's left of his career."

Spence just shakes his head. He's sitting next to me by the window, having been nice enough to trade seats with me after I explained that I get claustrophobic unless I'm by the aisle. (It makes me feel like I have to pee when I don't.) No doubt he's regretting his gallantry. The jet we're on is the kind with seats two to a row and zero legroom. With his tray lowered to hold his in-flight beverage, Spence looks like he's crammed into a child-size desk in a kindergarten classroom. I've never been more aware of how big he is than I am now. Wedged in next to him, I can feel the heat radiating from his six-foot-plus frame and smell his scent, a combination of starched shirt, breath mints, and clean sweat. I shift around in my seat, trying in vain to put some distance between us while holding on to the V-8 on my tray so it doesn't tip over.

"How's it going with you and your wife?" I inquire now that it's clear I'm not going to get any more out of him on the investigation.

He cuts me a sour glance. "Couldn't be better. Who wouldn't rather sleep alone and eat crap food when they could be curled up next to a warm body and enjoying home-cooked meals?"

"Welcome to my world."

"The difference is that I didn't choose this."

"Sorry. I didn't mean to bring up a sore subject."

"She's seeing someone," he says, after brooding in silence for a minute.

"Oh." I'm at a loss. "Well, that sucks."

He stares out the porthole on his side at the clouds skimming past. "We were talking about taking the kids to Disneyland this summer. The next thing I know, Barb is in tears, saying it's no use pretending. She's seeing someone." His expression is sad and defeated when he brings his gaze back to me.

"Is . . . Um, is it anyone you know?" I'm careful not to be gender specific. You never know these days.

"No. Barb met him at the gym." He says this as though he almost wished it had been a friend so he would have had an excuse to plow his fist into the guy's face. "He's in finance and his name's Keith, that's all I know. She says he's showing her how to 'capitalize her assets.'" He makes air quotes with his fingers. "Meanwhile, my stock is at an all-time low."

"Well, at least now you know."

"Yeah. It's all over but for the shouting, and I hope it doesn't come to that for the kids' sake. The question is where do I go from here. I don't know who I am apart from being a husband and dad."

"You're a cop."

"I can't remember a time when I didn't want to be a cop. I'm talking about how I want to live my life as a man. I don't see myself hanging out in bars hitting on women ten years from now."

"Is that what you're doing?"

"No. I was merely making a point."

"That you're not in the habit of hitting on women in bars? I didn't think so. Not since you ditched those tinted contacts. They didn't make you look like Brad Pitt, by the way. I like you better in glasses."

"Thanks, I guess."

"It was a compliment."

"I'm never sure with you."

I shrug and shift my body, angling it away from him when I notice that my kneecaps are brushing against his. "You go around complimenting people all the time, it can get boring."

"Boring," Spence says with a smile playing at his lips, "is not a word I'd ever use to describe you, Tish." He pushes his seat back as far as it will go and closes his eyes. I hear him snoring softly a minute later.

*   *   *   *

It's dark out by the time we land at Yellowstone International Airport. A short while later, we emerge from the terminal into the cool air of summer in the high country, and a man with a friendly face wreathed in lines below a ten-gallon hat climbs from the official vehicle that's idling at the curb and walks over to greet us. His uniform and badge identify him as the sheriff of Gallatin County. I'm relieved that he came alone and not with his deputies. "Detective Breedlove? Cal Jarvis." The two men shake hands before Jarvis turns toward me. "You must be Miss Ballard."

"Nice to meet you." I shake his hand and brace myself for the inevitable questions about my brother. I don't doubt that Jarvis will want to know what he could potentially be walking into.

But the sheriff only nods toward my bag. "Help you with that?"

I smile and hand him my overnight bag. Spence is carrying only his wallet. Typical guy.

On the drive to the ranch, Sheriff Jarvis gives us some background information on Lexie MacAllister. "Her husband, Craig, died of cancer a couple years back, but Lexie kept the ranch going. Don't ask me how. We're talking a thousand head of cattle, and it's just her and her foreman, Roberto. I grew up on a ranch and became a lawman, which tells you all you need to know about cattle ranching. It's always something. Last thing Lexie MacAllister needs is more trouble."

"I don't expect any trouble," Spence says. "The suspect isn't known to be armed or dangerous."

"That would be my brother," I pipe up from the backseat in a testy voice, "and he's innocent."

"That so?" Sheriff Jarvis darts me a mildly curious look in the rearview mirror.

An hour later, we turn from US 191 onto a two-lane rural highway traveling in a northeasterly direction. The black outlines of mountains rise in the distance, shouldering the sky, which is a mass of stars in which a crescent moon hangs. Fields sprawl in every direction with buildings scattered here and there. It's ten o'clock by the time the sheriff makes a right turn onto a gravel road where we pass through a set of metal gates. We drive for another mile or so, through fenced pastures and past cattle sheds, before we finally arrive at the house. A two-story wooden structure with board-and-batten siding, it stands against a backdrop of aspens and evergreens. Parked in front of us in the driveway are an older-model blue Ford Taurus—the getaway car, I surmise, from its California plates and the road dust it's covered in—and a newer-model red Mercedes-Benz coupe.

Spence jerks his chin toward the Benz. "Looks like we've got company."

CHAPTER NINETEEN

The air is fragrant with the woodsy scent of evergreens and the smoke rising from the chimney. A flagstone walk curves invitingly toward the front entrance, where I step onto a covered porch lit by the glow from the pair of coach lamps that flanks the door. The door swings open within seconds of Jarvis's knock and a black Lab comes bounding out, its owner not far behind, a woman with shoulder-length brown hair who grabs its collar as it jumps up on the sheriff.

"Bucky, *down*," she commands, and the Lab sinks onto its haunches. The woman straightens, smiling, and I see that it's Lexie—I recognize her from her Facebook page. Early thirties with a lean, athletic build and brown eyes that are crinkled at the corners. "Hey, Cal. Sorry, he's usually better behaved. Must be all the excitement. It's been quite the scene since Mom and Uncle Howard got here. Well, don't just stand there, come on in."

My heart sinks at the mention of Howard Sedgwick. So he's joined the party? Great. Just what we need. Lexie steps back, holding the door open to let us in. "Tish, we meet at last! And you must be Detective Breedlove." She kisses me on the cheek and shakes Spence's hand, and when she leans in to whisper as she ushers us into the living room, "Don't worry. His bark is worse than his bite," I know that she's referring to her uncle and not the dog. I can see Howard Sedgwick up ahead, jabbing at a log in the fireplace with a poker. He wears navy slacks and a cotton sweater in a shade of cranberry that matches his flushed face. His bald crown gleams with reflected firelight.

I enter a large, open-beamed room paneled in barn wood and dominated by the stone fireplace. My brother sits next to Gladys on the cowhide sofa opposite the fireplace, wearing a checked flannel shirt and jeans. He looks surprised to see me, while Gladys, bright and shiny as a new penny with her henna hair, wearing a coral twin-set and pearls, beams with delight. Seated in the leather armchair to their right is a trim, blond woman, dressed in belted jeans and a pink button-down with a red cashmere sweater draped over her shoulders, who could only be Gladys's daughter and Lexie's mother, Kate. Howard Sedgwick straightens, still holding the poker.

"Cal," he greets Jarvis, then his gaze shifts to Spence. "Gentlemen, is this really necessary? Detective Breedlove, you've come a long way when I could have told you over the phone my mother is safe and sound, as you can see." He motions toward Gladys, who frowns at him.

"I'm afraid we're here on another matter," Jarvis informs him in a serious voice. He looks at Arthur. "Son, Detective Breedlove would like to have a word with you." Arthur freezes like a deer caught in headlights. Gladys reaches over to give his hand a motherly pat.

"What's this all about?" demands Howard.

"Tish?" Arthur looks at me, worry and confusion written all over his face.

I wish I could go to him and make it all better, but I can't. "It's okay," I tell him, hoping I don't sound as disheartened as I feel. "Just do as they say, and we'll see if we can get this straightened out."

Spence crosses the room toward him, and I experience a moment of panic, picturing the sheriff rushing in to cuff my brother and read him his rights while Spence pats him down, but neither of those things happen. Instead, Spence says, in a kind voice, "Arthur, why don't you and I talk in private." Arthur nods and rises unsteadily to his feet. His eyes are huge behind his Clark Kent glasses.

"I'll show you to the study," Lexie says, and they follow her down the hallway to the rear of the house.

For several beats, no one says a word. There's just the crackling of the blaze in the fireplace and the sound of Bucky's leg thumping against the floor by the hearth as he scratches himself. Finally, I feel compelled to offer some sort of explanation. "It seems that certain evidence has come to light that . . . that implicates Arthur in the murder of Delilah Ward." There's a gasp from Gladys. Lexie's mother stares at me wide-eyed. "Of course he's innocent! That's why we're here. So Spe—Um, Detective Breedlove can take him in for questioning and get it sorted out."

"So what you're saying is that he's here to arrest him," Howard says, bluntly.

"No, not at all." I dart a glance at Sheriff Jarvis. I'm aware that I'm standing on a technicality, since he'll be the one making the arrest, but he's nice enough not to correct me. "And I'd appreciate it if you would refrain from making any more false allegations about my brother."

My words are the verbal equivalent of a matador's pick stabbing a bull's neck. "Allegations?" Howard erupts. "Dear God, I didn't know the half of it! I thought my mother had been taken in by a con man when in fact she was in the clutches of a dangerous psychopath!"

Gladys speaks sharply to him. "For heaven's sake, Howie, put that down." She gestures toward the poker he's brandishing, and he quickly lowers it before dropping it in the bucket of fire tools on the hearth. "I won't have you talking that way about Arthur. Why, he wouldn't hurt a fly."

"A warrant for his arrest says otherwise!" bellows Howard.

Lexie reappears just then. "What's all this? Uncle Howard, if you're going to shout, take it outside." Good for her. She has her grandmother's gumption. Lexie turns to me. "Tish, I don't believe you've met my mother. Tish, this is my mom, Kate. Mom, this is Tish." The older woman stands to shake my hand. Her expression is strained, but she rises to the occasion and smiles.

"I'm sorry if Arthur got into trouble because of what my brother told the police." Kate shoots Howard a look of reproach. "It's just that we were worried about Mom. We had no idea where she was headed or what kind of person she was with. But of course now that we've met Arthur . . ." She trails off as if not sure she should be saying anything nice about a murder suspect.

"I appreciate that," I reply. "And I can assure you that your mother was never in any danger."

"The very idea!" exclaims Gladys. "We were having a perfectly nice time, and it's not as though I need permission from either of you." Her gaze shifts between Howard and Kate. "Did it ever occur to you that the reason I didn't inform you of my plans was because I knew this was how you'd react?"

Howard adopts a placating tone. "If Kate and I were worried, Mother, it was only because we care. We wouldn't want anything to happen to you. At your age with a heart condition . . ."

"It's called angina and it's nothing a pill can't fix," Gladys snaps. "You, on the other hand, I'm not so sure about. I thought I raised you better. When did you get to be so damned pompous?"

"Now, Mother—"

She cuts him off. "Howie, there's something I've been wanting to say to you that you need to hear."

"What?" he asks apprehensively.

"Put a sock in it!"

From behind me, I hear a muffled giggle from Lexie and a snort from Jarvis. Howard flushes, his face suffused with color from his cheeks to his bald crown. I see a flash of admiration in Kate's eyes. She goes over and sits down next to her mother on the sofa. "Of course you don't need our permission, Mom. I only wish you'd called to let us know you were okay."

"Why? So I could get an earful?" replies Gladys.

Kate gives a rueful grimace. "I'm sorry if I ever made you feel like you needed my permission. Next time you decide to go on a trip, I'll come help you pack, as long as you promise not to leave without telling us where you're going."

"Fair enough." Gladys's angry expression softens. "Meanwhile, poor Arthur! I don't understand how the police could think he was in any way connected with the murder of that actress."

"It would help if he had a solid alibi," I say. "He says he was home alone, working at his computer, on the morning of the murder, but no one can corroborate it. None of his neighbors saw him."

"Morning, you say it was?" Gladys frowns in confusion. "That can't be right. I don't know why Arthur would have told you that. We always go power walking in the mornings." My pulse quickens as I realize this might be what I was praying for: Arthur's Get Out of Jail Free card.

"Every morning?" I ask.

"Without fail, unless it's pouring rain." I remember that it was sunny on the day of the murder, which was why Delilah had been lying by the pool. "Once around the park and—"

"Breakfast at the Bluejay Café," I fill in the rest of the sentence, recalling Gladys's words from when she invited me to join them. "Which means other people saw you."

"Yes, of course. We always sit at the same table. Everyone knows us there. Emily—she's our waitress—she doesn't even bother with menus anymore, she just brings us our usual. Scrambled eggs and bacon for me, the blueberry pancakes for Arthur." Her frown of confusion deepens. "What I don't understand is why he would have told you he was home when he wasn't."

"I think I know why." I feel ashamed at the realization. "He was worried I'd get the wrong impression if I knew he was seeing you. Not that there's anything wrong with . . . What I mean to say is"—I break into a sheepish smile—"I guess I need to put a sock in it sometimes, too." This elicits a chorus of chuckles from Gladys, Kate, Lexie, and Sheriff Jarvis. Howard harrumphs.

Gladys jumps to her feet. "I need to speak with Detective Breed-love!" With that, she goes dashing down the hall, the low-heeled black patent-leather shoes she wears tip-tapping against the floor.

Lexie collapses onto the sofa, and I sink down next to her. "What a night!" she exclaims. "I wouldn't be surprised if a meteor came crashing through my roof next." She glances up at the ceiling as if she half expects it to happen. "I can't believe we thought Grandma and Arthur were an item," she says to me, adding with a twinkle in her eye, "though you have to admit they make a cute couple."

"Except your grandma was saving Arthur for you," I remind her.

"Well, she was too late because I'm already engaged." Lexie ducks her head, blushing as she says this.

"You're *what*?" Howard stares at her.

"Congratulations," says the sheriff, grinning. "Who's the lucky fellow?"

"Roberto." I recall Sheriff Jarvis's mentioning a ranch foreman named Roberto. "We were going to wait until the Fourth of July barbecue to make the announcement, but being as you're all here now . . ."

Kate beams as she hugs Lexie. "Sweetie, this is wonderful!"

"You're not mad that I didn't tell you sooner?" Lexie asks her.

"Not at all. I couldn't be more delighted. You know how we feel about Roberto." Kate looks over at me. "Not that we wouldn't have grown to love Arthur. He seems like a nice young man."

I smile at her. "He is. But somehow I can't picture him as a cattle rancher." Turning to Lexie, I offer my congratulations. "When's the wedding?"

"We haven't set a date yet," she answers. "Maybe in the fall.

We're thinking an outdoor wedding. You're invited. You and Arthur. Please say you'll come." She reaches over to take my hand.

"I'd love to," I tell her. *If I'm not dead by then.*

Howard declares, "Well, it's about time we had some good news in this family!" Bucky the Lab, who's stretched out on the braided rug in front of the fireplace, raises his head to look up at him. Howard bends down to scratch him behind the ears, and Bucky grins and wags his tail.

I'm thinking maybe this will all work out, that I won't be murdered or have to visit my brother in prison, when I hear the crack of a gunshot from outside.

CHAPTER TWENTY

I start, my heart racing. Then I hear the sound of the front door opening, and a gust of cool air blows in before the door is slammed shut. "Damn coyotes." A man's voice carries from the entryway.

The man appears before us momentarily. Medium height with a stocky build, wearing jeans and a cowboy hat. He has brown eyes and skin the color of the wooden stock of the rifle he carries. I jump up to introduce myself with more enthusiasm than I normally would have shown, I'm so relieved that he's not pointing the rifle at me. "You must be Roberto. Hi, I'm Tish."

Lexie's fiancé breaks into a grin as we shake hands. Late thirties or early forties with a nice face and a smile that could bring the cows home without aid of a sheepdog. I can see why Lexie fell for him. "The famous Tish? Well, this is a nice surprise. I didn't know you were coming."

"I didn't know, either, until a little while ago."

"I don't shoot to kill, only to scare 'em off," he explains when my gaze drops to the rifle.

"Glad to hear it." *You have no idea.*

"Roberto! Lexie just told us the good news!" Kate comes flying across the room to throw her arms around her future son-in-law. Roberto casts a questioning look over her shoulder at Lexie.

She shrugs and says, "It sort of slipped out."

I know that it was Lexie's idea and not Roberto's to keep their engagement a secret when he says, "Does this mean I finally get to see that ring on your finger?" Lexie blows him a kiss.

Jarvis pumps Roberto's hand, congratulating him. Howard offers his own congratulations, giving the younger man a hearty clap on the back. Spence reappears with Arthur and Gladys as Lexie is uncorking a bottle of wine. "Mr. Ballard and Mrs. Sedgwick have agreed to come to the station with us," he informs the sheriff, suggesting that it was voluntary on the part of Arthur. Spence looks at me as he goes on, "If Arthur's alibi checks out, I don't think we'll need to hold him." I'm flooded with relief, and I can only nod in response, my throat is so tight.

I hug Arthur as they're leaving, cautioning, "Just tell the truth. If you'd told me you were with Gladys that day . . ." I stop myself before I say something that will make a hypocrite of me. "Okay, so I probably would've fainted with shock that you'd taken up power walking, but other than that . . ." I glance over at Gladys. "I think it's wonderful that you made such a good friend."

Arthur nods, wearing a sheepish expression. "You're not mad that I left town without telling you?"

"That," I reply, injecting a stern note into my voice, "is a whole separate matter. If Detective Breedlove decides to go easy on you, don't expect the same from me. Dude, you are so dead."

I lightly punch my brother's arm, and he rubs it, making a face as if I'd hurt him, like he always does, before he breaks into a grin. My heart is full as I stand in the doorway watching him and Gladys and the two lawmen drive off in the sheriff's cruiser.

"Don't think I'm not appreciative," I say to Spence later on, after everyone else has gone to bed. We're sitting on the sofa drinking coffee, warmed by the glowing embers in the fireplace. Lexie invited us to stay the night, and as the nearest motel is forty miles away, we readily accepted.

"Even though your brother has to spend the night in jail?" Spence asks.

"As long as he's not under arrest." Chief Sanderson had agreed to hold off on that, but his orders were that Arthur be held in custody until his alibi checked out. The CBPD was already at work finding witnesses who could verify Arthur's whereabouts on the morning of the murder.

"The accommodations aren't too bad," Spence assures me. "Jarvis was calling in an order for chicken-fried steaks from the local diner as I was leaving." He smiles as he sips his coffee.

"I hope Arthur realizes how lucky he is, and not just because he's eating chicken-fried steak tonight instead of a bologna sandwich." I cut Spence a glance, adding shyly, "If you hadn't stepped up . . ."

"Just doing my job," he says gruffly.

"No, it was more than that. And it wasn't the first time. All those years ago, you could have pressed charges against me, and you didn't." I take a deep breath before saying what I should have said four years ago when I was making my AA amends. "I want you to know that I'm sorry I torched your car."

"Am I dreaming, or did you just apologize?" We're sitting close enough so that I can almost count the hairs in his raised eyebrows.

I punch his arm lightly. "Shut up, or I'll take it back."

"No way. You're not taking it back. I only waited twenty years to hear you say that."

"If I'd known then what I know now, you'd still be driving that car."

He takes my hand, and I start to stiffen, at the strangeness of it, before I surrender to the pleasurable sensation of his warm fingers curled around mine. "What do you know now that you didn't know then?"

"That you're not such a bad guy."

"True, but I still should've busted Nate's chops for talking trash about you back then." Nate Hofstadter was his best friend in high school—and my chief tormentor after Spence made the mistake of confiding in him. "And it wasn't just Nate. I knew which guys wrote that stuff on your locker, and I didn't confront them, either."

I had blamed Spence for pretty much everything that was wrong in my life back then, and now, hearing that he blamed himself, too—even though his sins were but a fraction of the ones that I'd heaped on him—I realize the time had come to let go of all that. "We were both young and stupid."

"So you forgive me?" he asks, wearing a hopeful look.

I smile at him. "If you can forgive me for destroying your car, I can forgive you for not defending me."

He looks relieved, but I can tell that he's still troubled by something. After a minute, he says quietly, "Tish, there's something I need to ask you. All these years, I've wondered . . ." He hesitates before the question bursts forth on an expelled breath. "Did I force you that night?"

I stare at him in surprise. Had I been asked to come up with ten questions that I was mostly likely to be asked by Spence Breedlove, that would not have been one of them. "You don't remember?"

He grimaces. "You weren't the only one who had too much to drink."

"No." I look him in the eye. "You didn't force me."

I feel the tension go out of him as if a tremendous weight has been lifted from his shoulders. He holds my gaze for several beats, then almost before I know it's happening, he leans in to kiss me. A light kiss that increases in intensity, sparking a fire that quickly spreads throughout my body. The heat builds and next thing I know, Spence is lying on top of me on the sofa. I can't stop kissing him even though I can hardly catch my breath with the weight of his six-foot-plus frame pressing into my diaphragm. I can feel his erection through his jeans. He pushes his hand under my turtleneck as I tug his shirt from his waistband. Every inch of me is alive with sensation, even with six layers of clothing between us. I'm made aware of his own desire with each thrust of his tongue and the urgency with which he fumbles with the clasp on my bra.

Spence has my bra unclasped, and I'm wrestling with the zipper on his jeans, when we both freeze at the sound of a floorboard creaking overhead. I quickly come to my senses, remembering that we're not alone in the house. I glance nervously toward the landing at the top of stairs, which is where the noise had seemed to come from, and whisper, "Do you think . . . ?"

"Nobody saw us," he whispers back. I feel like a teenager making out with her boyfriend while her parents are upstairs. I start to giggle, and he puts his finger against my lips. "*Shhhh . . .*" Then I feel his body shaking with soundless laughter against mine before he finally climbs off me.

I pull myself into an upright position and run my fingers through my hair. He zips his fly, then hunts for his glasses before finding them under a sofa cushion. By the time decorum is restored, a certain awkwardness has set in. Spence leans forward, resting his elbows on his knees as he stares into the dying embers of the fireplace, reflected firelight dancing across the lenses of his wire-rims. He clears his throat. "Look, Tish, it's been a while for me, so if I came on too strong . . ."

"We both got a little carried away. It doesn't have to be a big deal," I reply, keeping it light. "We're not in high school anymore. And, apparently, it wasn't a big deal to you back then." I thought I had buried the hatchet, but I guess I didn't bury it deep enough. A hurt look crosses his face.

This was a mistake. It wouldn't have happened if we hadn't been victims of circumstance, thrown together at a time when he was hurting and we were both lonely. If his wife hadn't told him she was seeing someone else, and if my boyfriend and I weren't separated by an ocean . . .

"Shall we call it a night?" Spence says. I nod and rise. A glance at the regulator clock on the mantel tells me it's midnight, long past my bedtime, though I don't feel sleepy in the least. We go upstairs, and as we part to head to our separate guest accommodations, Spence kisses me on the cheek and whispers, "Good night." I feel a pang of regret, wishing we were sharing a room.

I spend a restless night drifting in and out of sleep. I wake when it's barely light out. Kate, who I'm sharing a room with, is still asleep in the twin bed next to mine. I grab my clothes and tiptoe down the hallway to the bathroom, where I shower and dress, putting on the jeans that I'd worn yesterday and the blue fleece pullover that I packed for the trip, before I head downstairs. My stomach grumbles at the mingled aromas of coffee and bacon frying.

I walk into a kitchen that's roomy with hardwood flooring, country-style cupboards, and a glassed-in breakfast nook that looks out on a view of evergreens with snowcapped mountaintops in the distance. Lexie stands at the Wolf range, turning strips of bacon in a cast-iron skillet, while Roberto drinks coffee and reads the paper at the pine table in the breakfast nook. They're both dressed in jeans and dark-green sweatshirts with IRON SPRINGS RANCH in white letters on the front. Roberto looks up from his paper to smile at me.

"Morning. Sleep okay?" Lexie greets me.

"Like a rock." Make that a volcanic rock, smoking as it cools.

"I heard you when I got up to use the bathroom," Lexie says as she flips bacon strips in the skillet with a long-handled fork. "Help yourself." She gestures toward the pot of coffee by the stove.

"Spence . . . um, Detective Breedlove, and I were up late talking." I pour myself some coffee, hoping she hadn't noticed the blush rising in my cheeks. "I hope we didn't disturb you."

She gives me a wry, sidelong glance that tells me she's on to me. "Not in the least. Apart from getting up to pee, I wouldn't have woken if a meteor actually had crashed through the roof."

"That's because I'd have been the one fixing the hole," remarks Roberto from behind his paper.

Spence strolls in, dressed in the clothes he wore yesterday. His hair is damp from the shower and he smells of soap and minty toothpaste. "Morning, ladies. Roberto. Something sure smells good." There's nothing in his demeanor to suggest that we were intimate the night before.

"I hope you have time for breakfast," says Lexie.

"I was counting on it." Spence pours coffee into one of the splatterware mugs from the row on hooks over the counter. He hungrily eyes the bacon, which Lexie is transferring to a paper towel–lined plate. "Sheriff won't be by for another half hour." He had offered to take us to the airport.

"What about Arthur?" I ask anxiously.

"Your brother"—Spence looks up at me, breaking into a grin, as he stirs milk into his coffee—"is a free man." Weak with relief, I lean against the tiled counter and close my eyes in a silent prayer of thanks. "I just got off the phone with Chief Sanderson. Arthur's alibi checks out. A number of people recall seeing him that morning. Emily Ames—the waitress from the Bluejay—for one. She said, and I quote, 'The only thing that boy ever slaughtered was a stack of pancakes.'"

Roberto chuckles. "Thank you, Lord," says Lexie, echoing my own sentiments.

Minutes later, we're sitting down to a breakfast of fried eggs and bacon, and sourdough toast with homemade strawberry preserves. I can't remember the last time I ate so much or tasted food this good. As I'm popping the last bite of toast into my mouth, I hear the sound of a car engine and look out the window to see the sheriff's cruiser pull into the driveway with my brother riding shotgun.

Two hours later, we're taxiing down the runway at the airport. When we reach cruising altitude, I look out at the sea of evergreens below, rolling toward the snow-dusted peaks of the Rocky

Mountains. Arthur is seated in the window seat next to me, while Spence has the whole aisle across from us.

"How was the chicken-fried steak?" I ask.

"It could have used a touch more salt," my brother answers with his customary dry wit. We exchange a grin. He wears the flannel shirt he had on yesterday that belonged to Lexie's husband—the closest Arthur will ever get to cattle ranching, thankfully.

"Thank God for Gladys. She saved the day."

Arthur's smile gives way to a contrite look. "I'm sorry, Tish. I should have told you the truth."

"I'm sorry, too. You know, if I made you feel like you couldn't. You don't have to be embarrassed about wanting a girlfriend. I promise, no Journey." When he had a crush on Melanie Faber in eighth grade, I teased him by humming "Lovin', Touchin', Squeezin'" whenever he was within hearing range.

"It wasn't my idea. Gladys thought if Lexie and I met . . ." He trails off with a shrug.

"So you don't like Lexie?"

"Not that way. She's nice, but she's not really my type."

I smile at this. I'm glad my brother feels he's in a position to be choosy. The truth is that Arthur has a lot to offer. He's smart, handsome, funny, and has a big heart. If half the guys I dated in my younger years had had that much to offer, I'd probably be married to one of them by now. "Well, she has Roberto, so it's just as well." I pat his arm. "You'll find someone of your own someday."

"Yeah, I guess." He doesn't seem too eager. "But I'll be pretty busy with my job, and Ray and I are working on this new computer game, so I won't have much time for dating."

"Please tell me this game doesn't have Phantasmagora in it."

"No. It's about space invaders from another galaxy battling zombies from a zombie apocalypse." He speaks excitedly as he sketches it out for me. But Arthur's shifts in mood are like the weather. A minute later, he sounds worried as he asks, "Do you really think I would have gone to prison?"

It would freak him out if he knew how real a possibility it had been, so I only say, "Dude, what juror would ever think a guy who can't keep his shoelaces tied could shoot straight?" I look pointedly down at his feet.

My brother bends down to retie the shoelaces on one of his sneakers. When he straightens, he still looks worried. "You're not going to make me go back to the puff, are you?"

"When have I ever made you do anything?"

"You're not an easy person to say no to."

"You're probably right about that," I admit. "But no, I don't think you need to go to the puff. Not unless you do something stupid again. You know, like decide to take up cattle ranching."

This gets a smile out of him. "Thanks for coming to get me."

"You can thank Detective Breedlove." I glance over at Spence, who seems to fill most of the row across the aisle with his tall, muscular frame. I watch him leaf through the magazine he's reading, thinking of ways in which I'd like to show my own gratitude, none of them G-rated like the in-flight movie that's playing on the screen overhead. I ought to have my own head examined.

CHAPTER TWENTY-ONE

There are two new voicemail messages on my phone when we land, one from McGee saying that he has information on "the bunny boiler"(a.k.a. Olivia Harding), and the other from Greta Nyland wanting to know when would be a good time for her to collect Delilah's belongings. I call Greta from Spence's car on the way back to Cypress Bay and arrange for her to meet me at Casa Linda Estates tomorrow morning at nine. I decide to hold off on returning McGee's call. I don't want Spence to know what I'm up to until I have actual dirt on Olivia Harding.

I phone Ivy next, and she's relieved to hear that Arthur is no longer a suspect. "Tell him I DVRed the episode of *Game of Thrones* that was on while he was away," she says.

"He'll be thrilled." Arthur lives for *GoT*. "Did you and Rajeev . . . ?"

"No." She sighs. I'd urged her to make it clear to her boyfriend that she doesn't see marriage in her future before he pops the question. "He was supposed to come over last night, but he ended up having to work late. He's taking me to dinner tomorrow night, to make up for it. I'll talk to him then."

"How's it going with Brianna? Or should I ask." I'm not sure I'll recognize my house after she stayed the night.

A pause at the other end. "I have two words for you: scented candles."

"Why would I need scented candles?"

"They mask the smell of Pine-Sol."

We drop Arthur off at his place, then head over to mine. The sun is shining as we turn onto Seabright Avenue. My elderly neighbor, Mrs. Caswell, is pruning the rosebushes in front of her house, while next door, seventeen-year-old Jeremy Nuyen hoses down his Jeep Cherokee. A surfer, clad in a wetsuit and toting his surfboard, ambles in the direction of the beach. Another ordinary day of people going about their business while my own world has been rocked. In the past twenty-four hours alone, I visited a film set where I encountered a possible murderer, my brother narrowly escaped arrest, and I tangled with the law in a way that has me blushing as I think of it now.

"You're awfully quiet," Spence observes. "Everything okay?"

"Sure. Why wouldn't it be?"

"Just making sure we're good."

"We're good," I say, though I'm not sure what "good" is anymore. Forgiving each other our transgressions doesn't make us friends. Nor are we lovers. When we arrive at my house, we don't kiss good-bye or even shake hands, though I'm sincere when I tell him, "Thanks. I owe you." I know it's better this way, but I'm left with a hollow feeling inside as I trudge up my front walk.

The air is redolent of Pine-Sol when I walk in the door. Brianna emerges from the laundry room as I enter the kitchen. The house is spotless and she's carrying my laundry basket, filled with folded clothes, only she doesn't look like I do after I've been cleaning. She looks like an actress playing a housewife in a Tide commercial, dressed in pleated fawn slacks and a white knit top, not a hair out of place or a chip in her nail polish. "I see you've been busy while I was away," I note. Every surface gleams. The appliances sparkle. A bowl on the counter is filled with fresh fruit.

"I tidied up a bit." Brianna sets the laundry basket down, then brushes an invisible crumb from the table. "I also took care of everything on the list. Nothing new to report except a gutter at the Coughlins' house that needs fixing. Did your brother get home okay?" I'd texted her with an update while en route. "He's enjoying a tearful reunion with his hamster as we speak." Before I can ask about my own pets, I hear the skittering of claws on floorboards from the next room. As I step into the living room, Prince comes streaking from the hallway, chased by my cat. Except that Hercules doesn't appear to be terrorizing him. On the contrary, it seems—I can hardly believe my eyes—*they're playing.* I watch in amazement as the Yorkie runs in excited circles around the living room while my cat takes a playful swipe at him from under the sofa whenever he comes within striking range. "What on Earth . . . ?" I turn to Brianna. "You didn't tell me you were a cat whisperer."

She laughs. "I'm not, but I know a few tricks."

"Such as?"

"Fish sticks."

"I'll have to remember that."

"Oh, before I forget, my uncle wants you to call him," she informs me. "Apparently, he couldn't get through to you when he tried your number. He said he left a message on your voicemail."

"I know. I'll get back to him." Bartosz called while I was in Montana, but I'd been too busy to return his call. I wonder what he wants—he didn't say in his message. "First, I need to speak with McGee. He said he had some dirt on Olivia Harding." I feel my pulse quicken as I head for my office to place the call, leaving my cat and the dog to frolic and Brianna to stare after me, wide-eyed.

"She's a piece of work, that one." McGee sounds almost cheerful as he reports on Olivia Harding. He's back in the groove, doing what he loves best. "Maiden name, Godowsky. She grew up in Milwaukee. Dad's a bricklayer. Mom died when she was eight. No criminal record, but when she was sixteen, she was expelled from school for threatening another student. Girl's parents got a restraining order."

"What did she do to make Olivia so angry?"

"Stole her boyfriend apparently." A chill trickles down my spine. "Olivia ran away from home after that, then turned up at a hospital with her wrists slashed a few months later. That got her transferred to the psych ward for ninety days before she was deemed no longer a threat to herself."

"Or to society," I mutter. "What about homicidal tendencies?" If the incident that got her expelled from school was part of a pattern of behavior, that would make her a likely suspect for Delilah's murder.

"If it's in her medical records, you'll need a court order to get access. But if this was my case? I'd take a closer look at her alibi and also pull her phone and bank records, find out if she's been in touch with any unsavory characters, or if she made any large cash withdrawals in recent weeks."

"You think she hired a professional?"

"Sure looks that way, based on your description of the crime scene. You should also talk with your client, Russo. See if he knows Mrs. Harding and if there's any connection between them."

"Don't start with that again," I warn. "What is it with you? It's like you're obsessed with the man."

"Where there's smoke, there's fire," says McGee in an ominous tone while I take in the newly uncluttered surface of my desk and the lush philodendron on the windowsill that's replaced the old, scraggly one. I'm afraid to look in my drawers or file cabinet. I can only hope I'll still be able to find my way around my own office now that Brianna's organized it.

"Do you have anything on Olivia that's more recent?" I ask, eager to get off the subject of Russo.

"She sees a shrink."

"A lot of people see shrinks." My brother for one.

"Sure, but not twice a week."

"Well, clearly she has some issues." If she thought marrying Brent Harding would solve her problems, it would explain why she was still messed up. "Let me know if you find out anything else."

"Keep your doors locked in the meantime," McGee says with a rasp before he hangs up.

My next call is to Bartosz, who wants to know if I'm free for dinner tomorrow evening. "I booked a table at the Shady Brook Inn, and I was hoping you could join me. I could use your input on the menu for my dinner party," he explains. In scoring him a booking at the Shady Brook Inn through my connection with the owner, Steve Hanson, a former classmate of mine, I seem to have become Bartosz's party planner. Either that, or he's using it as an excuse to get in my pants.

Whatever. I see it as an opportunity to pick his brain about Delilah. "As it so happens, I'm free then," I tell him. "I'd love to have dinner with you. Anything I can do to help," I hasten to add.

"Excellent. I look forward to it. The reservation is for eight, so I'll pick you up at seven forty."

I give him my address, then it occurs to me Bartosz might already have known where I live and I feel a light chill of apprehension. He isn't high on my list of suspects, but I can't rule him out. If he's the one who drugged me at his party, a table for two could become a table for one at the morgue.

The following morning, Brianna drives me to Casa Linda Estates for my meeting with Greta Nyland. Greta is waiting when we pull up to the gates at nine o'clock. She stands at the fence by the entrance, gazing at the offerings from Delilah's fans. They seem to have doubled in number since the last time I was here. I climb out and walk over to her while Brianna waits in the car.

Greta gestures toward the pile of candles and bouquets and stuffed animals. "I saw it on the news, but I . . . I wasn't prepared."

She bows her head as if overcome, her auburn hair gleaming in the sun that peeks through the clouds overhead.

"It must be some consolation to know she was loved by so many." I don't mention the complaint from the president of the homeowners association who'd called the makeshift memorial an "eyesore."

"When I lost Eric, I didn't think I would ever know such grief again, but this is worse because now they're both gone." Greta bends to pick up a teddy bear with a photo of Delilah in a cheap plastic frame on a ribbon around its neck. She hugs it to her chest before placing it back on the pile.

"Take your time," I whisper, but when I turn to head back to my SUV, she falls into step with me.

Brianna drives me to the house, while Greta follows in her rental car, a blue Nissan compact. When we arrive, I send Brianna on her way with a list of items to buy at Costco, instructing her to pick me up in an hour. Esmeralda's older-model red Toyota Camry is parked in the driveway, and I hear the distant droning of the vacuum cleaner as Greta and I enter the house. "Why don't you make yourself at home? I'll go see if Esmeralda's done packing up her things," I say. Greta nods and wanders into the great room, drawn by the ocean view from the floor-to-ceiling windows.

I find Esmeralda in the master suite, pushing the vacuum over the carpet. She doesn't see me when I walk in, nor can she hear me with the vacuum running, and she straightens with a startled yelp when I step into her line of sight. She thumbs the off switch. "*Dios mio!* I thought you were a—"

"Ghost?" I finish, and she produces a wan smile. She looks as if she'd stepped from the pages of a Land's End catalog, wearing a striped Breton jersey and cropped jeans, a pair of hot pink, lace-up espadrilles on her feet. You'd never guess she gets up before dawn every morning to clean other people's houses after getting her kids off to school. My gaze travels to the set of Louis Vuitton luggage that stands by the walk-in closet. "Thanks for taking care of that."

"Such beautiful clothes," Esmeralda says mournfully. "It's sad to think she will never wear them again."

"It is. Though some of us will never be a size four or be able to afford such things, so at least she got to enjoy that." I walk over to the closet, where an item of clothing covered in dry-cleaner's plastic hangs from the door. A mink-lined raincoat, I see when I lift the plastic. "Nice. Must've cost a fortune."

"*Sí*. The man, he charge extra."

"What man?" I turn to look at Esmeralda.

She explains that Delilah had given her the money to have the coat professionally cleaned. Esmeralda had dropped it off at the dry cleaner's the day Delilah was killed, then forgot about it in the aftermath of the murder until she happened to come across the ticket in her purse this morning.

I notice a piece of paper folded inside a Ziploc bag that's pinned to the hanger as I'm smoothing the plastic over the garment. It must have been in one of the pockets. I pull it out and see that it's a note handwritten on hotel stationery, embossed with the letterhead for the Peninsula Hotel in New York City. I recall Brianna's mentioning that Delilah had flown to New York on business the week before she arrived in Cypress Bay. The opening line jumps out at me.

Dearest Greta,
If you're reading this, it means I'm already dead.

CHAPTER TWENTY-TWO

It appears to be a suicide note. I read on, curious to know what had driven Delilah to such despair.

I can't live with the guilt any longer. It was my fault that Eric died. He went flying that day because I goaded him into it. I said I hoped his plane would crash, that it would save me the trouble of divorcing him. I didn't mean it. We'd been fighting and I was angry. But I also knew what he was like. I knew he would do it just to prove he could. And now he's dead. I hope you'll find it in your heart to forgive me, even if I can't forgive myself.

Ever Yours,
Delilah

I don't know quite what to make of her words, though I can imagine the circumstances in which they were written. I picture Delilah alone in a hotel room with a minibar, grieving and racked with guilt. When you drink alone, small problems can seem big, and big problems can seem insurmountable. The unthinkable becomes the inevitable. Obviously, she'd had a change of heart—after sleeping on it, if she was like most drunks—or it would have been a hotel employee, and not me, who'd found her dead body. What's a mystery is why someone else had wanted her dead.

"It was good she did not do this terrible thing," says Esmeralda, after she reads the note. She makes the sign of the cross before fingering the gold crucifix that's nestled in the hollow of her throat.

"Except for the fact that she's dead."

"*Sí*, but she is in heaven."

Esmeralda is a devout Catholic, and taking one's own life, as every devout Catholic knows, is a mortal sin. Better a bullet in the head than an eternity in purgatory. I don't agree with that thinking—one of the reasons that I left the church—but there are times when I envy Esmeralda the simple conviction of her faith.

I fold the note and tuck it in the back pocket of my jeans, wondering what Greta will make of it.

"Poor Delilah. I wish she'd come to me." Greta sits on the sofa in the great room, holding the note that's addressed to her, her face as pale as the fog that's rolling in outside. She clearly had no idea the note existed until I showed it to her just now. "As if I could ever hate her!"

"Seems like she hated herself enough for the two of you."

Greta's eyes well with tears. "The truth is, Eric had only himself to blame. He knew better—there was a weather advisory. But he thought he was invincible. He was always taking risks, even as a child. When he was five, he broke his arm jumping from a tree, pretending to be Superman."

"So even if he and Delilah hadn't been fighting . . ."

"He still would've gone up."

"Do you know what their fight was about?"

"No, but I can guess. The only thing they ever fought about was money. Eric would rack up these enormous credit-card bills, and Delilah would throw a fit. She was poor growing up, and part of her never stopped feeling poor. Eric was the opposite—to him every dollar was two dollars."

"He sounds like my brother. You'd think Arthur was stocking up for the End of Days when he goes grocery shopping."

Greta smiles thinly. "With Eric it was big-ticket items and thousand-dollar bottles of champagne. He would have appreciated the irony of a charity in his memory." She lapses into thought for a moment before remembering to ask, "And your brother? Is he all right? Did you find him?"

"Yes, and he was cleared as a suspect."

"Thank God. You must be so relieved."

"You don't know the half of it." I gesture toward the note. "I think Detective Breedlove will want to see that. I don't know if it's relevant to the case, but why don't we let him be the judge."

"Of course." Greta hands me back the note, locking eyes with me as she adds, "I don't have to tell you what the press would do with this. It would be twisted into something lurid and ugly. I'd hate for that to happen, for them to be robbed of their dignity even in death. It would be too cruel."

"I'm the soul of discretion," I assure her.

"You're a good person." She squeezes my hand, wearing a look of gratitude that's disproportionate to what I consider a normal reaction on my part. It tells me Delilah had been burned in the past by people she had trusted. The vacuum cleaner stops droning and then there's only the distant sound of breaking waves. Greta rises to her feet, her movements heavy as though she had aged twenty years since she'd sat down. "I should go. If you'll show me where her things are . . ."

We carry the Louis Vuitton luggage packed with Delilah's belongings to Greta's rental car. By the time the last suitcase has been loaded in the trunk, fog has crept in to cover the landscape except where the outlines of trees and buildings are sketched. Greta hugs me as she's leaving. "Tish, I'm sorry you were dragged into this, but I have to say I'm glad it was you and not someone else."

I smile. "I don't know that I can say the same, but I'll take it as a compliment."

"Perhaps it was all meant to be."

"What makes you think that?"

"You clearly have a nose for this sort of thing." Greta taps her own nose in the universal gesture of sleuths picking up a scent. "You found the note. Who knows what else you'll find."

Brianna returns at 10:15, precisely one hour from the time she'd dropped me off. If I didn't know better, I'd think she was ex-military—she operates on oh-one-hundred time. "I got everything on the list." She gestures toward the supplies that are stowed in back: jumbo packs of paper towels and toilet paper, cleaning products and lightbulbs. "Oh, and I also bought a step stool."

"I didn't know I needed one."

"For when you're knocking cobwebs from ceilings, so you won't hurt yourself falling off a chair."

"That was thoughtful of you." At her concern for my safety, I feel guilty I ever suspected her of murdering her previous employer. She's an odd duck, but her heart seems to be in the right place.

"I also have some ideas on how we can improve efficiency."

We? When did she and I become a team? "And I'd love to hear them," I reply, buckling my seat belt as she backs out of the driveway. "But if you don't slow down, you'll run out of jobs to do."

"I hope you're not suggesting I slack off?" Brianna replies coolly.

"I wouldn't dream of it." Outside, the Spanish-style villas of the gated community glide past, ghostly amid the fog, as we drive to our next stop. Life here seems to have returned to normal since the excitement over the murder, but maybe that's only because here, where privacy is evident in the deep setbacks and the tall fences that separate the homes, life seems to happen mostly behind closed doors. "But it wouldn't hurt to occasionally show you're human like the rest of us."

"Fine. Then I'm not going to pretend it isn't totally weird that you're going on a date with my uncle."

"It's not a date!" I cry before I almost lose a tooth as we go flying over a speed bump. "I told you. He asked for my help. You know, with the menu for his dinner party. I could hardly refuse."

"Few do."

"What's that supposed to mean?" I demand.

"You met him—he's very charming. That and he has no scruples when it comes to getting what—or who—he wants." She brakes at a stop sign, and a hardbodied mom in Spandex pushing a jogging stroller zips past us along the crosswalk. "Also, it's been six months since he broke up with his last blonde—that starlet who's in the new Adam Sandler movie—so the hunt for a replacement is heating up."

"I'm hardly one of the glamour girls he's used to."

"No, but you're his type."

"Right hair color, wrong girl. I'm not an actress looking to make a name for herself and I don't have daddy issues." Never mind my father was an absentee parent except for the fact that he lived with us—after my mother went missing, when I was in grade school, he was never the same. "I think it's safe to say I won't be walking down the red carpet with your uncle at the next Oscars."

Brianna slows as we exit through the gates. She makes the right turn onto Seashell Drive, swinging wide to avoid hitting the UPS truck that's double-parked in front of the condo building on the corner. "Okay, but fair warning: He doesn't give up easily."

"I'm pretty sure I'm immune to his charms."

"That won't stop him."

"Are you saying I should cancel my d— um, meeting with him?"

"Actually, I have a better idea." She cuts me a sly glance. "You know that Rajeev is taking Ivy out to dinner tonight?"

"She mentioned it, yes."

"Well, I suggested they book a table at the Shady Brook Inn. That way, if you need backup . . ."

"You," I say, breaking into a grin, "are evil."

"I learned from the best," Brianna replies with a modest shrug.

CHAPTER TWENTY-THREE

That evening, Karol Bartosz arrives to pick me up at seven forty sharp. As I walk toward the black Escalade that's idling in my driveway—the same one I noticed at Casa Linda Estates on the day of the murder—my sense of unease returns. Maybe this wasn't such a good idea after all. Because blondes don't always have more fun. Some, like Delilah Ward, wind up dead.

"You're a vision, my dear," Bartosz says as I slide in next to him in the backseat. The driver is the bull-necked security guard, who's become a familiar figure, though we've never exchanged more than a few words.

"You wouldn't have said that if you'd seen me when I got off work. I was covered in termite droppings." The infestation at the Oliveiras' house had their wooden ceiling raining tiny brown pellets that stuck to my sweaty skin—I looked like a poppy seed bagel by the time I left to go home. But if I hoped to dispel his "vision" of me, my efforts were in vain. He continues to eye me in my basic black dress as if I were encased in Spandex. Bartosz himself is the picture of old-world elegance, wearing a charcoal bespoke suit that disguises his girth, a striped shirt with French cuffs, and an Hermès necktie in a subtle lavender-and-plum pattern. The white silk handkerchief that protrudes from his breast pocket compliments his cockatoo's crest.

"Women are at their most beautiful when they're not trying to look beautiful," he replies, smiling.

Brianna was right. There's no discouraging this guy.

Fifteen minutes later, we're pulling up at the Shady Brook Inn. Located in the hills northeast of town, the restaurant overlooks a wooded ravine with a creek running through it. Its romantic setting and two Michelin stars make it a popular wedding as well as dining destination. I think of Delilah's "fairy-tale" marriage that wasn't so perfect—I've thought of little else since I discovered the note she wrote—as I walk past the photos of bridal couples that cover the walls of the entryway.

The main dining room has walls paneled in fir, an open-beamed ceiling hung with copper-and-oak Craftsman chandeliers, and etched-glass panels depicting woodland scenes that divide what would otherwise seem a cavernous space, giving it a more intimate feel. Arrangements of curly willow and evergreen boughs studded with flowers and dried persimmons and pomegranates in pottery bowls made by local artisans add the perfect grace notes. "You chose well," Bartosz remarks as he looks around in appreciation. "It's exactly what I had in mind."

"Come, I'll introduce you." I wave to the owner, Steve Hanson, who's having a word with the hostess, a beautiful redhead named Jill, who also happens to be his wife and the mother of their three children. Steve looks like your typical surfer dude with his deep tan and sun-bleached, longish blond hair, but he has an MBA from Stanford and has been in the family business since he was thirteen. He was my supervisor when Ivy and I both had summer jobs at the Shady Brook during our junior and senior years, when his parents owned the restaurant.

"It's an honor, Mr. Bartosz," Steve says after I've made the introductions. "I've seen all your movies. In fact I took my wife to see *The Night Watchman* on our first date."

"And she married you anyway?" Bartosz seems amused.

"It wasn't what I would call a date-night movie," Steve admits. "But it was brilliant."

I remember that the movie was so bloody that I had nightmares after I watched it. I'd forgotten about that, or maybe I'd blocked it from my memory. But it's coming back to me now, and I cast a nervous glance at Bartosz, wondering if it was autobiographical like some of his other films.

"One more and we could call it a class reunion," Ivy remarks when we stop to greet her and Rajeev, who are seated at a two-top by the sliders to the deck, as Steve is showing us to our table. She glows in a silk wrap dress the same aquamarine color as her eyes. Rajeev, in a coat and tie, looks Bollywood-worthy as ever.

"Then we'd have to wear name tags," Steve says with a laugh.

"And pretend we like people we used to hate," I say.

Ivy tips me a wink as Bartosz and Rajeev exchange pleasantries. We have a secret pact. Through the years, it has led to numerous dates from hell being mercifully cut short when one or the other was summoned to some fictitious family emergency following an SOS text. Between the two of us, Ivy and I had lost six sets of grandparents and countless pets to sudden, tragic deaths.

Tonight, she's my wingwoman.

Finally, we sit down at our table. Our server, a salt-and-pepper-haired man named Frank who's been waiting tables at the Shady Brook Inn since I worked here, brings us menus. Bartosz asks if I would prefer red or white wine. I order a Perrier with lime, explaining that I don't drink, and suggest that he might enjoy the Bonny Doon pinot grigio from one of our local wineries. "For someone who doesn't drink, you certainly know your wine," he comments when he's sampled it.

I take a sip of my Perrier. "A little too well, I'm afraid."

He nods in understanding. "Here's to new beginnings." He raises his wineglass, holding my gaze a beat too long.

I grab my menu, and say, in an effort to set a businesslike tone,

"Why don't we go over this before we get distracted? You know, for your dinner party. I highly recommend the smoked trout appetizer. Also, the goat cheese tart with braised leeks, and the carrot soup with fennel. As for the entrees . . ."

"You don't really think I asked you here to discuss menu items?"

I look up at the sound of his voice to find him regarding me with wry amusement. I feel my cheeks warm. "I normally take someone at their word, yes. If you had some ulterior motive—"

"Only this." He places his hand over mine. "The pleasure of your company."

"You should have said so in the first place," I reply testily.

"And what would you have told me?"

I withdraw my hand. "That I have a boyfriend."

Bartosz responds with a philosophical shrug. "I have a wife. And yet here we are, enjoying a lovely evening together. Where's the harm in that? If I find you attractive, Tish, I can hardly be blamed. I only want what every man in this room is envying me at this moment."

Oh, he's good. I'll give him that. The line is a new one on me, and I thought I'd heard them all from when I used to get hit on by men in bars. But I'm not easily swayed by flattery. "I don't appreciate being lured into having dinner with you under a false pretext."

He puts on an expression of mock contrition. "Then allow me to redeem myself by humbly begging your pardon and formally requesting that you do me the honor of dining with me."

"Fine," I relent. "As long it's just dinner."

Over our appetizers of warm duck salad and Arctic char with sea beans, we finally get around to discussing his dinner party, which is in honor of Delilah, I learn. He explains that, with the date for her memorial still months away—it had been set for the middle of September—he felt the need to mark her passing in some way. "In Hollywood, this is what passes for sitting shiva," he says.

"Does that mean everyone will be wearing black?" I know little of the Jewish custom, only that it's an open house for people to pay their respects to the families of deceased loved ones.

He smiles. "Not unless it's black tie. And no covering of mirrors."

"I'll be the only person who didn't know Delilah."

"But you met her?"

"Once, briefly."

"And what was your impression?" Bartosz's brown eyes study me below his thick, black brows that are in stark contrast to his snowy mane.

"She was more down-to-earth than I expected," I reply as I bring a forkful of char laced with *uni* foam to my mouth. "I think we could have become friends if we'd met under different circumstances."

"Yes, she was good at that."

"What?"

"Being whoever you wanted her to be," he answers, leaving me to wonder what he means.

The evening is more pleasant than I expected. Bartosz entertains me with his stories. If Brianna's are of a "Hollyweird" peopled with poseurs with skewed values and ruthless ambitions, his are of a glamorous world filled with glamorous people doing exciting things. He tells me about the party he attended at "Bob" Redford's ranch when he was at last year's Sundance Film Festival, and about cruising the Mediterranean with "George and Amal" aboard his leased yacht during a recent trip to Italy. I quiz him about the goings-on behind the scenes of the movie he's currently filming, but he doesn't divulge much more than what I already know. Brent Harding has "an eye for the ladies." Liam Brady is a "prankster." Taylor Ramsey is a "little vixen."

We're tucking into our desserts of *tarte tatin* and blackberry shortcake when I become aware of movement over at Ivy and Rajeev's table. I look over to see Rajeev getting down on one knee before Ivy. My heart sinks when I realize what's happening. *Oh, no.*

No. Please don't. I watch in dismay as he pulls a jeweler's box from his pocket, smiling up at Ivy as she stares at him in shock. In the hush that's fallen, I hear him speak the words that my best friend dreads most.

"Ivy, will you marry me?"

Ivy bolts like a fox at the braying of a hound, leaving Rajeev to stare after her in disbelief, the cries of delight and applause from other diners dying in her wake. After a stunned moment, he goes after her. I follow, catching up with him in the hallway outside the restrooms.

"What just happened? Why did she run off?" he asks, looking hurt and confused.

Dude, what were you thinking? Any man who's been with Ivy as long as he has ought to have known better than to propose in a crowded restaurant. I chalk it up to the fact that beneath his Bollywood exterior lies the soul of a computer nerd who's inexperienced in the ways of women. I could have told him she'd run as if from a live grenade. But the damage is done, so I temper my response. "Maybe if you'd waited until you were alone before you proposed?" I suggest gently.

"I want to make a life with her. How is that a bad thing?" he whispers plaintively, still clutching the jeweler's box in his hand. "I thought she knew that I would propose. She met my parents. Does she think I would not have asked her to marry me had they not approved?"

"No. It's not that. It's just . . . Look, you should be discussing this with her, not me."

Rajeev stares at the closed door to the ladies' room. "How can I when she refuses to show her face?"

He has a point. Which places me in an awkward position. "You never talked to her about it before? The subject of marriage and kids never came up?" I lower my voice as a heavily perfumed woman with a helmet of blond hair sidles past us before she disappears into the ladies' room.

"Yes, of course." He runs his fingers through his thick, glossy hair before he slumps against the wall between two sconces. "When we were first dating. She told me she didn't see herself as a wife or mother. And I said I wasn't ready to be a husband. But that was before our feelings for each other had grown. Before my parents came to meet her." He eyes me dejectedly. "We don't have to decide about children right away. If she doesn't want children, I could live with that."

If this were a Bollywood musical, Ivy would have popped out of the ladies' room at that moment, tears of joy running down her cheeks at having come to the realization that her love for Rajeev was strong enough to overcome any doubts or fears. Everyone would be singing and dancing while music played. Instead, Rajeev sighs to the soundtrack of a toilet flushing.

"Sounds like you two have more talking to do. In the meantime, hold that thought." I tap the jeweler's box. He looks down as if he forgot he was holding it, then straightens and slips it in his pocket.

"Yes, we need to talk, but not tonight." Rajeev's expression hardens into one of grim resolve. "Now I should go home before I say something I'll regret. Will you let her know?"

"Of course. She can ride home with me."

Rajeev quirks an eyebrow at me. "Your friend, Mr. Bartosz, won't mind?"

"Are you kidding? Knowing him, he'll try to rope us into a threesome," I reply just as the blond lady emerges in a cloud of perfume. She gives me a scandalized look.

"I don't want to discuss it." Ivy's voice floats toward me, disembodied.

"Fine. But I'm not leaving until you come out." I cross my arms over my chest and lean back against the row of sinks set in granite that stands opposite the stall where my best friend is holed up.

Thirty seconds pass before the door to the stall swings open and Ivy steps out. She looks as if she's been crying. She walks over to one of the sinks and cranks on the tap. "I didn't handle that very well."

"You think?"

She turns to glare at me as she washes her hands. "No need to rub it in."

"Looks like you're doing a good job of it yourself."

She grabs a paper towel, embossed with the Shady Brook Inn logo of ferns in a laurel wreath pattern, from the stack on the counter and uses it to wipe mascara from under her eyes after she's dried her hands. "How bad, on a scale of one to ten?" The question we've been asking each other through the years, with every breakup or dating disaster, every foolish move in the name of love.

"I can't say until you give him an answer."

"Oh, God." Ivy buries her face in the paper towel.

"You better hurry, because he's leaving."

"Without me?" Her head jerks up. She looks stricken.

"I'm sure he took care of the bill." Even though she broke his heart and humiliated him in front of everyone, Rajeev is, above all else, a gentleman. "I told him you could ride home with us."

"I don't care about that!" Ivy whisper-shrieks. "How did he seem?"

"Confused, hurt. Couldn't you have told him you'd think about it at least?"

"I panicked," she moans.

"I noticed." Unfortunately, so had everyone else in the restaurant. "On the bright side, he didn't take it as a no. He's hoping you'll come around, even if he doesn't want to talk to you right now."

"I can't marry him."

"Why? Because you always said you'd never get married? Or because you've seriously considered and rejected the idea of marrying a man who loves you and who you claim to love? A decision,

I might add, that would have women on two continents scrambling to be next in line."

"You think I should marry him." She narrows her puffy eyes at me in reproach.

"As I told you before, I think you should keep an open mind."

She crumples the towel and tosses it in the bin. "Keep talking, and I'll make it the ugliest bridesmaid dress you've ever seen. Pink satin with ruffles and bows and ginormous puffy sleeves."

I grin at her. "I'd walk down the aisle naked if that's what it took."

"Then he'd think he was marrying the wrong girl."

We start to giggle, and soon we're laughing so hard, tears are streaming down our cheeks. It breaks the tension, and possibly a fingernail when an older lady comes in to use the bathroom and then can't exit fast enough after she's done. She must have thought we were drunk. "We should get back, or Bartosz will think I'm talking you off the ledge," I say when our giggles subside.

She sighs as I lean in to pluck a stray eyelash from her cheek. "And I was supposed to rescue *you*."

"That won't be necessary. Bartosz is behaving himself. He's actually quite charming."

"The night is young." She waggles her eyebrows suggestively.

CHAPTER TWENTY-FOUR

Later that night, I Skype with Bradley. We haven't spoken in days—he's currently in the Arghandab district of Afghanistan, covering some heavy military action—so there's a lot to catch him up on, starting with my trip to Montana (the expurgated version) and ending with Rajeev's ill-fated marriage proposal. "It was awful," I say. "There he was down on one knee with everyone watching, and Ivy . . . You'd have thought she was running from a burning building."

"Poor guy." Bradley's face creases in sympathy. "Though I have to say, he brought it on himself."

"You mean he shouldn't have popped the question in front of all those people?"

"Well, yeah. But he also broke the cardinal rule."

"And what's the cardinal rule for proposing to one's girlfriend?"

"Don't, unless you're sure of what her answer will be."

I arch my eyebrows at him. I'm reclining on my bed, wearing my Angry Bird pj's, with my head propped against the headboard and my legs stretched in front of me. Hercules and Prince are curled on either side of me and my Mac Pro is nested on the pillow that covers my lap, the only thing warming my lady parts. "And how does a confirmed bachelor like yourself know so much?"

Bradley ended his previous relationship with an orthopedic

surgeon named Genevieve when she wanted to take it to the next level. Never mind that she was perfect for him: smart, talented, gorgeous, and with a gazillion frequent flier miles from her volunteer work for Doctors Without Borders. His attitude was, *Why ruin a good thing by putting a ring on it?* (Bradley and Ivy would make a good couple.) Naturally, I supported his decision, but now that I'm the girlfriend, I see it more from Genevieve's point of view. Recently, she emailed Bradley with the news that she was engaged to be married. I was happy for her, but it left me feeling hollow inside, wondering if this is all I'm ever going to have: a long-distance relationship in different time zones.

"How do you think I got to be a confirmed bachelor?" he replies lightly. Bradley thinks we're on the same page, for which I have only myself to blame—I may have given him that impression initially and I haven't disabused him of it since. In truth, the reason I'm still single at the age of thirty-six is because I have yet to fall in love with a man who's the marrying kind, and I won't settle.

"His heart was in the right place," I say in defense of Rajeev.

"So how was it left?"

"That remains to be seen."

"Marriage isn't for everyone."

"I'm well aware of that." An edge creeps into my voice. "But how can Ivy know if it's right for her if they've never even lived together?"

"Let's say they move in together. What happens when she realizes it was a mistake six months or a year from now? They'll both be worse off than they were before."

"That's *if* and not *when*. Sometimes these things work out."

"And a lot of the time, they don't."

Why are you so damn pessimistic? I almost snap before I remember that I have no business being annoyed at my boyfriend. He's always been honest with me and, in fact, he warned me in the beginning that he wasn't the white-picket-fence, two-car-garage kind of guy. I change the subject before the debate can turn ugly. I tell him about my dinner with Bartosz. "He's hoping I'll do him the honor of becoming his next blonde. Good thing Ivy was with us on the ride home. I only had to fend him off for the five minutes it took us to get to my house after we dropped her off."

"If he laid a hand on you . . ." Bradley's voice deepens to a growl.

"Oh, he laid a hand on me all right. Four fingers of which are still intact." I'm exaggerating. Fortunately for us both, I turned my head when Bartosz was kissing me good night, and what was shaping up to be a wet one landed on my cheek instead.

Bradley's face relaxes in a smile. "Pity the poor man who messes with you."

"And you have the scars to show for it." Bradley and I had a "meet cute," as they say in Hollywood. I mistook him for a squatter at one of my properties and hurled a vase at him as he was coming out of the shower, only to discover afterward he was the visiting son of the owners, not a homeless man. It didn't result in bodily harm only because of Bradley's quick reflexes.

It's 12:30 a.m. by the time we sign off. I nudge Prince to get him to scoot over so I can crawl under the covers, and he rolls onto his back, inviting me to scratch his belly. I oblige, muttering, "Men. You think all we're good for is to keep you happy." I lie awake in the dark long after I've put out the light, reflecting on my pitiful love life. I've forgotten what it feels like to have Bradley's arms around me, while the memory of my night in Montana with Spence is all too vivid. I grow aroused at the memory of his lips on mine, our bodies tangled together on the sofa. Combustible is the only word for it. Sort of like when I set fire to his Camaro.

I'm awakened in the middle of night by the sound of Prince growling beside me. Then I hear another, fainter sound: the creaking of floorboards in the hallway. I bolt upright, wide awake, my heart pounding. *Someone is in the house.* I break out in goose bumps.

Prince is still growling. My cat's yellow eyes glow in the dark. "Who's there?" My voice emerges as a faint whisper.

I fumble for my phone on the nightstand. It's not there. Of course it's not there. It's plugged into its charger in my office. What now? I can't call 911. And my gun is in my office along with my cell phone. Did I remember to set the house alarm before I went to bed? I think so, but I'm not sure. I cock my head, listening. I'm not hearing the sound now. I slip out of bed to investigate, while Prince and Hercules both wisely opt to stay put. The recent attempt on my life is uppermost in my mind as I peer into the darkness, looking for something I can use as a weapon. The lamp on my nightstand? No. I'd have to pull the bed away from the wall to unplug it, which would alert the intruder—if it *is* an intruder—to the fact that I'm awake. The pottery candlestick on my dresser? Not heavy enough. In movies, there's usually a baseball bat handy in situations such as this, but I don't play baseball. I do work out on occasion, however, which reminds me of the body bar that's in my closet. Double the length of my arm and weighing ten pounds, it could inflict some damage.

I ease open the door of the closet and wince at the creaking of its hinges. Craftsman bungalows don't have walk-in closets unless they were remodeled at some later date, and mine is no exception. As a result, it's crammed full with clothes, shoes and boots, an old tennis racket, a plastic bin that holds gift-wrapping paper . . . Shoes in shoeboxes are stacked on the shelf along with boxes of old photos. I wriggle my hand through the tightly packed clothing that hangs from the clothes rod, groping for the body bar that I dimly recall having propped against the wall in back. I freeze when I hear the creaking sound again. Not my imagination. And not the noise of an old house settling.

Someone is out there.

My heart climbs into my throat, and a chunk of ice lodges itself in the pit of my stomach. I reach deeper into the closet, thrusting my head in among the dresses and slacks and blouses on hangers that smell of deodorant and fabric softener. Where the hell is that body bar? Has it really been that long since I last worked out? Yeah, this is what happens when you let yourself go. You die.

I hear the snick of a door latch and feel a gust of cooler air from the hallway. Prince erupts in a fit of barking. (Too bad he's not a Rottweiler.) I drop into a crouch, the beating of my heart matched by the frantic barking of the dog. I have only a few seconds before the intruder notices that my bed is empty and that the closet door is standing open, by which he'll cleverly deduce my whereabouts. Do I make a run for it? Something tells me I wouldn't get very far and that I would fare better if I were face-to-face with the intruder. But how can I defend myself without a weapon? I'm wearing my big-girl panties, but fortitude alone isn't enough, especially when you're so scared you're about to pee those panties. I'm shaking with fright. The blood roaring in my ears seems loud enough to wake the dead, the ranks of which it appears I'll soon be joining.

An image of Delilah's dead body flashes through my mind, and I summon the courage to rise from my crouch. If I can't die with my boots on, I can die on my feet surrounded by boots at the very least. I thrust my hand deep into the recesses of my closet . . . and feel my fingers close, blessedly, around the body bar. I wrestle it free from the folds of clothing that it's caught on, and in a bold move, I leap from behind the door while simultaneously taking a swing aimed at the intruder, whom I can't see but who I know is nearby from the proximity of the creaking noises. The bar whistles through the air instead of connecting with flesh. I see a blur of movement in the darkness—a fleeting impression of a figure clad in dark clothing and a ski mask—before I'm knocked off my feet by a hard kick to my kneecaps. Then suddenly all hell breaks loose. I'm lying on the floor when my cat and dog launch themselves at the intruder in a fury of barking, hissing, and spitting. I hear a grunt, as if at the pain of sharp teeth sinking into an ankle. I let out a scream loud enough for the neighbors two doors down to hear. Over the chorus of barking, yowling, and shrieking, I hear the percussive note of footsteps thudding as the intruder beats a hasty retreat, followed by the sound of the front door slamming shut.

I curl up in the fetal position on the braided rug that covers the floor, where I remain huddled until I feel rough tongues licking me. I drag myself upright. Prince wriggles onto my lap and Hercules meows loudly as he winds back and forth, rubbing his body against mine. "Good dog. Good kitty," I whisper, my fingers tangled in the Yorkie's fur as I stroke my cat with my other hand.

Finally, I get up. I go to my office down the hall and get my phone. I don't call 911, though. Instead, I dial a number from my contact list. A sleepy male voice answers. "Tish? What's wrong?"

I start to cry. "S-somebody just t-tried to k-kill me," I manage to get out between gasping breaths.

"Do you need me to call an ambulance?" The voice is alert now. Calm and controlled, buffering my hysteria.

"No. I . . . I'm okay."

"Where are you?"

"Home. I'm home. Can you come?" I squeak.

"I'm on my way," says Spence.

CHAPTER TWENTY-FIVE

Spence arrives just as the uniforms are pulling up in front of my house—he must have called them en route. He asks questions, then leaves the uniforms to fill out their report while he canvasses the premises inside and out. Whoever the intruder was, he (or possibly she) knew his way around home-security systems because mine had been disabled. There's no other sign of disturbance. "We'll do a door-to-door as soon as it's light out," Spence says. "One of your neighbors might have noticed something." But if my screams had roused the Nuyens or Mrs. Caswell, what would they have seen except a masked figure fleeing? If the intruder was smart enough to disable my alarm, he would have parked someplace where his or her vehicle wouldn't be spotted.

It's after three A.M. by the time the uniforms leave. I'm so wiped out I don't protest when Spence leads me back to bed and lies down next to me with his body spooned against mine. Secretly, I'm glad for his arms that hold me tight until I've stopped shivering and have drifted off to sleep.

When I wake the next morning, he's gone. On the nightstand is a note. *I asked Frontpoint*—the home-security company that installed my system—*to send someone. Keep your doors locked in the meantime.*

I call Ivy, and she insists on coming over. She fixes me breakfast between gasps of horror and exclamations as I describe the scare I had last night. "Could you tell if it was a man or a woman?" She puts a plate of scrambled eggs and toast in front of me. The toast is slightly burned and the eggs are rubbery—Ivy is not the greatest cook—but she's here, which is all that matters.

"No, it was too dark." I shudder at the memory and pull my robe more tightly around me. "It wasn't Olivia Harding, though. I don't think anyone who was eight months pregnant would be that nimble."

"She could have an accomplice. Her husband or someone who was working for her." Ivy sits down opposite me, helping herself to a triangle of my slightly burned toast when she notices I'm not eating. She nibbles it while Hercules and Prince sit at her feet, looking up at her expectantly. You'd never guess from the way they're licking their chops that they had their fill of treats earlier, as a reward for saving my life last night. Prince may be the size of Toto, but he has the soul of Lassie. As for Hercules, I never doubted his fearlessness or the deadly aim of his claws. "But why *you*, that's what I don't get. You're not a material witness, so you're no threat to anyone."

I consider this as I sip my coffee. "No, but I've been asking questions. Also, at Bartosz's party, I hinted I knew something about Delilah's murder that I wasn't at liberty to disclose," I remind her.

"Do you think it was Brent Harding that attacked you? It would make sense, if he's an accessory after the fact in Delilah's murder."

"Maybe. I can't be sure. I didn't see his face."

"Did you tell Spence what you told me—that you suspect Olivia and Brent?"

"Yeah, but he didn't take it seriously. He thinks the only thing that's creepy about Brent Harding is his face work."

"He may see it differently after what happened last night."

"He came right over when I called. That's something." I warm at the memory of his body spooned against mine. I felt safe in his arms, knowing nothing else bad could happen as long as he was with me.

"He cares about you."

There was a time I would have protested heatedly. But if actions speak louder than words, Spence's actions last night—and prior to that, I realize looking back—had disproven the old adage, that a leopard doesn't change its spots, to which I'd clung. "Either he's changed, or I've mellowed."

"Or maybe he was always a nice guy, and you pushed his buttons so you wouldn't have to see it."

"What is this, Psych 101? Speaking of nice guys . . ."

Ivy's face falls at the reference to Rajeev. "No, he hasn't called. And he hasn't returned any of the eight hundred messages I left." She sighs and breaks what's left of her toast triangle in two pieces, feeding them to the dog and cat. Prince inhales his half, while Hercules licks the butter from his.

"A man has his pride."

Ivy sighs again, staring glumly into her coffee cup.

We're interrupted by the bleating of the ringtone on my phone. It's Brianna. It seems she's left several messages on my voicemail and she became concerned when I didn't call her back. I explain that I slept in, and when I tell her why, she makes all the right noises, fretting aloud like an elderly maiden aunt until she's assured that all the doors and windows in the house are secured. She tells me not to worry about a thing on the work front, she's got it covered. That I don't doubt. She orders me to take the rest of the day off. "Yes, boss," I reply with a small smile.

The guy from the home-security company shows up as Ivy is leaving to go to work. He makes the necessary repairs, but even with my system up and running again, I don't feel safe. It's horrible knowing you're not safe even in your own home. I can't go on living in fear, I realize, seeing the bogeyman in every shadow.

Because the next attempt on my life might succeed. *Think, Tish.* I sit for a long while, still in my pajamas, drinking my umpteenth cup of coffee as I stare sightlessly out the window at the backyard, lost in thought, until an idea forms. By the time I've showered and dressed, I have the outline of a plan.

I leave a message on Spence's voicemail before calling the number for the station, where the desk sergeant informs me he's at the hospital. Visiting the officer who was wounded in the armed robbery that went down earlier in the week, I imagine. Twenty minutes later, I'm pulling up to Dominican Hospital in a cab. I feel as though I'm treading a well-worn path as I cross the atrium-style lobby, remembering my daily trips to see my father when he was in the oncology ward on the fourth floor. But that was then, and this is now. There had been no hope for my dad. But my situation isn't hopeless, not if I *do* something rather than wait for the killer to make his next move.

My pulse quickens at the bold plan I have in mind.

As luck would have it, Spence steps from one of the elevators as I'm approaching. But he's not wearing a visitor's badge. He's holding the hand of a little girl with his blond hair and blue eyes who could only be his daughter. He seems surprised to see me before concern registers on his face.

"Tish, what are you doing here? Is everything all right?"

"I'm fine. I was looking for you, actually, but I see I caught you at a bad time." I smile down at his little girl. She has a bandage on her chin and a bloodstain on the Hello Kitty T-shirt she's wearing.

"My daughter had a little accident," he explains.

I bend down so that I'm eye level with her. "Hi. My name's Tish. What's yours?"

"Katie," she says brightly. "I got stitches!" She points to the gauze covering her chin. "Colby pushed me, and I fell on my *face*. There was blood *everywhere*. Daddy took me to the doctor to get fixed. Look what I got!" She shows off the Beanie Baby she's holding, a purple frog.

"One of the bigger kids got a little rough on the playground at school," Spence explains.

"Did you arrest the kid?"

He smiles. "I will if he ever pulls a stunt like that again."

"Noooo, Daddy," Katie corrects him. "I *told* you, we were *playing*. Colby's my *friend*." To me she says, "I didn't cry. Only a little. I'm not a crybaby like Ryan." Ryan is her little brother, I recall.

"That's right, sweetie. And when Ryan's your age, he'll be just as brave as his big sister." Spence strokes Katie's small blond head, and she looks up at him adoringly. I feel a pang, witnessing the tender moment between father and daughter, wishing I'd had that with my own dad. "Is there something you want to talk to me about?" he asks in a low voice as I walk out with him.

"Yes, but . . ." I cast a meaningful glance at his daughter.

"We can talk after I drop Katie off, if you want to ride with us."

On the drive to her house, Katie chatters on about how brave she was, and how she won't cry when she gets her ears pierced on her birthday. "Because then Mommy won't let me," she adds solemnly.

"We told her she had to wait until her next birthday," Spence explains when Katie becomes engrossed in playing with her Beanie Baby. "I still say she's too young, but Barb says if we make a big deal of it she'll do it on her own when she's older and it won't just be her ears that are pierced."

"In other words, you caved."

He gives a rueful chuckle. "It was the threat of a belly ring that did it."

"When did you become Ward Cleaver?"

"When I became a parent. I don't want my kids doing the same dumb stuff I did."

We arrive at the house, a modest ranch painted beige with coffee trim, situated on a quiet, tree-lined street south of town, and I wait while he takes his daughter inside. He appears tense when he climbs back in the car. He starts the engine, then stares straight ahead as it idles. "God, I hate this. Every time I walk through that door . . ." He shakes his head, looking bereft. "My kids used to ask when I was coming home. They've stopped asking. I don't know which is worse."

"You'll always be their dad. That will never change."

Spence smiles wanly. "Feel like taking a walk?" he asks as he's backing out of the driveway. I nod, and he drives to where his street dead-ends at a cliff that looks out on the ocean. We get out and follow a footpath that leads to a beach access. We make our way down the wooden staircase to find the beach deserted except for a lone fisherman and a woman walking her dog. Surfers ride the waves, and farther out at sea, sailboats glide. We take our shoes off and stroll along the packed sand by the water's edge, the surf washing over our feet with each wave that rolls in.

"The guy from the security company came," I inform him. "Thanks for thinking of that."

"I wish there was more I could do." He sounds frustrated.

"Any luck with the neighbors?"

"Lady next door, Mrs. Caswell, heard your screams. She thought she saw someone when she looked out her window, but she didn't get a good look, so she couldn't give us a description."

Just as I suspected. "Dark clothes, ski mask. Not much to go on, even if she'd gotten a better look."

"I haven't given up."

"Yeah, but what are the chances? If it's the same person who killed Delilah, he's as good as gone. Or he's hiding in plain sight."

"It's still an active investigation."

"Which is rapidly becoming a cold case." He doesn't contradict me, which emboldens me to go on, "What if there was another way?"

"Like what?" He cuts me a wary look.

"What if you were to set a trap?"

"A trap?" he repeats, frowning.

I sketch out my plan, which seems more far-fetched as I voice it than when I was formulating it in my head. "I'm invited to a dinner party Bartosz is hosting next Friday, and chances are Delilah's killer will be there, too, if it's the same person who drugged me at his last party." I step over strands of kelp that form a braid along the tide line. The sand is cold against the soles of my feet, but that's not why I'm shivering. "Let's say I was to hint that I know something about Delilah's murder."

"Didn't you already do that?"

"Yes, but I kept it vague. This time I'd say it was information vital to the case."

"I'd have made the arrest by now if you had vital information."

"Not if you were holding off until you had the evidence to back it up."

"Good point." He nods, and I see the respect in his eyes. He's starting to realize I'm more than a pain in the ass—the pest who shows up at crime scenes—that I actually have a knack for this.

"The killer would be desperate. He, assuming it's a man, has already come after me on two separate occasions. He'll try again, possibly even that night, if he's spooked enough. Which is where you come in. As soon he makes his move, you move in and make the arrest."

Spence stops and turns to face me, the wind that's blowing off the ocean flattening his short blond hair on that side of his head. The lenses of his wire-rims are lightly misted with sea spray, but I can see the concern in his eyes. "You'd be taking a huge risk. I couldn't ask that of you."

"You're not asking. I'm offering."

He shakes his head. "It's still a risk. I couldn't guarantee your safety even with police protection."

"I'd be safer than I am at home," I point out. "And from what you've told me, the chief is desperate enough to try anything. Let's face it, it's not like you have a whole lot of other options."

"You don't know that."

"Yeah, I do. Or you'd have a suspect in custody by now. Come on. What do you have to lose?"

I'm surprised and touched when he answers in a soft voice, "You."

My throat tight, we walk in silence to where the beach ends in a rock jetty before we head back. Sandpipers scatter at our approach, whole flocks moving as one like the shadows cast by the clouds that scud overhead. Spence stops to douse a burned-down campfire that is still smoldering. We pause to watch as the fisherman reels in his catch and a surfer glides gracefully into shore on his board. The climb up the steep wooden steps has me panting by the time I reach the top.

I pause to catch my breath. "I'm getting old."

"With any luck," Spence mutters.

I refrain from commenting. Patience isn't my strong suit, but I can see from the expression on Spence's face, as we walk back to his car, that he's debating with himself, so I wait for him to come to a decision. "All right," he says at last. "I'll run it by the chief, see what he has to say." He pauses when we reach his car. "In the meantime . . ." He pulls out his wallet, from which he extracts a driver's license—mine, I see when he hands it to me. "I believe this belongs to you."

"Oh, my God. Thank you!" I throw my arms around him, kissing him on the cheek. When I start to draw back, I feel his own arms tighten around me. Then we're kissing for real. I catch a faint whiff of smoke from the campfire he'd put out, along with the masculine scent that is his alone. His lips are salty with sea spray, and their warmth travels through me as if I'd gulped a hot beverage. "Thank you," I say again when we finally stop kissing, murmuring it this time.

"I'm not sure I'm doing you any favors." Spence's voice rumbles up from his chest as he holds me close, my head against his shoulder. "Something tells me you'd be better off locked up."

CHAPTER TWENTY-SIX

Spence drops me off at the Russo house, where I'd arranged to meet up with Brianna. I'm surprised to find a cement truck parked in the driveway. Normally, the owners of my properties inform me in advance of any home improvement projects. I wonder why nothing was said about this one. I walk around in back, where I find my client Mr. Russo overseeing a crew of workers who are pouring a foundation by the six-foot privacy fence. There's no sign of Brianna. She must be inside.

"I would have called ahead if I'd known you were in town," I apologize, after we've exchanged greetings. "What's all this?" I gesture toward the construction site, which covers an area roughly equal in dimension to the swimming pool. The four workers are smoothing the freshly poured cement with concrete trowels. Building materials are stacked on the lawn around it.

Russo's brown eyes dance with merriment as he presses his finger to his lips in a shushing motion. "It's a surprise, so don't say anything to Lydia. She thinks I'm in Palm Springs on business."

"What's the occasion?"

"Our fiftieth." His and his wife's golden anniversary is next month. They're celebrating with a party here at the house. They sent me an invitation. "I couldn't think what to get her—she says she has more jewelry than she could ever wear—then I remembered she's always wanted a greenhouse."

"She'll love it." Mrs. Russo is more the Smith Hawken than the Cartier type. Her hobby is orchids, and she's running out of places in the house to put them. "I promise I won't breathe a word."

He tips me a wink. "You know where all the bodies are buried, eh, Tish?" He's referring to the indiscretions of my other clients about which I keep mum, but at the mention of bodies, coupled with the sight of wet cement and Russo's rumored mob ties, I feel a little queasy all of a sudden.

Not that Victor Russo seems threatening. With his golf tan and the khaki trousers and V-necked sweater he's wearing, he could be mistaken for a retired banker or an insurance executive. His face is even featured below a balding crown, and nothing like the swarthy ones you see in *The Godfather*. You would never guess from looking at him that he owned a casino. Except for his watchful gaze. Occasionally, I'll catch him studying me as if I were on a CCTV monitor at his casino.

"Don't mention the word *bodies*," I reply with a groan.

"Ah, yes. Terrible business, that. I knew her—Miss Ward," he adds, and in my mind's eye, I see the picture of Russo and Delilah together at his casino. My discomfort intensifies.

"Really?" I feign surprise.

"She and her husband were regulars at the casino," Russo explains. "He liked to gamble. She went along to keep an eye on him. She was a real sweetheart—always went out of her way to personally thank me whenever I comped them a meal—though I can't say the same for him. He didn't deserve her, if you ask me." The look of contempt on his face at the mention of Eric Nyland softens into one of reflection. "She was that rarest of creatures—exquisite with a heart of gold. She could light up a room just by walking into it. No other woman could compare and there wasn't a man—"

Our conversation is interrupted by a familiar female voice

chirping, "Lemonade, anyone?" I turn to see Brianna stepping out from inside, carrying a bamboo tray that holds tall, frosty glasses of lemonade topped with sprigs of mint. Like she's the lady of the house. Unbelievable. Russo helps himself to a lemonade while I just stare at her.

"What do you think you're doing?" I whisper when Russo moves to the other end of the patio to take a call on his cell phone.

"I thought the men would like some refreshments," she answers pleasantly, moving past me onto the lawn. She chats with the workers while they thirstily gulp their lemonades. Knowing her, it was made from lemons that she picked herself. The lemon trees bordering the patio are loaded with them.

"Did you bake bread while you were at it?" I ask when she rejoins me.

"I'm glad to see you haven't lost your sense of humor," she replies tartly before her expression softens with concern. "Are you okay? You look like you didn't get much sleep last night."

"So would you if you'd almost been killed in your bed by a masked intruder." I feel a chill go through me, remembering. "I'm lucky to still be alive. If it hadn't been for Prince . . . He woke me up with his growling, then he defended me like he was a trained attack dog."

"So does this mean . . . ?"

"Yep. He can stay." Like there was any question after he saved my life. "Oh, and thanks for filling in for me. It's been a crazy week—I don't know how I'd have managed without you."

"Just doing my job," she replies, matter-of-fact. "Speaking of which, while I was inside . . ."

"Squeezing lemons?" I prompt, arching an eyebrow.

"That was just an excuse. I wanted to have a look around, and I figured the door to the den wouldn't be locked if Mr. Russo was home. I was right." A sly smile steals across her pretty face.

Crafty girl. I should have known. "And?"

Brianna darts a glance at Russo, who's still on his phone at the other end of the patio, before she leans in to whisper, "I checked out his ego wall. The photo of him and Delilah? It wasn't there."

I don't know what to make of it. Why would Russo remove the picture of him and Delilah from his ego wall? Was it to keep from being reminded that her life had been cruelly taken, or so as not to draw attention to his connection with her? If it was the latter, why would he care unless he had something to hide? He certainly wasn't shy about mentioning Delilah to me.

The questions keep piling up, but so far I have no answers.

I don't hear back from Spence about my proposed plan until two days later. He calls me, fittingly enough, as I'm driving to Casa Blanca with a welcome basket for the new renters—a family of six from Michigan who are neither ghouls nor tabloid stringers posing as vacationers—after having left Brianna at the Keyses' beach cottage, on Seascape Drive, to meet with the contractor who's to replace the rotting fence. "It's a go." Spence's voice is grim. "The chief gave it the green light."

My heart starts to pound. This is huge. My one shot at flushing out Delilah's murderer and my would-be killer. "You don't sound too happy about it," I remark. "This could be your big break."

"Or your funeral," he growls. "The chief wasn't happy about it either. He wouldn't have agreed to it if he weren't desperate. Apparently, his concern for his own reputation takes precedence over any concerns about tying up departmental resources . . . or putting you at risk."

He details the plan of action as I drive south on Highway One. "I'll have a surveillance team posted outside the restaurant and two undercover officers on the inside, but you won't be in their line of sight every minute."

"I won't be alone, either. I'll be with other people besides the killer," I remind him. "If he . . . or she . . . tries to lure me away, I'll know it's a trap. And you can be damn sure I won't walk into it."

"'The best-laid plans . . .'" he intones darkly.

"If you quote Robert Burns, I'm hanging up."

"If a poem from a century ago is still being taught in schools, it means there's truth in it."

"Whatever." Butterflies flutter in my stomach, and my heart is pounding. What have I gotten myself into? Is this really such a good idea? I make light of the situation to keep my fears at bay. "Now I just need to find something to wear. Do you think red would send the wrong signal?"

CHAPTER TWENTY-SEVEN

The rest of the week is blessedly uneventful. The only corpse I find is a fish floating belly-up in the Chens' koi pond, the only drama one involving clients (Mrs. Miller discovered that Mr. Miller was cheating on her). Nonetheless, I'm a nervous wreck as I count down the days to Operation Red Carpet—the code name assigned by the police to their sting operation—because I know that, unlike on detective shows, there's a chance I won't come out of it alive.

And I used to think the worst thing about black-tie affairs was pantyhose and high heels.

When the day finally arrives, my fingernails are so bitten, they elicit a despairing head shake from the manicurist. Who has time for a manicure anyhow? I had to squeeze the appointment into my packed workweek. Then, as if the Millers' marriage being on the rocks weren't enough, I arrive at their house—my last stop on Friday—to find a leaky pipe had flooded their kitchen.

It seems a bad omen.

We're running fifteen minutes late when Brianna and I arrive at the Shady Brook Inn for her uncle's party. I circle the upper lot a couple times in my Explorer before I finally find a parking space in the lower lot. Minutes later, we're pulling up to the restaurant in the Shady Brook Inn shuttle, a London cab painted pistachio green and emblazoned with its logo. My stomach is in knots, and

I've sweated through a double layer of antiperspirant. But I can't let on—Brianna doesn't know about Operation Red Carpet; I told only my two trusted associates, Ivy and McGee—which is making me even more tense. I'm somewhat calmed when I see the unmarked van belonging to the police surveillance team parked across the street. *You're covered. Nothing can go wrong.* Also, my phone has been equipped with a transmitter, in case I should be in need of assistance at any time. There's also Spence, who is coordinating the efforts from police headquarters.

Inside, every table is filled, and through the glass sliders to the deck I see that the outdoor seating area, which is lit by the glow from the fairy lights that lace the branches of the trees beyond, is at full capacity as well. As I look around, I wonder which of the diners are the undercover cops, but no one stands out. The only visible security presence is the pair of bodyguards that flank the entrance to the private dining room to which we're escorted. Both men wear dark suits and earpieces. The taller of the two is the bull-necked security guy who works for Bartosz. The other guy, medium height and scrappy-looking, is all too familiar. I frown as I approach him.

"What are you doing here?" I hiss at McGee, while Bull Neck is occupied checking IDs.

"What it looks like." McGee motions toward his sidekick. "Jimmy here got me the gig after this other guy, Eddie, was fired on account of fraternizing with what's-her-name. The redhead who looks like a porn star? They weren't rehearsing her lines, if you get my drift. Figured I could use the extra cash."

"Likely story," I reply with a roll of my eyes.

He shrugs. "Somebody's gotta look out for you, Ballard."

I glance over my shoulder to see that Brianna has moved into the dining room. Bull Neck is busy with two more late arrivals, Rick McVittie and his date. I drop my voice nonetheless. "I have undercover cops and a surveillance team for that."

McGee snorts. "Amateurs. And I see you ain't packing." His

gaze skims over the gown I'm wearing, a vintage Halston with a fitted bodice and a skirt made up of layers of emerald and turquoise silk chiffon in a swirly pattern. I bought it at the consignment shop that Ivy frequents, two doors down from the Gilded Lily—the only place in town where you can purchase haute couture at affordable prices—but it fits like it was made for me. "Unless you got it where the sun don't shine."

"The invitation said black tie, not black ops."

"And I'm your plus one." He grins at me. In his dark suit with his hair scraped back in his usual ponytail, he looks more like a character from *Breaking Bad* than someone whose job it is to protect.

"Don't blow my cover, that's all I ask."

He places his hand over his heart. "I solemnly swear I won't shoot till I see the whites of their eyes."

I move past him and down a short flight of stone steps to the dining room, which is actually the wine cellar—it does double duty when the two designated private dining rooms are booked—where the other guests are gathered. When I used to work here, it was kept locked and only the owners, Mr. and Mrs. Hanson, and the sommelier had keys. I'd peeked in a few times, but now I pause to look around, taking in the exposed brick walls, stone floor, and low, curved ceiling clad in barrel oak. Rows of wine bottles cover each wall. At the center, there is a harvest table set with Provence linens in a muted botanical print, pewter cutlery and chasers, and jugs of flowers and potted herbs from the restaurant's garden that reflect the Shady Brook Inn's farm-to-table ethos. It seems ironic that an occasion to mark the passing of a woman who struggled with her sobriety should take place in a wine cellar, but fitting in a way, though I know it wasn't intended as such.

Bartosz walks over to greet me. "Crisis resolved?" he inquires after he kisses me on both cheeks. Brianna had texted him when we were en route.

"If you can call a leaky pipe a crisis." I put on a smile. I'm sweating despite the thermostat in the cellar being set at a relatively cool sixty-four degrees. "The owners of the house have bigger worries at the moment. She found out he was cheating on her. Which I could have told her."

"But you didn't," Bartosz replies with a knowing smile. He's elegantly attired in old-world European fashion, wearing a tuxedo with a velvet shawl collar and a shirt with rows of tiny ruffles.

"I'm paid to be discreet."

"And do you reserve judgment as well?"

I shrug. "People have a right to do as they please in their own homes as long as they're not hurting anyone. Besides, we all have secrets." I wonder what his are. If Bartosz is the murderer, what better way to appear above suspicion than to host a party in remembrance of his victim?

"Indeed we do." He smiles slyly. "Though I dare say there are some here whose secrets would shock even you." I already know that Brent Harding is a philanderer who's also into bondage, that his wife is a hot mess, and that Liam Brady is in recovery, so if Bartosz is referring to secrets of that nature, I could probably tell him a thing or two. The question is, who is a murderer?

After Bartosz has moved to greet Rick and his girlfriend, I observe the others as I sip my Perrier with lime brought by one of the servers. The men in their tuxedos look like the extras in Bond movies playing roulette at casinos in Monte Carlo. The women all have hair worthy of shampoo commercials and perfect bodies— or gravity-defying flesh in the case of the more mature ladies— showcased by the couture gowns they wear. The collective glow from all the cosmetically whitened teeth and porcelain veneers is as dazzling as that of the bling worn by the ladies.

I don't see the spiky-haired blonde, but that's probably because Olivia Harding is in attendance. In her beaded amber maternity gown, she glows like the gold Rolex on her husband's wrist. You would never know to look at them that she'd caught him cheating on her. Olivia is all smiles tonight, and if Brent's smile seems fixed, it could be because he's lost the ability to move his mouth from all the cosmetic surgery he's had. Liam Brady is his usual animated self as he flirts outrageously with his costar, Taylor Ramsey. I watch Rick McVittie inhale a canapé that's roughly the same size as his date. Mandy Drexler and Jillian Lassiter are in the corner where an antique wine press stands, Jillian's ginger curls contrasting with Mandy's flat-ironed black locks as they stand with their heads bent together in private conversation.

Which one of you killed Delilah Ward? I feel a prickling along my spine, recalling my own, near-fatal encounter with the killer. It's like a game of three-dimensional Clue with flesh-and-blood characters. I try to picture them in dark clothing and a ski mask, as one by one my gaze lights on each of the other guests before finally coming to rest on Brent and Olivia Harding. They look innocent as they stand chatting with Brianna and Greta Nyland, but appearances can be deceiving. Am I looking at a murderer and her accomplice?

"Thank you all for coming," begins our host when we're all seated at the table, Olivia on my right and Bartosz at the head of the table on my left. "We're fewer in number, having lost our beloved friend and colleague, Delilah, but let us not mourn," he intones in his theatrical baritone. "Tonight let us remember the shining star that she was. A star who shone both on and off the screen. Her life was cut short, tragically, but she lived life to the fullest, and that we can celebrate." He stands and raises his glass in a toast. "To Delilah." Then the only sound is that of glasses clinking together. Bartosz's eyes are moist as he concludes, in a cracked voice, "I miss her, dammit."

"She was some woman," Brent pipes up, apparently oblivious to the dark glance his wife shoots him.

"We *all* miss her," says Jillian Lassiter with seemingly heartfelt emotion. She earns a laugh from the others when she adds, "And I never thought I'd say that about a rival actress."

Over the appetizer course of poached quail eggs and slivers of quail confit on wood-roasted oyster mushrooms, memories of Delilah are shared around the table. Liam, who looks like a bad boy even in his tuxedo with his hair rumpled as if he rode here on a motorcycle, tells a story from when he and Delilah were filming *Return of Laserman*. "Beastly day it was, and I was flat-out, but Delilah insisted we visit a little boy in hospital whose fondest wish was to meet his idol. That would be Delilah, not I," he adds, eliciting chuckles. "We were the hit of the cancer ward until we were tossed out for overexciting the kiddies." He concludes, on a more solemn note, with a line from a poem. "'I cannot say and I will not say that she is dead, she is just far away.'"

Taylor Ramsey tells about when Delilah took her aside for a heart-to-heart at a People's Choice Awards ceremony. It was during Taylor's teen years, when she was behaving like a "spoiled brat," by her own admission. Delilah advised her to start acting like an adult or she wouldn't have a career. "Just like a big sister would." Taylor brushes a tear from her eye. "I can't believe she's gone." You would never know from the sad look she wears that she benefited from Delilah's death.

Rick McVittie talks about the time he and Delilah performed a skit together on *Saturday Night Live*, which is funnier in his recounting than it was when I watched it on TV. He has everyone cracking up, even his date who seems as lacking in personality as she is in body fat (apparently she's decided that putting blue streaks in her dyed-black hair makes enough of a statement). When laughter turns to tears that have several people dabbing at their eyes, Rick jokes, in a voice throaty with emotion, "Lighten up, people. For fuck's sake, you'd think somebody died."

"She was a devil, that one. Always with the pranks," recalls an older actress named Irina Chayefsky. Irina tells an amusing anecdote from when she and Delilah were making a picture together. Delilah had come to the set one day disguised in a wig and glasses, passing herself off as a production assistant. As Irina flings out her hand in reenacting the moment in which Delilah tore off her disguise to reveal her true identity, she accidentally smacks her husband—Kent? Keith?—in the face. A failed screenwriter fifteen years her junior—also number five in her hit parade of husbands—he squirms, wearing a pained smile, as Irina fusses over him, making sure he's all right.

Brianna, looking demure in a dusk-pink crepe de chine gown that brings out the rosiness in her cheeks, says a few words about how Delilah was as much a friend to her as a boss. Greta, wearing a navy gown with a high collar and cap sleeves, speaks movingly of her bond with her brother's wife, repeating what she'd told me at Bartosz's last party. "Delilah was the sister I never had."

Bartosz speaks of his "enduring" friendship with Delilah, which began with the first picture they made together when she was nineteen. Knowing that he has a thing for blondes, I wonder if there was ever a time when he and Delilah had been more than friends. His only reference to her drinking is to say, "She battled her demons, and the demons got the better of her at times."

Jillian recalls Delilah's graciousness in congratulating her the year they were both nominated for the Golden Globe for Best Supporting Actress and Jillian won. "You know, I think she actually meant it when she said the nomination was as good as winning," Jillian adds upon reflection.

Mandy Drexler portrays a Delilah who was outspoken in her support of racial diversity in Hollywood. "I was there when she put Bernie Waxman in his place," she says, naming a big-shot Hollywood producer. "We were at a party at his house and he made one of his obnoxious Bernie remarks. And Delilah says to him, sweet as pie, as she's looking around the room at all the white faces, 'If blacks are the new Jews of Hollywood, does that mean I'm at the wrong party?'" Everyone else laughs, a bit too loudly it seems, as servers pour more wine and clear away our plates.

The memory shared by Brent Harding is from when he and Delilah were filming the picture they'd made together in London. "So Delilah's stuck in her hotel suite—inner door was jammed— and we're due on the set. At the front desk they're running around like chickens with their heads cut off, except this one bellhop, a Pakistani kid. He barely spoke English, but he'd seen every *Mission Impossible* movie, like, twenty times. So he climbs the front of the building with a screwdriver between his teeth like he's some ninja and gets in through the balcony. Fucking epic!"

The frozen smile worn by Olivia Harding tells me she's thinking the same thing that I am: Brent must have been with Delilah in her hotel suite at the time to recall the incident in such detail. I hear her mutter to herself, "The bitch deserved to die," and feel a chill as if from a sudden draft.

"No one deserves that." I speak in a low voice as Brent, who appears oblivious to his wife's displeasure, holds forth. "You know. Except Hitler if you could go back in time."

"Excuse me?" Olivia turns to look at me.

"I'm just saying."

She stares at me with her wide green eyes. "I'm sorry. What did you say your name was?"

"Tish Ballard. We met the other day on the set." I refresh her memory.

Olivia's blank look gives way to a smile. "Oh, yes, I remember now. You were kind enough to walk me to my car after I twisted my ankle." I'm stunned speechless. It was her marriage, and not her ankle, that had taken a bad turn that day, yet she seems to have erased the memory along with that of having unburdened herself to me. Is she putting on an act? Or is she really that crazy?

"Pardon me, ladies."

I look up at the familiar voice from above, startled to find Ivy standing over me wearing the sage green uniform of the Shady Brook waitstaff and holding a steaming plate in each hand.

CHAPTER TWENTY-EIGHT

W hat the hell is going on?" I confront Ivy when we're alone. We're in the ladies' room. I slipped away to meet with her in private as soon as she was on her break. "Are you and McGee in cahoots?"

"As if." Ivy looks up from rubbing at a grease spot on her uniform shirt with a moistened paper towel. "I was as surprised to see him as you were. I guess he had the same idea that I did."

"Which was what, exactly?"

"I figured you'd be safer if you had someone on the inside who was looking out for you."

"Does Steve know?" I ask, feeling a dart of worry. For security reasons, no one was supposed to know about Operation Red Carpet, not even the restaurant's owner. Spence would be upset with me if he knew that I'd taken Ivy and McGee into my confidence. Rightfully so, I now see.

"No, but I heard he was short-staffed—apparently there's a bug going around—so I offered to fill in for tonight's dinner service." Since Ivy and I had both waited tables at the Shady Brook Inn during high school, she has the experience. She looks up at me again, this time to grin. "Getting him to assign me to your party was a cinch. He knows he can count on me to be discreet."

"Did it ever occur to you that someone might recognize you from when we visited the set?"

"You know as well as I do the waitstaff is invisible at functions like these." Apparently such is the case at this one because no one has remarked on Ivy's presence thus far. I suspect it's also due to the drab colors of her uniform and the fact that her normally riotous hair is pulled back in a neat bun.

"Don't do anything to blow your cover, in that case. The last thing I need is to worry about you on top of worrying about my own survival." Secretly, I'm glad she has my back, but I can't let her know that—she's prone to heroics. "Couldn't you have settled on a rerun of *Murder, She Wrote*?"

"Why should I sit home when I could be out having fun?" She pretends to pout.

"You wouldn't be sitting home if you hadn't screwed things up with Rajeev." He and Ivy are talking again, but so far that's all they are doing. "Besides which, I didn't ask you to stick your neck out."

Her grin fades at the mention of Rajeev, but she doesn't go there. She puts her hand on my arm, looking me in the eye as she says, "I'm your best friend, Tish. This is what best friends do."

"You couldn't have sponsored me for an AIDS walk?"

"Since when do you go on AIDS walks? You always say you'd rather give by writing a check." She watches as I pull up my pantyhose, and when I'm done, she says, with an amused expression, "Yeah. You definitely need me to watch your back." She points behind me to where the hem of my gown is caught in my pantyhose, bunched up like an ostrich tail. We both crack up.

"Fine." I relent, after our laughter has subsided and I've corrected my wardrobe malfunction. "But no heroics, please."

"I have no intention of becoming a human shield," she assures me.

"Some friend you are," I say with a huff.

"I love you, Tish, but not that much." She laughs and hooks her arm through mine as we exit the ladies' room, she to head back to her station and me to rejoin my party. "I'll signal you if I notice anyone acting nervous," she whispers, and I feel a flutter of anxiety. The time has come for me to set my trap.

"Anything strike you as suspicious so far?" I ask.

"Other than some boobs that I'm not sure are real? No," she says, then pauses, frowning in thought, before she adds, "There is one thing. . . . I don't know if it means anything, but your client, Mr. Russo, is here." She motions toward the main dining area at the other end of the hallway.

"Mr. Russo? Are you sure?"

"Of course I'm sure. I never forget a face." I recall that I introduced Ivy to Russo when we ran into him at the Trader Joe's near his house a while back. "And those rumors about him must be true."

"What makes you say that?"

"He's with a guy in a rubout suit." She pulls me to the end of the hallway where we can see the table at which the two men are seated.

It's Russo all right, and the man he's with is the wiseguy from central casting: midforties and built like a Subzero with a low brow and dark hair that's slicked back goombah style, wearing a shiny gray suit and an open-collared pink shirt that displays the gold chain glinting on his furry chest. Russo's muscle? If so, is it a mere coincidence that he's dining with Russo tonight . . . or are they plotting something together? Could Russo have gotten wind of Operation Red Carpet? I suppose it's possible, though I can't think what his angle might be in interfering it.

Lost in thought, I don't see Liam until I almost bump into him as I'm headed back to the party, after Ivy and I have parted ways. He had gone outside for a smoke when I went to use the restroom. "We have to stop meeting like this. People will talk," he murmurs seductively as he falls into step with me.

I pause to smile at him. "And what will they say?"

He gives me a sly smile and leans in to whisper, smelling of cigarette smoke and expensive aftershave, "That I'm making a play for Karol Bartosz's woman."

"I'm nobody's woman." Sadly, this is true. I'm separated from Bradley by an ocean and he seems in no hurry to be reunited with me, which makes him my boyfriend in name only.

"More's the pity." Liam shakes his head. "I must say, you look very sexy in that gown."

"Are you flirting with me, Mr. Brady?" I run my finger over a row of pleats on his tuxedo shirt. *There's one sure way to find out if he's gay or straight*, I think, lowering my eyelids and tipping my head back invitingly.

Liam cups my chin, and his cobalt eyes lock onto mine. Then my only thought is, *Holy crap. I'm about to be kissed by the world's biggest box-office star.* My lady parts stir to life. But before I can get too excited, he drops his hand and takes a step back, saying, as if with regret, "I still have some scruples, love. Not many, but enough to know where my bread is buttered." The closest we get to a PDA is when he puts his arm around my waist as he escorts me back to the wine cellar.

The mood at the table is more relaxed now that the solemn portion of the evening is behind us. As we dine on duck breast and wild-rice pilaf, eggplant three ways for the vegetarians, Rick has everyone in stitches with a funny anecdote about a trained chimp that went AWOL during the making of his most recent beer-and-bong comedy. "They found him raiding the closet in Sierra's trailer." He winks. "Best-kept secret in Hollywood. Not even his trainer knew."

I seize the opportunity to bait my trap. "If only animals could talk. Imagine what Delilah's dog would say—the only witness to her murder." I pause a moment, as if debating with myself whether to go on, before I add, in a confidential tone, "Actually, he may not have been the only witness."

My "revelation" is met with gasps and startled exclamations. Bartosz stares at me from the head of the table, his gaze dark and impenetrable. "If you know something we don't, perhaps you would care to enlighten us, Tish."

"I may have seen something, I'm not sure. I was in shock at the time, so my mind was kind of a blank when the police questioned me. But lately I've been getting these . . . I don't know what to call it exactly . . . flashbacks, I guess."

"Flashbacks?" Jillian's eyes widen.

"Just bits and pieces. Nothing you could call an actual, you know, memory."

"Do the police know about this?" Brent asks sharply.

"Yes. I'm working with them to—" I break off. "Look, I shouldn't be discussing this. They asked me not to. It's just . . . I can see how much you all cared for her. I want you to know it isn't hopeless."

Brianna stares at me with narrowed eyes as if she can see through my ruse.

"So you're saying you may have caught a glimpse of the killer before he fled?" Brent leans forward on his elbows. His face has all the animation of a bank robber's mask, but his eyes glitter with avid interest as they fix on me. He doesn't seem aware of Ivy reaching past him to refill his wineglass. I notice she's been liberal with the pouring of the wine tonight. *In vino veritas.*

"Possibly." I put on a troubled look, which isn't entirely an act. I can feel the food I ate inching its way back up my throat, I'm so nervous. "I should know one way or the other after tomorrow. Detective Breedlove arranged for me to see a psychiatrist who specializes in hypnotherapy," I explain. "She works mainly with kids who've been sexually abused. She helps them recover their memories, and we're hoping she can do the same for me. I'm told she has a very high success rate. Thanks to her, a number of those abusers were convicted and sent to prison."

Greta's eyes shine with excitement. "I've been praying for a break in the case. This could be it!"

"Don't get your hopes up just yet." I'm careful not to overplay my hand. "We'll see what comes of it."

"Oh, man. The dude's gonna fry." Rick mimes a death-row

electrocution, rolling his eyes back in his head and jerking his body around in his chair. Gallows humor in aspic. This time no one laughs.

Rick's girlfriend gives him a vaguely disgusted look from under her wispy black-and-blue bangs. "The death penalty isn't exercised in California. Not since 2006," she informs us in a low, husky voice that's completely at odds with her birdlike appearance. I realize this is the first time I've heard her speak.

Silence descends again. There's just the clink of plates being cleared from the table and the sigh of air from the vents that keep the cellar at an even, cool temperature. Then a female voice cries, "Nobody move!"

CHAPTER TWENTY-NINE

I freeze, expecting to see a gun. Instead, I see Jillian Lassiter drop to her knees. "I lost a contact lens!" her muffled voice calls from under the table where she's crawled. Irina and Rick, who are seated on either side of her, join the search. There's a muffled "ouch" as they bump heads. One of them knocks against a table leg—Rick from the seismic shudder that overturns my water glass. As Ivy rushes in with a napkin to mop up the spill, I see Brent Harding slip away out of the corner of my eye, his wife following suit a moment later. I don't think twice before I go after them.

I ignore the questioning look McGee shoots me as I fly by him. There's no time to explain. I have to keep the Hardings in my sights, and Brent is moving at a fast pace, Olivia trailing at a discreet distance. At first, I had thought they were planning to meet in private—perhaps to plot my imminent demise—but that doesn't appear to be the case. Brent seems unaware that he's being followed. I watch him turn into the service passageway at the end of the hallway, shadowed by Olivia. The usual cacophony of kitchen sounds assails me as I hurry after them—voices shouting in two languages, pots clattering, pans sizzling. I almost collide with a busboy carrying a plastic bin of dishes when I step out onto the deck . . . just in time to see Olivia descending the wooden steps to the path that leads to the ravine, along which Brent now strides. I note that she's amazingly light on her feet for a woman who's eight months pregnant, with twins no less, and I wonder what her secret is—yoga? Pilates?—as I follow behind, careful to stay far enough back so as not to be noticed. The mingled voices of diners from above grow more faint, and the rushing water of the creek at the bottom of the ravine grows louder as I make my way down the terraced steps of the path, guided by the glow from Brent's cell phone up ahead.

His shadowy figure emerges from the shadows of the trees into the moonlit clearing where the path ends. The clearing, which looks out over the creek, is where Shady Brook's outdoor events, primarily weddings, are held. The greenery here is tended and the grass is bordered in flowerbeds. A white Victorian-style gazebo sits on a rise at the water's edge. You'd be hard-pressed to find a more romantic spot for a wedding. After dark, it's apparently the ideal spot for an assignation.

"Tara?" Brent calls softly.

The slender figure of a woman steps from the gazebo and walks to meet him, their elongated shadows blending into one as they embrace. A tender moment that's cut short when Olivia bursts into the open with a cry so primal it raises the tiny hairs on the back of my neck. She might have been a wild beast charging its prey. She streaks across the clearing, faster than I would have imagined a heavily pregnant woman could move. Except beasts don't carry guns. I feel a lurch of panic when I see the small pistol she pulled from her handbag—I wondered about the unfashionably large purse when I noticed it earlier in the evening—which she points at Brent and the spiky-haired blonde. They freeze, holding themselves as still as the stone statue of a pair of lovers that stands behind them. I hang back at the edge of the clearing where I'm hidden from view. My heart is beating rapidly, and I seem to have sprung a dozen new pulse points. Fortunately, I have my phone with me. I use it to signal the cops, if they're not already on their way.

"You lying sack of shit!" Olivia snarls at Brent. "I should have known you were lying when you swore it was over. Every fucking word out of your mouth has been a lie since day one."

"Baby, please. Give me the gun. Before somebody gets hurt. Then we can sit down and talk this over. I can explain everything." Brent speaks in a calming voice, not letting his panic show. I never thought much of him as an actor, but his performance is worthy of an Oscar.

Olivia gives a shrill laugh. "You think I'm stupid? You think I don't know what's going on?" Tara starts to whimper, and Olivia snaps at her, "You mean nothing to him. I hope you know that. He'll toss you aside like a gum wrapper when he's done with you. Though I ought to save him the trouble." Olivia advances a step, and I hear the click of the safety on her gun. Tara lets out a terrified shriek and ducks behind Brent, who sidesteps her, unlike his alter ego Casey Steele, who never hesitates to throw himself between a bullet and a woman in peril.

"Baby, sweetie, please." He extends his arms towards his wife in supplication. "Look, I know I screwed up, and you have every right to be angry. But I swear it's not what it looks like. I came to tell Tara it was over."

This is news to Tara apparently. She whirls around to confront him, her hands clenched into fists. "You *asshole*. You told me you were getting a divorce. You told me we'd be together. Your wife is right. You *are* a fucking liar." She starts pummeling him with her fists.

Olivia barks out a laugh. "Well, well. Seems you've stepped in it, dear."

"Baby, please . . ."

"He'd be doing you a favor if he dumped you," Olivia says to Tara. "Too bad you won't be around long enough to find that out for yourself." She raises the gun to take aim.

"No!" Brent cries in a belated show of gallantry as he takes a lurching step toward Olivia with his arms still outstretched. "Sweetie, please, I'm begging you. Don't do anything you'll regret."

"Too late," she snarls. "I have nothing *but* regrets. My biggest one? That I married you."

"You want a divorce? Fine. I'll give you whatever you want—the house, the condo in Aspen, the money, you name it." He sounds desperate. "Just don't do this. You don't want to go to prison, do you? Think of our babies. I know you don't want them growing up without a mother."

"Like you care. Where were you when I was suffering through those infertility treatments? When I was throwing up all day every day with morning sickness? I had to *email* you my sonogram. Because you were too busy fucking Delilah to go with me to the doctor's. She's another one," Olivia spits out. "She pretended to be my friend. But it was only so I wouldn't notice what was really going on. You know what? I'm *glad* she's dead. I only wish I could have made her suffer like she made me suffer."

"Liv, what are you saying?" Brent stares at his own wife as if she were a stranger. I hardly recognize the glowing mother-to-be who'd been on his arm earlier. The woman pointing a gun at him, her face distorted with rage, might have been her evil twin. "You didn't—"

"Kill her?" Olivia gives a shrill laugh. "Yes, I killed her. I put a bullet in her head and I smiled when I did it. Just like I'm going to put bullets in you and your little friend here."

I stifle a gasp as I crouch in my hiding spot. Her confession comes as no surprise, but hearing it causes my stomach to wrench. I think about sixteen-year-old Olivia, who didn't get the help she needed after she was expelled from school for threatening another girl—or who was possibly beyond help even then—as I look at the woman she's become, all grown up and crazier than ever. I can't wait for the cops to get here, I realize. I have to stop her before she hurts someone else. But how? I don't have a weapon at my disposal, and

I'm not going to risk my own life to save Brent's or his girlfriend's. I'm not that noble. I do have one advantage, however. I know how to talk to a crazy person. I've had lots of practice. "Olivia?" I call from the shadows. "It's me, Tish. Why don't we go inside where we can talk. Just the two of us, like we did after you . . . um, twisted your ankle. You can tell me all about it."

Startled, Olivia swings around awkwardly at the sound of my voice, and the gun goes off—I don't think it was on purpose; she's shaking all over in her agitation—sending bits of bark flying at me like shrapnel as the bullet buries itself in the tree trunk behind me. I drop into a crouch, my heart hammering, my breath whistling in and out of my lungs. Time seems to stand still for a beat before Olivia shrieks, "Go away! Leave me alone! This isn't any of your business."

"You're right, it isn't," I call out, after I've regained some measure of composure. "But, believe me, I know what you're going through. I know what it's like to be so mad at a guy you'd do anything to get back at him, even if it hurts you as much as it hurts him. I once torched a guy's car."

This gives her pause. "You . . . You did?"

"He totally had it coming." *Or so I thought at the time.* "But still. It was wrong, and I've regretted it ever since. It only made the situation ten times worse. Don't make the same mistake I did." Never mind she'd already racked up one victim, namely Delilah Ward, and possibly others.

"Listen to her!" shrills Tara in a frantic bid to save herself. "He's not worth it! Why ruin your own life when you could divorce him and take him to the cleaners? I . . . I'd even testify against him in court if it came to that. I can't believe I fell for his lies. I wish now I'd never met him!"

"Women. You're all alike," Brent grumbles loudly.

He should have kept his mouth shut. With a growl, Olivia turns on him. At which point he belatedly mans up and launches himself at her. She doesn't go down easily, though. If hell hath no fury like a woman scorned, you can make that times two with the pregnant Olivia. She transforms into a hissing, spitting wildcat. They grapple briefly, and he wrestles the gun away from her before finally shoving her away from him and onto the ground. A second later, another shot rings out, and this time it's Brent who goes down. The spiky-haired blonde screams. Olivia starts to wail.

I hear voices and turn to see several figures racing in my direction along the path. In the moonlight that penetrates the shadows of the trees, I'm able to make out a stocky man, another man and a woman trailing behind him at a short distance. It's Russo's goon in the lead, I see when he bursts into the clearing. I assume he was the one who shot Brent, since he's holding a gun. Seconds later, the other man and the woman appear, identifying themselves as police officers. They must be the undercover cops from the way they're dressed, like a couple on a date.

"You okay, ma'am?" Russo's goon helps me to my feet with a meaty hand clamped around my arm, while the cops rush to tend to the injured Brent.

"Yeah," I answer shakily. "But I'm not so sure about him." I point to where Brent lies motionless, cradled in his wife's arms as she rocks from side to side, keening. You would never know to look at her that she'd been holding him at gunpoint a minute ago and threatening to blow a hole in him.

"He'll live," the goon assures me. "It's only a flesh wound."

I watch the female cop, a slender brunette, pry Olivia from Brent, allowing her partner to assess Brent's injuries. The wounded actor stirs feebly as he regains consciousness. Olivia is sobbing hysterically, while Tara shrieks at the top of her lungs, "Arrest her! She killed Delilah and she was going to kill us!"

The EMTs arrive on the scene along with a pair of uniforms. Brent and Olivia Harding are taken away, he on a stretcher and she in handcuffs loudly professing her innocence. "I wasn't going to shoot him! And I didn't kill Delilah! I only said that to get back

at him. I didn't mean it! I'm not a murderer. Do I look like a murderer?" No one appears to be buying her story, least of all me.

The plainclotheswoman takes Tara inside for questioning. The
plainclothesman questions me and Russo's goon, whose name is
Dom and who, it turns out, isn't a goon but Russo's nephew and
chief of security at his casino. Which explains why he was packing. He heard the shot fired by Olivia, after he'd gone outside for a
smoke, and came running. Except what he witnessed was very different from what actually occurred: an altercation between a man
and a pregnant woman that ended with the man standing over the
woman, brandishing a gun at her as she lay whimpering on the
ground. Dom, a former cop, did what he was trained to do: He
disabled the "assailant," in this case Brent, by pumping a bullet into
his leg as soon as he had a clear shot. "Christ, if I'd known . . ." Dom
shakes his head, wearing a pained expression. "Poor bastard."

I recall the shocked look on Brent's face—I wouldn't have
believed him capable of such an animated expression if I hadn't
seen it with my own eyes—when Olivia confessed to the murder
of Delilah Ward. Seems I'd been wrong about one thing: He hadn't
been covering up for his wife. Which means that Olivia had an
accomplice, presumably the same person who broke into my house
the other night. What I don't know is why she wanted me dead or
who drugged me the night of Bartosz's party. I'm pondering this
when we run into Russo as we're headed back inside. After I tell
him what happened, he squeezes Dom's Hormel ham–size bicep,
exclaiming, "Good man." Never mind Dom shot and wounded
an innocent man. To me he says, "Now the poor girl can rest in
peace." I realize he's talking about Delilah, and relief washes over
me, knowing I can finally rest in peace as well—in my own bed.

Phones glow on the deck, those of diners calling or texting
the shocking news of Olivia Harding's arrest and the wounding
of "Casey Steele." By tomorrow, the story will have gone viral,
complete with YouTube videos. The whole world will know who

shot Delilah Ward. McGee accosts me, scowling, as soon as I step inside. "Christ, Ballard. How many times I gotta tell you? Never—"

"Go in without backup," I finish for him. "I know, I should've listened."

"Next time, maybe you will."

"There isn't going to be a next time." I wrap my arms around myself to ward off the chill I seem to have caught. "I'm staying out of trouble from now on."

McGee gives a scornful snort. "Good luck with that."

I go in search of Ivy and find her doing double duty, having taken over for another waitress, who fled in panic when she heard the gunshots. Ivy pauses to hug me tightly as she's hurrying to the kitchen pass. "Tish! Thank God you're all right. So is it true? Is Olivia under arrest?"

"On multiple counts. Assault with a deadly weapon for one." I give her a quick account of the events that resulted in Olivia's arrest. "She's also facing a murder charge. She confessed to killing Delilah. She actually *bragged* about it, if you can believe it. Which goes to show how crazy she is."

Ivy's eyes widen. "Oh, my God. You totally had her number."

"I sensed something off about her from the get-go. Though it seems I was wrong about Brent. He didn't know Olivia was the culprit. You should have seen his reaction when she confessed. He couldn't have been faking it—he's not that good an actor."

"Then who—?" Before Ivy can pose the question that's nagging at me, a male voice bellows from the kitchen that the food on the pass is getting cold. Ivy growls in frustration. "Gotta run. Later, okay?"

I see drawn faces and people huddled together when I rejoin the party. No one seems to know whether to go or to stay. Brianna rushes over to me. "Tish, are you okay? I was so worried!"

I can't believe that I ever suspected her of being a murderer. She's a kind person for all her annoying traits. "Not sure, to be honest. Ask me again when the shock wears off."

"My uncle seems pretty shook up, too."

I follow her gaze to where Bartosz stands alone, looking dazed. When I first met him, he seemed to possess the vigor of a man half his age; now he seems old. "You should go check on him."

Brianna nods and leaves me to attend to her uncle.

I head for the table to pour myself a glass of water, and I'm joined by Greta. "What a night!" she declares. "I thought this kind of thing only happened in movies. Who would have thought Olivia Harding . . ." She trails off, eyeing me with concern. "You look pale. Are you all right?"

"I . . . I think I need to sit down." The floor is rocking like a pontoon. I plop into the nearest chair.

"Lie down more like it. Why don't you let me take you home?"

I shake my head. "I can't leave until Sp—Detective Breedlove gets here."

"He can question you at home as easily as he can here."

"I guess." I'm too drained to argue. "But you don't have to take me. I have my own car."

"You're in no condition to drive," Greta says firmly.

I used to get that a lot back in my drinking days. Bartenders would confiscate my car keys or concerned friends would insist on driving me home. Drunk, I was belligerent; now I nod wearily. "You're probably right. But Brianna can take me. I wouldn't want you to have to go out of your way."

"I expect she's needed here." Her gaze travels to where Brianna stands, holding a glass of water at the ready, as her uncle pries the lid from a prescription vial. I watch him pop a pill and wash it down. Then Greta helps me to my feet, guiding me toward the door. "Let's get you home to bed."

CHAPTER THIRTY

I'm nodding off by the time we reach the freeway exit, lulled by the purring of the car engine. When I wake, groggy and bleary-eyed, I see we've left the freeway. We're driving south along the old coast highway, miles from where I live, in the bedroom community of Seascape. Greta must have taken a wrong turn or gotten mixed up on the directions. "This isn't the way to my house," I croak.

"You're awake," Greta replies in a pleasant voice. "Did you have a nice snooze?"

"How long was I asleep?"

"Long enough. We're almost there."

"But . . ."

"I thought we'd stop at my place first. There's someone I'd like you to meet."

"If you don't mind, I'm kind of tired." I yawn. I need more sleep, not small talk. Frankly, I don't know why Greta would even suggest it. She was the one who'd insisted on getting me home.

"We won't be long," she assures me.

"Who is this person?" I know from the photos on the Full Bucket Web site that Greta's charity work has her rubbing elbows with ambassadors, heads of state, African royalty—I recall seeing a shot of her posing with Oprah at a fund-raiser—so I imagine the mystery guest is a visiting dignitary.

She smiles. "It's a surprise."

Seascape is the last freeway exit before the farms and orchards of Pajaro Valley. It's also the least touristy of the coastal communities directly to the north and south of Cypress Bay. A mom-and-pop grocery store, a drugstore, a liquor store, and a gas station, all contained within an unobtrusive and attractively designed mall, compose the business district, such as it is. The nearest supermarket is a twenty-minute drive, but you won't hear a resident complain about the inconvenience. In fact, they rigorously maintain it with draconian zoning regulations. I recall the public outcry when an empty storefront became the proposed site of a Starbucks franchise. The proposal was shot down by the community board like a drone in enemy territory. Bed-and-breakfasts here cater to tourists who prefer bird-watching and nature walks to shopping and dining out.

Greta is staying at one of the more upscale bed-and-breakfasts. Located on the tip of a peninsula, Land's End boasts unparalleled ocean views as well as views of the state park that abuts the peninsula. The main building is a beautifully restored Craftsman mansion, and it has three kitchen cottages, each with its own unique character and each named after a different seabird. Greta pulls into the crushed-shell driveway of Pelican's Roost, the most exclusive and private of the cottages. Clad in cedar shakes weathered the silvery tan of driftwood, it looks inviting with the light from inside casting a warm glow over the stone path and flowering shrubs in front.

"Here we are, my home away from home," Greta announces cheerily.

We climb out. A cold wind is blowing, bringing the briny smell of the ocean. The moon plays hide-and-seek with the clouds that scud overhead. Moonlight gleams on the swells out at sea. Closer to shore, waves boom like thunder as they crash against the cliffs below. More faintly, I hear the strains of classical music from inside.

We follow the path to the front door and enter a cozy room paneled in beadboard with hardwood flooring and a stone fireplace. The armchairs and sofa are upholstered in beachy fabrics, the walls hung with Audubon prints and watercolors painted by local artists. A man in jeans and an Irish fisherman's sweater stands facing the picture window, his face a ghostly reflection in the glass. Lean with an athletic build and dark hair that brushes his earlobes, he seems vaguely familiar from behind.

"Lovely evening," he remarks, his voice deep and pleasant sounding. "I prefer a cooler climate. In the tropics, every day is a sunny day, which can become boring. Like people who smile all the time."

"You live in the tropics?" I inquire politely. He nods but doesn't reply. I wonder why he still hasn't shown his face or introduced himself. This mystery-guest thing has gone from intriguing to creepy. I forge on, "Are you involved with Full Bucket? Is that how you know Greta?"

"In a way." The man's ghost reflection smiles, sending a chill through me. But that's nothing compared to the cold shock wave that hits me when he turns around and I find myself face-to-face with a dead man.

Delilah's dead husband to be precise. Who, it seems, isn't dead after all.

"Tish, meet my brother, Eric. Eric, this is Tish." Greta's voice seems to come from far away. I stand there, stupefied, my hand automatically floating up when he extends his. Eric's grip is cool and dry, and he wears a smile that's all teeth and no warmth. I note in a detached way that he's even better looking in person than in the photos I've seen of him. He and his sister both have the same dark-lashed hazel eyes, pronounced jaw, and prominent nose, features that combine to make Eric's face a strikingly handsome one while merely lending character to Greta's.

"I'm sure you have questions," he says. "We'll do our best to answer them. Please, have a seat." He motions toward the sofa and armchairs opposite the fireplace, where a blaze crackles, though it might have been one of those fake fires in the Santa's Village that's staged at the Harborview Plaza each year during the Christmas season for all the warmth it seems to generate. I suddenly feel chilled, as though I had turned down the frozen food aisle of a supermarket. Except I can't just grab the ice cream or the frozen waffles and move on to the next aisle. I take a step backward.

"Love to, but can we make it another time? I'm pretty beat. Don't trouble yourself, I can call a cab," I say to Greta, wearing a smile that feels carved into my face. She doesn't respond. There's no need. Her brother steps around me to block my passage as I'm making my way to the door.

"Sit," he orders.

"We don't bite," Greta says, her voice sweet and lilting.

I trudge across the room, my heart pounding high in my chest, to sink down on the Ralph Lauren Home Collection plaid sofa. "What do you want with me?" I force the words out through numb lips.

"You're a smart girl. Figure it out." Eric sits in the armchair that's kitty-corner to the sofa.

"You need a third for Scrabble?"

He chuckles. "Good one. You're clever, Tish. Too clever for your own good."

"May I offer you some hot cocoa?" Greta plays the good hostess. I don't answer, which she seems to take as a yes. She shrugs off her coat, while I shiver in mine, and heads to the kitchen area, which has marine-varnished wooden countertops and an old-fashioned brass ship's porthole for a window. She pours milk into a saucepan and sets it on the stovetop to heat, then spoons cocoa mix from a tin into three mugs. "I always find I sleep better after a nice mug of cocoa."

"Especially when it's doctored with Valium," I reply sarcastically.

The puzzle pieces are falling into place in my mind. "You were the one who drugged me at Bartosz's party, weren't you?"

She frowns. "That was a mistake."

"I almost drove over a cliff!"

"That wasn't my intention—I only meant to deter you. I was the one who alerted the highway patrol." She sighs. "That, too, was a mistake. If you *had* gone over a cliff, it would have saved us all a lot of grief."

"Let me guess. You were also the one who broke into my house."

"That would be me," Eric says.

I glare at him. "Why? So you could murder me in my sleep?" Like they had with Delilah. If I didn't see it before, it was only because Greta had an alibi and I had no clue of Eric's existence.

He confirms my suspicion with his next words. "Too bad you weren't as . . . compliant as Delilah."

"Sorry to spoil your fun," I snap. He glares at me, clearly put out that he didn't succeed in killing me. I derive a glimmer of pleasure thinking of my cat's claws and my dog's teeth leaving their marks.

"We're not enjoying this," Greta says, sounding irritated, whether at me or her brother, I can't tell. "Any more than we enjoyed killing Delilah. Her death was a necessity. She'd become a liability."

My terror gives way to anger in that moment. I'm angry about what these two did to Delilah, who'd been tormented by her guilt, believing she was responsible for her husband's death when in fact he was alive, presumably living under an assumed name. I ask Eric, "How did it feel to pull the trigger on your own wife? Hardly sporting, sneaking up on her while she was asleep."

"Better for her that way." Eric defends his actions. "She never even saw me coming."

"Like a ghost." One of flesh and blood, in his case. "You were as quiet as one, too."

"I used a silencer so the neighbors wouldn't hear the shot."

"Why did she have to die? I know it wasn't for the money. Brianna said she left everything to Full Bucket."

"Of which I'm the director," Greta reminds me. "And with Delilah out of the picture, I now have full authority. The board won't interfere. I've seen to that. I was careful about who I appointed."

"I see." Another puzzle piece falls into place. "You were embezzling, is that it? What, did Delilah catch you?"

"No, but it was only a matter of time. Our bookkeeper noticed some discrepancies in the expense reports, and he brought them to Delilah's attention. She was going to have an independent audit done." Greta smiles grimly. "I'll tell you something about Delilah that most people don't know. She played the dumb blonde, but she was smart. She didn't go to college, but she was good with numbers, gifted, like people who pick up languages easily or can play a musical instrument without lessons. It's a shame, really. She'd still be alive if she'd been one of those airheaded celebrities content to let their business managers handle their affairs as long as they have unlimited credit on Rodeo Drive." I see Greta's contempt for those people on her face.

"Too bad she wasn't as good a judge of character as she was at managing her finances, or she'd have seen you and your brother for the snakes in the grass that you are," I comment in disgust.

Greta's expression clouds over. "I'm sorry to have given you that impression. I genuinely cared for Delilah. She was a mess, but her heart was in the right place. She felt so guilty about Eric."

"If she could've seen him lounging in a hammock by the seashore, drinking piña coladas, she might have felt differently." I feel nauseated thinking about it. "I don't get it. Why fake your death?" I ask Eric.

"He was in a terrible bind, and Delilah was threatening to divorce him," Greta answers for him. "He owed a great deal of money to people who . . . let's just say they weren't the sort you could repay on the installment plan. They would have had him killed if he and I hadn't arranged for him to 'die.'" I recall that Eric's body was never recovered, only the wreckage from his plane.

"Wouldn't it have been simpler to get divorced?"

"Yes, but he signed a prenup that would have left him with very little."

"She said I was the only man she ever loved. She said there would never be anyone else," Eric recalls bitterly, sounding more like a pouty little boy than a grown man. "So who's the liar?"

I cast him a scathing look. "Blame the victim, why don't you?"

"The charitable organization was my idea," says Greta. "It was a way to finance my brother's new life abroad. He needed a place where he could hole up, and private estates don't come cheap even in Central America. There was also the matter of creating a new identity for him, which is quite costly as it turns out. The beauty of it was that I was also honoring his memory."

"The memory of a man who wasn't dead. Nice."

"Delilah loved the idea," Greta goes on. "It was a way to ease her conscience. And with her involved, raising money wasn't a problem. If I skimmed, there was more than enough to go around."

"In other words, you stole from poor people."

"That's one way to look at it," she says. "Another is to look at all the lives we've saved. Lives that might otherwise have been lost. I'm not exaggerating when I say this. A clean source of water can mean the difference between life or death in parts of the world where disease, starvation, and crop failure are everyday realities. And our good work will continue even without Delilah."

"While you go on skimming."

Greta pours the heated milk into the mugs with the cocoa mix and places them on a tray, which she carries to the coffee table. "Don't be so quick to judge, Tish. Black and white is only in movies. In real life, morality isn't so clear-cut. Eric and I were victims, too. We didn't have it easy growing up."

"That's your excuse? You had a tough childhood?" I sneer.

Greta settles in the armchair opposite Eric with her cocoa. "The best I can say about it is that we weren't orphans. We had a mother, for what it was worth. Mom's welfare checks went toward booze and cigarettes. There was never enough to eat, and when back rent was owed, we moved—I was never in any one school long enough to make friends. I was more mother than sister to my little brother. Whatever I couldn't beg, borrow, or steal, I sold. . . . My blood, my body if that's what it took." There is no shame in her voice as she says this; she speaks with pride. "I made sure Eric never went without, that there was always enough money for food or clothes or class trips. I've always looked after him, and I always will." They exchange a look that speaks of their devotion to each other. It's chilling because that's how I feel about my own brother.

Except I wouldn't kill for him.

"Touching," I remark. "I might even feel sorry for you, if you hadn't murdered an innocent woman to get what you want. And how convenient to have a dead man as your accomplice."

Eric smiles. "Being 'dead' has its advantages. It gave my sister an alibi. She could be in New York at the time of the murder. Who would ever suspect her? Or a dead man, for that matter?"

"It was risky even so," I point out. "Someone might have recognized you."

"I came by boat," he explains. "I have my own, and I know which ports to avoid—the ones where the sorts of people who might have recognized me tend to anchor. I've been staying out of sight since I got here. Aside from paying Delilah a visit . . . and dropping in on you the other night."

"Congratulations. You got away with it." I'm freaking out on the inside, and it's all I can do to keep it together outwardly. "And how convenient that Olivia Harding confessed."

A smile flits across Greta's face. She looks like the Wicked Queen from Disney's *Snow White* in her high-collared, austere navy gown, backlit by the moonlight that's coming through the porthole. "Yes, although I doubt Olivia's confession will hold up. She's always been a little . . ." She twirls her finger next to her temple in the universal gesture for crazy. "It should buy us enough time to get Eric out of the country, but that still leaves the problem of what to do with you, Tish."

Icy fingers seem to clamp around my gut, twisting. It feels like I'm being strangled from the inside. My fingers and toes go numb. "If you kill me, you won't get away with it. I was seen leaving with you."

"Which is why your death will be made to look like an accident."

Dire scenarios flit through my mind. They'll take me home . . . and then what? A house fire with me trapped inside? A "fall" that has me hitting my head at the precise wrong angle? A blow-dryer that "slips" into the tub while I'm bathing? My one hope is Spence. He has to be looking for me by now, and the tracking device on my phone will give him my location. But will he find me in time? I shudder to think of what will happen if he doesn't. "You're both monsters. You know that, don't you?" The words, spoken in a calm voice, seem to come from someone else's mouth. Someone who isn't terrified, whose heart isn't thumping like an overloaded clothes washer.

I'm on my feet a second later, bolting for the door in a blind panic. But Eric is too quick for me. He leaps forward to grab me by the arm. I struggle to free myself, but he's too strong. I feel his hot, cocoa-scented breath on my face as he growls, "You're only making it harder on yourself." The realization seizes me like the fingers that are digging into my arm: *I'm going to die.*

I feel a surge of hope when I hear the sound of a car engine approaching and see the glare of headlights splash across the picture window. *Spence.* He came for me. Except neither Greta nor Eric appear to be worried. Greta peers out the window, saying, "Ah, there she is. As prompt as ever."

CHAPTER THIRTY-ONE

A minute later, I hear the sound of footsteps approaching briskly along the front walk. Greta calls out a greeting from the open doorway where she stands. "Brianna, thanks for getting here so quickly."

Brianna? Is she working with them? Oh, God. I feel like I'm going to throw up. Has she been plotting against me all this time? I thought it was too good to be true when she took the job. I should have trusted my instincts. *Are they paying her? Or did she have her own reasons for wanting Delilah dead?* Like with the roommate who was killed in a hit-and-run after she screwed her over.

"No problem," Brianna chirps. "Anything I can do to help."

"That's my girl," says Greta.

My girl? I'll kill her. I swear I will. If I make it out of here alive, that is.

Then I hear Brianna ask sweetly, "Are you feeling any better?"

"A little. It must have been something I ate," Greta says.

She doesn't know. Realizing I was wrong about Brianna, I'm at once relieved and terrified. Because she's walking into a trap, and I can't warn her. Eric is holding me pinned to the wall, his body pressed against mine, his hand clamped over my mouth. I struggle to free myself, and the pressure against my mouth eases a fraction, just enough for me to bite down on the fleshy part of his palm.

"Run!" I yell loudly when he jerks his hand from my mouth with a grunt of pain.

Too late. Eric is out the door in a flash, and with a hard push from him, Brianna is inside with me seconds later. "Eric?" Her jaw drops. "I don't understand. . . . How can you . . . You . . . You're *dead*."

He grins. "Apparently not. Hello, Bree. Nice to see you. I'm glad you could join us."

"Greta texted me. She said she wasn't feeling well, and that Tish needed a ride home." Brianna speaks in a voice dull with shock. She stares at Eric as if at a ghost, which he is in a way.

"It was a trap." I state the obvious. "They killed Delilah. Now they're planning to kill me." What I don't understand is why they lured Brianna here. What could they possibly want with her?

"Why don't you ladies have a seat." Eric motions toward the sofa. He looks a little flushed, and he's rubbing his hand where I bit him. He glares at me when I don't obey.

"Pardon the theatrics." Greta produces a gun from the cherry console that stands against the wall by the door. "But I've found it pays to err on the side of caution. Now, please, do as you're told."

Brianna darts a panicked glance my way. I squeeze her hand. "Is it true? Did you kill Delilah?" Brianna asks when we're sitting down. From the look on her face, she already knows the answer.

"It was unavoidable, I'm afraid," Greta says. "She got in the way of our plans."

Brianna pales. "Oh, my God."

"I asked you here because your services are required," Greta goes on in the same mild tone. "You and Tish will ride home in her car. Tish will insist on driving because that's what drunks do. Tish, you see, had a bit of a . . . slip. She was so shook up after what happened earlier, she took the edge off with a drink—let's make it two. She insisted she was fine to drive, and you, the loyal assistant, went along. A bad decision on both your parts. Sadly, neither of you will survive the trip."

"It won't work!" I burst out. "No one who knows me would believe it!"

"That you're not a model of sobriety?" Greta smiles like an indulgent parent at the protestations of a child. "AA has a recidivism rate of eighty-five percent. Not the greatest odds, we can agree. I've done my homework, you see. And don't forget, Tish, you were recently pulled over."

"Because you drugged me!"

"There's no proof of that. By all appearances your 'accident' will be the sad but all too familiar tale of a drunk driver who exercised poor judgment in failing to hand over the keys. No one will question my story."

"So what does that make me? Collateral damage?" Brianna tips her chin up at Greta.

"That's one way of putting it." Greta shrugs. "You also managed Delilah's affairs and now you work for Tish. Knowing you, you'd find some inconsistency, and like the eager beaver you are, you'd keep digging until you had enough to take to the police. You and Tish are alike in that sense. Now"—Greta walks over to the rolling cart against the wall by the bookcase that holds an array of liquor bottles—"what shall it be, Tish? A Jameson neat? Or is vodka and tonic your pleasure?"

"I always knew you were a two-faced bitch!" Brianna bursts out. "My uncle and Liam, they tried to get Delilah back into rehab, but you only told her what she wanted to hear. 'You're not an alcoholic. You can cut back anytime you like. You don't need a bunch of losers telling you what to do.'" She mimics Greta's voice. "You were killing her then, only slowly. There's a special room in hell for people like you, and that's where you're going. Preferably by way of lethal injection."

I wish I'd known sooner how Brianna felt about Greta. Why hadn't she said something? Was it because she felt sorry for Greta in her bereavement? Ill-placed sympathy, as it turns out.

Greta replies irritably, "Did anyone ever tell you you're extremely annoying?"

Brianna ignores the insult. "You had Eric all to yourself before she came along. She broke up your love fest—I can't say what it rhymes with or I'll throw up—and you hated her for it."

Greta's eyes flash, her features twisting into an expression that has her morphing in that instant from the evil stepmother to the hag who offers Snow White the poisoned apple. "Don't be disgusting. I don't care who Eric sleeps with. Women have been throwing themselves at him since he was old enough to know where to put it. Starting with his ninth-grade English teacher." She sounds like a proud mom bragging about the achievements of a precocious child.

"Mrs. Mac." Eric's expression softens. "Yeah, she was hot. Couldn't get enough."

"Delilah wasn't like the others," Brianna goes on, undeterred. From the waxy pallor of her face, it seems she might actually be on the verge of throwing up. "She meant something to him once. That was the *real* reason you wanted her dead, wasn't it, Greta? Whatever excuse you gave."

Eric appears unsettled, which tells me there's some truth to what Brianna said—he must have loved Delilah at one time—while Greta looks furious enough to pull the trigger. For a breathless moment, it seems she might do just that. But the moment passes along with her fit of anger. She pours three fingers of Maker's Mark into a cut-glass tumbler and carries it over to me. "Here you go. Bottoms up."

I ignore her outstretched hand. "Thanks, but I'll pass."

"Take it," Eric growls.

I do as I'm told, only to set the drink down. "Go to hell."

Greta shrugs and sets the bottle on the coffee table next to my untouched drink. She hands the gun over to Eric and exits the room. When she reappears a few minutes later, I see that she's changed into a dark-gray tracksuit and athletic shoes. She stuffs the fifth of bourbon in the pocket of the windbreaker that she wears over her tracksuit. Eric dons a jacket from the row of pegs by the door that holds various items of outwear. He orders, "On your feet, ladies. Let's get a move on."

Except I can't move. I'm paralyzed with fright, reliving my near-death experience of last summer. Another night. Another gun. Another psycho who'd been bent on killing me. Brianna takes my hand, pulling me with her as she rises to her feet. The thought of Spence returns along with mobility to my limbs. I still have my phone, so all is not lost. *Hurry*, I mentally urge. *Before it's too l—*

Greta snatches my silver evening bag from my hand and extracts my phone from it. "You won't be needing that." She tosses it on the cherry console before she hands me back my bag. She's not taking any chances. She must watch the same detective shows that I do. She'll tell the police I accidentally left my phone behind in my "inebriated state." It will sound all too plausible.

"Where are they taking us?" Brianna whispers to me as we're marched outside at gunpoint.

"I don't know," I whisper back, "but you can bet it's someplace remote."

"You won't suffer," Greta says from behind. "It'll be quick."

Terror sits like a chunk of ice in my belly, sending cold trickles through my gut. Brianna tightens her grip on my hand as we make our way to my Explorer, which is parked in the driveway behind Greta's rented blue Nissan. Greta opens the driver's door. "Get in," she orders. I hesitate, thinking that if Eric were to shoot me on the spot, it wouldn't necessarily be fatal, and the shot would be heard by the owners of the bed-and-breakfast—better than my odds elsewhere. "You know," Greta says as if she read my mind, "Eric could just as easily kill you with his bare hands."

I climb in.

Brianna gets in on the passenger side and Eric climbs in back. "Drive," he commands when Greta is in her car with the engine running, and I feel the cold kiss of the gun barrel against the back of my neck. Despair settles over me, thick as the fog that's creeping in. I back out of the driveway and follow the glowing red taillights up ahead as they move in the direction of the main road.

We drive south along the old coast highway for several miles before we arrive at the entrance to Manresa State Park, where Greta makes the turn. I follow her car as it cruises slowly past the shuttered ranger's station. The park looks deserted. There are no vehicles in the parking lot, and the only thing that's stirring is the fog that drifts in ragged patches through the beams of my headlights. We wind through the park until we reach the first scenic overlook, where Greta pulls over. Prompted by a nudge from the gun barrel, I pull in behind her. In AA we're taught not to pray for specific things or outcomes. "Your higher power ain't no short-order cook," as one old-timer, Lennie O., put it. But now I pray for divine intervention, of the burning-bush variety, rather than God-give-me-strength kind, because only a miracle can save us.

I know this park well. I used to come here a lot with my ex-boyfriend Daniel, who's an assistant professor of marine biology at the university. We'd stroll along the rocky shore at low tide, pausing to peer into tide pools with Daniel pointing out the various forms of marine life. High tide, on the other hand, can be treacherous. You can quickly become trapped by rising waters. There are signs posted around the park, warning visitors, but every year some idiot ignores them and ends up having to be rescued. Or the person's body is recovered. Right now, I'm thinking about the latter. At the edge of the overlook is a drop of over a hundred feet. I can see Brianna and myself trapped inside my Explorer, Eric and Greta pushing from the outside. We crash through the guardrail and . . . I shudder, imagining our swift descent onto the rocks below.

I watch Greta get out of her car and cross through the beams of my headlights. She climbs in the backseat of my SUV and places the fifth of bourbon in the cup holder that normally holds my large coffees from the Daily Grind. "Let's get this party started," says Eric in a hearty voice.

"Be my guest," I tell him.

Brianna reaches for the bottle. "I, for one, could use a drink. Ouch, that hurts!" she cries when Eric grabs her by the wrist. I know she was only trying to protect me, and I feel a rush of affection for her. She yanks free of Eric's grasp and twists around to glare at him. "You're a fucking asshole. And you were a shitty husband. I don't know why she didn't divorce you while she had the chance."

He grins. "Wow. *F*-word and all. I'm impressed, Bree. Didn't know you had it in you." He picks up the bottle, and I notice he's donned a pair of calfskin driving gloves. Dead men don't leave prints. He thrusts the bottle into my hand. "Go on, Tish. Live a little." He chuckles at his own joke.

I stare at the bottle. Why not? It would ease my nerves and soften the blow of what's to come. The Grim Reaper would seem more like an old drinking buddy. But the thought is fleeting, like a twinge from a phantom limb. If I have to die, I'll die sober. "Go fuck yourself," I say pleasantly.

"Bitch," he snarls. "You'll goddamn do what—"

"Now, now. Temper," Greta chides, the way I imagine she did when they were kids and Eric pulled the wings from flies or beat up on other boys. She pokes my shoulder with her finger. "Do yourself a favor, Tish. Trust me, you don't want the alternative."

I feel Eric's knees through my seat as he shifts from side to side, trying to get comfortable. He has almost no legroom, he's so tall. Which gives me an idea. Not the most inspired idea I've ever had, but it's all I've got. I unscrew the cap from the bottle and accidentally on purpose let it slip through my fingers into the footwell. I bend as if to retrieve it and instead grab hold of the metal bar underneath my seat that's for adjusting the seat position. I release it from its locked mode, then as I straighten, I ram my seat back as far as it will go, throwing my full weight into it.

I hear a dull crunch as the seat drives into Eric's kneecaps. He roars in pain. "Mother*fucker!*"

When I glance in the rearview mirror, the gun is no longer in his hand. He must have dropped it when I rammed into him. While Greta is bending to retrieve it, and Eric is rubbing at his sore knees, I bring the bottle down on the back of her head. There's an equally satisfying crunch and broken glass flies everywhere. Greta slumps onto the seat, incapacitated for the moment, if not unconscious. I wrench my door open, heady with the thrill of my temporary advantage and the pungent fumes of alcohol that fill my nostrils, and leap out. Brianna does the same.

I make for the edge of the overlook, Brianna sprinting along-side me. The park campground is located less than a mile to the south. The quickest way to get there is by road, but Greta and Eric would pick us off like sitting ducks, so we have to go by shore, where they can only follow on foot. We have a head start and I'm familiar with the terrain, which gives us a slight advantage. But the odds aren't in our favor. Eric and Greta both appear to be in peak physical condition, and Eric was a stuntman. Still, a slim chance is better than none, I tell myself.

First, we have to descend the cliff, freestyle, which would be a daunting prospect even in daylight. But there's no time to think twice. I kick off my heels and hop over the guardrail. That's when I notice I'm still clutching the jagged neck of the bottle. I shove it in my coat pocket, unthinkingly, before I drop onto my belly. I scoot backward to lower myself over the edge of the cliff, using the stout vines of the ice plant, the kudzu of coastal California, that blankets the ground as a makeshift rope, spurred by the sounds of vehicle doors slamming, voices shouting.

I glance up at Brianna, who looks panicked. "Do like me, and you'll be fine," I whisper, and she nods.

I grope blindly for footholds as I make my descent, loose dirt and pebbles raining from above as Brianna makes her own descent. I balance on outcroppings the width of my palm and dig my toes into crannies. The ice plant that I'm using as a rope tears loose at one point, and I slide a few, terrifying feet before I regain my footing. I'm halfway down when I hear a popping noise from above, that of a gun equipped with a silencer being fired, and dirt and shale kick up near my face, stinging my cheeks and making my eyes water.

"Don't be stupid! There's no escape!" Greta's voice shouts.

I freeze like a plush kitty suctioned to a car window. Then a voice in my head says, calmly but firmly, *Keep moving.* The same voice that I used to hear whenever I was about to turn down the wine aisle of a supermarket during my first thirty days of sobriety when I was clawing my way up from the bottom of a barrel. I shake off my panic, pry myself loose, and continue on. When I'm nearing the bottom, I drop the last few feet onto the boulder below. I land at an awkward angle and give a muffled cry when I feel my right ankle twist, bringing a sharp stab of pain.

"You okay?" Brianna jumps nimbly down beside me.

I put my weight on my ankle, testing. It hurts like hell, but it doesn't feel like it's sprained or broken. I can still walk on it. "I'll live," I grit out through clenched teeth. *With any luck.*

The short distance to the campground might have been a hundred miles as I hobble in that direction. It's slow going, between my injured ankle and the rough terrain. This stretch of shoreline is more rocks than sand, and the rocks are partially submerged by the rising tide in spots. We splash through pools of icy seawater and slip and slide our way over boulders slick with algae. After we've gone maybe a couple hundred yards, I glance over my shoulder and see a pair of dark figures silhouetted against the face of the cliff in the moonlight, not inching their way downward as Brianna and I had but moving with the agility of mountain goats. A ball of panic lodges in my throat. For a second, I can't breathe. But I keep putting one foot in front of the other.

The throbbing in my ankle is matched by the pounding of my heart as I hobble along as fast as I can. Each breath is like sandpaper rasping against my dry throat. I stumble at one point and would have fallen on my face if Brianna hadn't grabbed my elbow, holding me upright as she must have done countless times with her former employer. The difference is I'm not drunk—I've never been more sober in my life, in fact—and it's not my dignity or career that's at stake but my life.

We reach a large rock formation that juts into the ocean, preventing us from going any farther. We'll have to swim around it. Fortunately, I'm a strong swimmer and the tide isn't yet at its peak. I shoot Brianna a questioning look, and she says briskly, "I'm a certified lifeguard." *Of course you are.* "I earned spending money for college working summers at my uncle's country club," she informs me as we slog through the churning surf into deeper water. "I never had to save anyone from drowning, but . . ." Her next words are swallowed by the wave that crashes over us.

It's rough going with the undertow alternately threatening to pull me under and dash me against the rocks. I feel as though I've swum the English Channel by the time I reach the other side. I stagger toward shore, only to have another wave snatch my feet out from under me. I go down with a splash. Brianna grabs my arm and pulls me to my feet. I peer at her through the salt water that's streaming down my face. She looks as bedraggled as I'm sure I do. Her hair hangs in wet strings around her face, and her gown looks like a wrinkly elephant skin where it's plastered to her body. She was smart enough to shed her coat, whereas my own, waterlogged one weighs on me like the lead apron you wear when having an x-ray at the dentist's. I'm also shivering in my drenched clothing, and if I can't feel my fingers or toes, it's only due to the fact that I'm numb with cold. "Go. I'm only slowing you down," I gasp as I limp alongside Brianna with her keeping a firm grip on my elbow.

"No way." She shakes her head, sending droplets of water flying from her hair onto my face.

"You work for me, remember? You have to do as I say."

"Fine. In that case, I quit."

"Have it your way," I reply through clenched teeth, though selfishly I'm glad she's being a pain in the ass.

A spark of light off in the distance catches my eye. A campfire glowing on the bluff where the campground is located. My heart leaps, only to sink at the splashing sounds from behind. Greta and Eric are rapidly gaining on us. It's no use. I can't outrun them. I hear the popping of the gun again, and Brianna staggers, letting go of my arm. She takes several lurching steps before she collapses in a heap. I scream and drop down beside her, flashing on the image of Delilah's dead body when I see she's not moving. *Please God, don't let her be dead.* I roll her over and my hand comes away sticky with blood. Most of the blood seems to be coming from where she hit her head when she fell on the rocks, I'm relieved to see, though I notice her right arm is bleeding, too. When I look up, Eric is closing in on us, Greta not far behind.

"You idiot! You ruined *everything*!" Greta shrieks at me.

Her words are like a pin pulled from a grenade. All at once, I'm subsumed by a blaze of fury. So this is *my* fault. Because I wouldn't surrender? Because I messed up her nice, neat murder plot? I surge to my feet, mindless of the threat as I fly to meet Eric headlong. In my drinking days, after I'd had one too many, I sometimes forgot I was the weaker sex. I once broke the nose of a guy who was twice my size and probably twice as drunk when he tried to grope me in the parking lot at the Tide's Inn. But it appears I'm just as reckless and mean-tempered sober as I was when drunk.

It proves to be my saving grace. Eric must have expected me to make a run for it or to cower like a scared rabbit, and he falters when I do neither. He sees the crazy lady coming at him but not the wave breaking behind him. A monster wave with a heart of glass and gnashing white teeth. It crashes over us, and we both go under. I feel a burning sensation in my scalp—my hair seems to be caught on something—and when my vision clears I see it's Eric's hand that's holding me tethered as the wave recedes. I flail about, trying to free myself, but it's no good; he's too strong, and I only end up losing strands of hair and taking water into my lungs. I sputter, coughing. Through the roaring of the surf and that of the blood in my ears I hear Greta's voice scream, "Don't kill her!" Incredibly, she still seems to think she can make my death look like an accident.

Eric has other ideas. He pushes my head underwater while I thrash about. I can't breathe, and as I struggle against him, I realize I'm only making it worse—in my panic I'm running out of oxygen quicker than if I were concentrating on holding my breath. I start to lose consciousness, my body weakening and black spots swarming behind my closed eyelids. I'm about to suck in a lungful of salt water when another wave slams into us. We're dragged apart by the undertow, and I surface seconds later to see Eric splashing his way toward me. I make haste in putting some distance between us, but I only get as far as the tide line before I'm tackled by Greta.

She hurls herself at me like a human cannonball, knocking me down. I don't have the strength to resist when she straddles me, pinning me down. *Game over*, I think. Then something strange happens. I've heard of people performing superhuman feats in life-or-death situations, like hoisting a car from someone who's trapped underneath it or carrying someone who outweighs them from a burning building, but I never imagined it could happen to me. Yet, suddenly, I'm Superwoman. In a burst of renewed strength, I take a swing at Greta with my fist, an uppercut that connects with her jaw and causes her head to snap back. Released from her grip, I roll out from under her and feel something sharp jabbing me through the sodden folds of my coat. I dig the broken bottleneck from my pocket, and when Eric lunges at me from behind, I use it to lash out at him.

"That was for Delilah," I cry, opening a gash in his cheek, "and this is for me!" I strike again before he can retreat. He screams in pain, reeling backward, clutching his right cheek where blood gushes. Greta lets out a howl like a mama bear and rushes to the aid of her wounded cub. She appears oblivious to all but her brother's distress. I seize the advantage.

"You bipolar *bitch*!" I cry, slashing at her face.

CHAPTER THIRTY-TWO

My higher power must be looking out for me after all. Either that, or we got lucky. Brianna regains consciousness as Greta and Eric are floundering. She finds the gun that Greta had put down before she tackled me. Her injures, it seems, aren't serious. She goes for help while I keep the gun pointed at Eric and Greta, both of whom are bleeding profusely and spewing profanities at me, until the cops arrive.

At the hospital, while Brianna and I are treated for our injuries, I learn that the campfire I had spotted earlier belonged to a Danish tourist who let Brianna borrow his phone to call 911. I've suffered a sprained ankle in addition to some scrapes and bruises. Brianna has sustained a flesh wound where Eric's bullet grazed her right arm and a bump on her forehead from when she fell. By the time we're released, Ivy is waiting down the hall to drive us back to her house.

Spence shows up as we're walking to meet her and insists on driving me home. "Would you rather I take you to the station for questioning?" he says sternly when I decline the offer.

"Fine," I tell him. I'm too spent to argue.

"I'll let Ivy know," says Brianna, shooting me a meaningful look before she peels away.

Spence blows his tough-cop stance by putting his arm around

me, inquiring in a solicitous tone as I limp alongside him, favoring my sore ankle, which is wrapped in an Ace bandage, "You have ibuprofen or should we stop at a drugstore?" He's equally insistent on staying the night when we get to my house. "You need someone to look after you until the swelling goes down."

"You do realize this is above and beyond," I say when he returns from fetching me an ice pack. I'm reclining on my living room sofa with my ankle propped on the pillow he placed on the coffee table. It's one o'clock in the morning. We ought to be in our own beds by now, but here he is fussing over me like a Jewish grandmother. Next, he'll be bringing me chicken soup.

Finally, he plops down next to me with an expelled breath. He looks tired, and more than a little rumpled in the off-white chinos and the red-checked button-down shirt he wears, both of which are creased as if from an all-night stakeout. Twin half-moons of sweat darken the shirt under his arms. Who knew he perspired? "Because I'll be sleeping on the world's most uncomfortable sofa bed . . . or because your cat might use me as a scratching post?" he asks, smiling. I warned him about both.

"I was referring to the call of duty."

"So? You're not the only one who makes your own rules." His blue-gray eyes crinkle with wry humor behind his wire-rim glasses. He puts his arm around me, and when my head drops onto his shoulder, it seems only natural. "Like it or not, you're stuck with me, Tish Ballard."

"Since when?"

"Since . . . I don't know. Kindergarten? Don't you remember, I used to pull your pigtails?"

"That was you?"

He heaves an exaggerated sigh. "How quickly they forget."

"I had a crush on you in high school." I glance up at him shyly. There was a time I'd sooner have stuck pins in my eyes than admit that to Spence, but I'm no longer embarrassed by it.

He seems surprised and disconcerted. "So the night we hooked up . . . ?"

"It meant something. To me, anyway."

He groans. "Now I feel like an even bigger jerk."

"You should. But I forgive you."

"Because you knew I was a good guy underneath?" he asks hopefully.

"More like I know the average teenage boy is thinking with the wrong head ninety percent of the time."

He doesn't dispute this. "Would it have helped if I'd said I was sorry?"

"Doubtful. But I wouldn't have torched your car, and you wouldn't have ended up hating me."

"I never hated you. I was pissed."

"You had every right. It was a rotten thing to do. You loved that car."

He replies wistfully, "Sweetest ride I ever had. 'A love like that comes but once in a lifetime.'"

"Ugh. I just threw up a little in my mouth." I sit up straight to give him a mock glare. "I don't know which is worse, you quoting *The Bridges of Madison County* or telling me that a car was the love of your life."

"You're jealous. Admit it," he says, grinning.

"Why would I be jealous?"

"I'm starting to think you like me, the way you keep turning up at crime scenes."

"It wasn't on purpose! Well, except that one time." When I was caught breaking and entering in the course of investigating my mom's murder. "Besides, you wouldn't have solved either case without my help."

He rolls his eyes. "There you go again, hogging all the credit."

"Not all, just some."

"You'd have made a good cop," he admits.

"Did you just pay me a compliment?" I stare at him in surprise.

"Don't let it go to your head. And don't," he adds, "ever scare me like that again. When I showed up at your house and you weren't there . . ." He trails off, his arm tightening around my shoulders.

"You came?"

He nods. "I traced your phone to the bed-and-breakfast, and when you weren't there, I went to your house. I didn't know where you'd gone or why you didn't have your phone with you. What in God's name were you thinking, going off like that without telling anyone?" he admonishes.

"You had a suspect in custody! How was I supposed to know Greta was the real culprit?"

"She had me fooled, too," he admits. "Though I had my doubts about Mrs. Harding's confession."

"Why, because she took it back?"

"That, and she doesn't fit the profile. Also, don't forget, her alibi checked out. Greta Nyland had a solid alibi, too, which is she why wasn't on my short list of suspects. I didn't see a motive, either. She wasn't named as a beneficiary in the will, and there was no life-insurance policy."

"She was benefiting in other ways. By embezzling funds that were supposed to go to poor people so her brother could live like a banana republic dictator." We'd been over it earlier, so Spence knows all this, but the scope of the depravity is so great, it brings a fresh grimace to his face.

"It doesn't get lower than that," he agrees.

"Other than homicide, you mean?" That goes without saying. "But look at the bright side. You now have, not one, but two suspects in custody. And before this, you were looking at a cold case."

"Better a cold case than a fresh corpse," he mutters darkly.

I shudder, thinking of my close call. "Don't worry. I'm sticking to my day job from now on."

Spence holds my gaze. "Is that a promise?"

"Cross my heart, hope to—" I break off before I can say the word. "May the only dead bodies I come across from now on be those of small critters." A fish that went belly-up or a mole that was decapitated by my cat. That I can handle. My gaze drops to my swollen ankle. "I just hope I can get around okay with this foot. When you're self-employed, you don't have the luxury of sick days."

"You have Brianna," he reminds me.

"Not for much longer. It was only a temp job while the investigation was ongoing," I remind him. I realize, to my surprise, I'll miss her when she's gone.

"Maybe you can get her to stay on."

I shake my head. "I couldn't afford to pay her what she's worth."

"There are other incentives."

"Like what?"

"You could make her a partner."

"Partner? Are you out of your mind?" I speak first before I pause to consider. "Actually, that's not a bad idea." If I had a partner, I could take on more clients. I could even take a vacation. "Except she's a total control freak. I wouldn't want her thinking she could boss me around."

"No one," says Spence, smiling, "could ever be the boss of you, Tish."

"I don't know that she'd agree to it. I'm sure she has bigger ambitions."

"It doesn't hurt to ask. She's the kind of person who'd see it as an opportunity to grow the business."

"Maybe. We'll see."

We lapse into companionable silence. The only sounds are the distant rumbling of the furnace in the basement and the clatter of the icemaker in the kitchen. Hercules and Prince are both asleep on the nubby green armchair opposite me, my cat draped across the backrest, my dog curled on the seat cushion. The cozy domestic scene is a reminder of another issue that needs to be resolved.

"Can I ask you something?" I venture.

"Shoot," he says.

"Any chance you and your wife will get back together?" My heart starts to beat faster, but I keep my voice light. Until I have his answer, I don't want him to know how much it matters to me.

When I sneak a glance at him, he's staring straight ahead, his brow creased in thought. My heart sinks because I can guess what his answer will be. It starts with *We were together a long time* and ends with *We talked it over and decided to give it another go.* He'll say they have the kids to think of, the life they built together. You don't walk away from that so fast.

But he doesn't say any of those things. "No," he answers. Just that one word. But if a picture tells a thousand words, one word can speak volumes. I release the pent-up breath in my lungs.

"Oh. Well. That's good. I mean it's good you know for sure."

"It is what it is." He seems resigned.

"So what happens next?"

"I made an appointment with a lawyer. Neither of us wants to drag the other through the mud, so we're hoping we can work it out without going to court. We agree on one thing. We both want what's best for the kids."

"How are they handling it?"

"Barb and I had a talk with them last night. We told them we'd always be their parents and we'd always love them, but we wouldn't ever be together again. They've had some time to get used to the idea, so they took it pretty well. Katie wanted to know if this means *two* trips to Disneyland."

I smile. "Divorce is not without its perks."

"I have to be careful not to spoil them."

"Good luck with that. Once they turn those puppy dog eyes on you . . ."

"Don't I know it." He chuckles. "Mainly, what they want is their dad. That much I can give them now that I'm cutting back on my hours."

"That's good. Kids need both their parents." I speak from experience.

Spence cuts me a sideways glance. "You never wanted kids?"

"More like I never found the right person to have them with."

"I take it your boyfriend's not the one."

"No." It's not just that Bradley isn't the marrying kind or that we live separate lives on different continents. I realize I'm not in love with him. I like him a lot and I won't deny that he stirs lust in me, but love needs sustenance to grow, and a long-distance relationship such as ours doesn't allow for that. "In fact, he's not my boyfriend anymore." If he ever really was.

"So it's over?" Spence eyes me anxiously and he looks relieved when I nod. The only thing that remains is to break it to Bradley. I don't think he'll be too heartbroken. "I was hoping you'd say that."

You would think that I was the most desirable woman in the world, not one with a puffy ankle who was plastered with bandages and wearing her most unflattering sweats, from the way Spence is gazing at me. His expression is soft, and the kiss he gives me is exquisitely tender. When we kissed before, there had been a frantic feel to it as if we'd been flung together by the winds of fate and we were holding on to each other for dear life. Now it's slow and deep and purposeful, as delicious as sinking into a shared hot tub. The bag of ice on my foot clunks to the floor when I shift positions to draw closer to him. The pain in my ankle is but a distant ache. I'm aware only of the pleasurable throbbing between my legs and the feel of his hands and lips on my body. He presses his mouth to the pulse beating at the base of my throat. I stroke the back of his neck with its fuzz of golden hair and work my way down, exploring other parts of his body. I reach below his belt buckle where his jeans have grown noticeably tight, and . . .

He pulls back abruptly, placing his hand over mine to still it. "Tish . . . no."

"What's wrong?" I ask in a breathless voice.

"Not now. Not like this. We should wait." From his pained expression I know it isn't an easy decision for him to make.

"Seriously? You're going to let a technicality get in the way? I don't care that you're still legally married. This is not the nineteenth century," I remind him.

"This isn't about me and Barb. This is about you and me. I want it to be right when we do this, and after all you've been through tonight, I don't think now's the time. Tish, I can't mess this up. I did once before, and you don't get many second chances in life. I don't want to blow this one." As I look into Spence's eyes, I see the man he's become wrestling with the teenage boy he was.

I nod slowly. My body might disagree, but I know he's right. We should wait until we're both rested to make love. Spence sees a future with me, that's what counts. "I promise I'm in full possession of my faculties, although I admit I'm not in the best of shape or at my most attractive."

"You are beautiful." He delivers a chaste but meaningful kiss to my lips. "When I think of how close I came to losing you tonight . . ." He trails off, and his voice is husky when he finishes, "I can't lose you, Tish. You're"—he pauses as if searching for the right word—"special."

Awash in tenderness, I feel my throat start to close up. "In AA we call it 'terminally unique.'"

Spence folds me in his arms. "Let's just go with *unique*, shall we?"

EPILOGUE

Nine months later

"Now this is what I call riding in style." McGee grins as he settles back in his leather seat on the Gulfstream Five that's flying us to L.A. for the red-carpet premiere of the long-awaited *Devil's Slide*.

When I first laid eyes on the private jet sitting on the tarmac at San Francisco International, I couldn't believe it was for us. It's more suitable for an Arab sheik traveling with his entourage and multiple wives than our party of eight, which includes McGee, Brianna, Ivy and Rajeev, Arthur and Gladys, and Spence and me. It's huge, and the cabin is grander and more luxurious than any I'd ever seen. Detailed in burled wood veneer, it has cushy, butter-colored leather seats set two to a row with tables in between, and a commodious service area in back, where a uniformed steward named Derek is preparing refreshments for us. I haven't checked out the bathroom yet, but I'm told it has a shower. The movie studio didn't stint.

"No going back to coach after this," Ivy agrees as she plops into a window seat. She's dressed in a stretchy black top paired with a peasant skirt and her pink Tony Lama cowboy boots.

"Marry a billionaire and you won't have to," I tease her.

"Can it wait until after the wedding?" Rajeev reaches for Ivy's hand after he takes the seat next to her. Six months ago, Rajeev left his previous job to take one at a Silicon Valley start-up that includes stock options that will potentially be worth a fortune when the company goes public in a few months. Ivy has mixed feelings about the prospect of being a rich man's wife. Her acceptance of Rajeev's marriage proposal was on the condition that she would never have to move out of her white elephant into a McMansion or trade her VW Beetle for a luxury vehicle. No bling, either—just the emerald-cut diamond that sparkles on her left hand. Knowing Rajeev, he won't let success go to his head. He wants the same things that Ivy does, and he loves her for who she is.

"This *is* nice." Gladys Sedgwick sighs contentedly as she stretches out in her seat next to Arthur—she'd have miles of legroom even in coach, she's so petite—looking younger than the last time I saw her, if that's possible. I attribute it to the fact that she now has a boyfriend, named Dave, a retired marketing firm CEO whom she'd met online. The romance seems to have given her a new lease on life. She ditched her Palm Beach matron duds in favor of more youthful attire like the white capris and a cropped, navy-checked jacket she has on, got a new hairstyle, and started dyeing her hair a more subtle shade of red. Her boyfriend is ten years her junior, but I imagine she'll wear him out. She has him taking tango lessons with her and they're booked for an African safari in the fall. Meanwhile, she and Arthur still go on their morning power walks together.

Arthur looks handsome in a Calvin Klein blazer, dark gray with muted stripes, paired with a navy-blue open-collared shirt, an outfit Gladys picked out for him when they went shopping last week. She's his new personal shopper, having assumed the role that was once mine. I used to have to drag Arthur to the mall, and getting him to part with so much as his not so tighty-whiteys required a combination of cajoling, bribes, and threats on my part. I see it as a positive sign in terms of his mental health that he's taking more of an interest in his appearance. He seems happier these days and stands taller, having grown in confidence with his job at the senior center.

"You can thank Uncle Karol for getting the studio to pony up," Brianna pipes up. She's standing in the aft of the cabin, where she's briefing Derek the steward on our individual dietary restrictions.

"I still don't get what we did to deserve it." I slide into the seat next to Spence, who sits opposite Ivy and Rajeev. He shoots me a wry glance. He's not used to my being so modest.

"We saved them a ton of money. The picture would've gone over budget if the investigation had dragged on any longer," Brianna reminds me.

Spence doesn't appear offended by Brianna's failure to credit him. He's too busy luxuriating in the legroom his seat affords him. But in fairness I point out, "If the investigation was dragging out, they had only themselves to blame. People who have people"—I use the Hollywood construction, not like in the song—"make it tough for the police to get anything done."

Brianna shrugs. She looks as crisp as the invitation to tonight's premiere—which arrived in the mail six weeks ago, engraved in black on heavy cream stock—in pressed charcoal jeans and an ecru linen top accented by the beaded ebony necklace that Ivy brought back from her most recent trip to Malawi. "No one in Hollywood cares about what really happened. They only care about the bottom line. Also, let's face it, our daring escape makes a way better story than boring police work."

McGee gives a derisive snort. "Next, you'll be selling movie rights."

McGee has an even dimmer view of Hollywood since he started moonlighting as a celebrity bodyguard, courtesy of his new friend Jimmy who's been throwing extra work his way. It didn't prevent him from accompanying us on this trip, however. I observe that he's again rocking the *Miami Vice* look in his tropical-weight off-white blazer and Hawaiian shirt. Wraparound shades and a Panama hat, tilted at a rakish angle on his ponytailed head, complete the ensemble.

"Did you know the Gulfstream G550 has a Rolls-Royce engine?" Arthur says to no one in particular. My brother, the king of the non sequitur. He goes on in greater detail about the G550 while we sip mimosas—virgin for me and McGee, who's ninety days sober and who now regularly attends AA meetings when he's not fending off paparazzi or busting chops (along with the odd camera) for his celebrity clients—from champagne flutes with the studio's logo of a gilded griffin.

Finally, Gladys interrupts him to exclaim, "My goodness, Art, the things you know!"

"Too much?" He eyes her anxiously.

"Not a bit. It's all very interesting." Gladys is more diplomatic than I am. My brother takes the hint and stops talking about stuff you'd need a degree in engineering to understand.

We taxi down the runway to a smooth takeoff. As we climb toward cruising altitude, Spence gives us the latest from the DA's office. "The judge denied the motion for a change of venue," he reports, referring to Greta Nyland's attorney's latest stall tactic. "Jury selection starts Monday of next week." Greta's trial date is slated for the end of March. Eric will be tried in April.

"You'd have to go to an Amish community or an FDLS compound to find jurors who haven't been exposed to the press coverage," I remark. The murder of Delilah Ward and the subsequent arrest of her husband and his sister sparked a media frenzy the likes of which hasn't been seen since the O. J. Simpson trial. It was made even more sensational by Eric Nyland's "return from the dead" and the fact that Greta Nyland was the director of the charitable organization in his name.

"If there's any justice, those two will spend the rest of their lives behind bars!" Gladys declares heatedly.

"In India, you can spend years in jail before your case even goes to trial," Rajeev comments. Ivy shoots me a meaningful look. She and Rajeev are getting married in December, and the wedding is to take place in Mumbai, where Rajeev's family lives. I know she's thinking that trouble has a way of finding me wherever I go. Good thing I'll have Spence to steer us clear of any dead bodies.

Spence puts our minds at rest. "Greta's attorney was angling to cut a deal since hers was the lesser charge, but the DA didn't bite." The charge was conspiracy to commit murder. Greta will be tried at a later date on the charges of kidnapping and attempted murder. "No plea bargain means the prosecution's case is airtight. I spoke with the DA myself. He's confident of a guilty verdict."

"Do they still have chain gangs?" Ivy asks hopefully.

"These days they're called work crews," McGee says with a rasp.

"As long as they're locked up where they can't hurt anyone else, I don't care if they're breaking rocks or making license plates," I say. A chill goes through me at the memory of my near death at their hands. I hope Greta and Eric think of me whenever they see their scarred faces in the mirror.

"Count on it." Spence puts his arm around my shoulders. These past months haven't been smooth sailing, between his divorce and the fact that his kids are still getting used to the idea of their dad having a girlfriend, but for the most part we're like any new couple. We hold hands a lot, have pet names for each other, and fight over who gets to use the TV remote. I try not to project too far into the future. When Spence returned from the final meeting with his wife and their respective attorneys, he declared in a grim voice, "I never want to go through *that* again." I didn't know whether he meant marriage or divorce, and I was afraid to ask. For the most part, I'm content. He sleeps over at my place on the nights his kids are with their mom, and I'm always welcome to join them when Katie and Ryan are with him. We go out for pizza or burgers, or eat in and watch a movie. On weekends, we go to the beach or to the playground in San Lorenzo

Park. I'm crazy about his kids, but I don't know if Spence and I will ever have a child of our own.

Derek comes around to pour more champagne and orange juice. I propose a toast. "We won't know till we've seen it how good this movie is, but I know one thing: It would have been better with Delilah in it." Taylor Ramsey is talented, but not as talented as Delilah was. "Hell, the *world* would be better with her in it." I raise my glass. "Here's to Delilah."

Brianna ducks her head, but not before I notice the overbrightness of her eyes.

Lunch is sliced papaya, crab salad with avocado, and sushi so fresh it's practically swimming, served on china plates with real forks and knives. Commercial air travel will never be the same after this. How will I go back to sporks and pretzels? Brianna and I talk shop while we enjoy our meal. Revenues for Rest Easy Property Management have doubled since I made Brianna a partner. Turns out she's a marketing whiz. She redesigned our Web site and posted a clever video she made on YouTube that has gotten over a hundred thousand views so far (it shows us doing *Mission Impossible*–style stunts such as spider-crawling across ceilings in getting to those hard-to-reach spots). We now have a dedicated office space—the attic floor we're renting at Ivy's—a company van, and an employee, a high school girl by the name of Natalie who works part-time.

"I read online there was a fourteen percent increase in the number of vacation rentals over the past year." Brianna uses her chopsticks to convey a piece of salmon dipped in soy sauce to her mouth without so much as a drop landing on her ecru linen top or the cloth napkin that covers her lap. "If we had another van, we could take on even more clients. So here's what I'm thinking . . ."

I suppress a sigh as she sketches out the latest plan for expansion. I owe her my life, but she'll be the death of me yet.

When we're done eating, I go over to McGee and slip into the empty seat next to his. "So what did you decide?"

"About what?" he replies, feigning ignorance.

"You know."

He grunts in response.

"It's a good offer," I point out.

The night of the shooting at the Shady Brook Inn, he became acquainted with my client Mr. Russo, and formed an unlikely friendship with him. Recently, Russo offered McGee a job at his casino working directly under his nephew, Dom, the chief of security. Between retirement pay and a salary he'd be sitting pretty, though McGee doesn't see it that way.

"I like being my own boss," he says.

"Which means way too much time on your hands, and you know what that leads to."

"Yeah, you nagging me."

I nudge him with my elbow. "I'll miss you when you're gone."

"I ain't gone yet." McGee isn't one for expressing sentiment, but I detect a faint smile hovering over his lips. He lowers his shades to peer at me over the tops. "You trying to get rid of me or something?"

I grin. "As if."

The subdivisions of greater Los Angeles appear below in miniature, dotted with swimming pools that stare up at the sky like unblinking blue eyes. I feel a flutter of anticipation thinking about tonight's event. I'm eager to see *Devil's Slide*, which was named after the very spot where I nearly lost my life and which now serves to remind me that, even though bad things happen to good people, good things can happen, too. I'm also looking forward to reconnecting with Liam Brady at the premiere. He flew in from Prague, where he's filming next summer's blockbuster in which he stars as a mortal for a change. We've kept in touch through Facebook messages. Liam is still sober, still kicking butt at the box office, and still straight, as far as I know. His current girlfriend is a Brazilian supermodel. As for the other cast members, I only know what's reported by the press.

The big story is that Brent Harding and his wife got back together. He had a change of heart when Olivia gave birth to their twins while awaiting trial on the charge of assault with a deadly weapon. He subsequently moved back into their Bel Air mansion and testified in her defense at her trial, admitting to his own misconduct and pleading for clemency. The judge sentenced Olivia to community service in lieu of jail time. They plan to renew their vows once she's served her sentence. I wish them all the happiness in the world. They deserve each other, if you ask me.

I return to my seat to find Ivy and Rajeev peering at his laptop, shaking their heads over the latest "suggestion" emailed by his mother. Rupa Jaswinder might have modern views on her son's choice of a bride, but she's determined to see Rajeev wed in a traditional Indian ceremony, complete with a guest list that numbers in the hundreds, a wedding feast fit for a king, and more than one form of hired entertainment. "You don't think professional dancers are a bit over the top?" Ivy asks apprehensively. The Bollywood-style extravaganza envisioned by her future mother-in-law has given her a new appreciation for her own mother's hands-off approach. Dr. Ladeaux bestowed her blessing on the union but has taken a backseat in regards to the wedding itself. Her sole contribution was to pay the air fare to Malta, where the newlyweds will honeymoon.

"I'll see if I can get mama-ji to tone it down," says Rajeev.

We circle LAX a couple times, then the jet is screaming down the runway. Instead of the interminable wait while other passengers wrestle carry-on luggage from overhead bins, I'm stepping from the open rear hatch a minute later. A stretch limo awaits us on the tarmac, sunlight reflecting from its shiny black exterior. A uniformed driver stands beside it, and he smiles and tips his chauffer's cap when he notices I'm staring. It seems like a dream, one that began as a nightmare—with Delilah Ward's dead body. I'm pretty sure I'm still dreaming when Spence, as we're making our way to the limo, squeezes my hand and whispers, "Marry me and I'll take you away from all this."

AUTHOR'S NOTE

I've led a storied life in more ways than one. I've gone places and done things that astound me, looking back on it. Where did I ever find the courage? The willpower? Much of it I would advise against, were I to go back in time and have a heart-to-heart with my younger self. But good or bad, it was all grist for the mill, so I regret none of it. (Though I feel fortunate not to be haunted by compromising photos of myself online, having come of age in the pre-Internet era). The beauty of fiction is you can reshape past events however you please. I wasn't popular in high school but got to hang out with the cool kids when I wrote for the phenomenally successful teen series Sweet Valley High in the early years of my career. Trust me, you wouldn't have wanted to live through some of what I lived through, but hopefully you've enjoyed the novels that came of it.

If you Google my name, you will see my Cinderella story: welfare mom to millionaire. Every word is true, though the reality is I was a starving artist for a much longer period of time than I was on welfare. With two young children to support on my own, I often had to forgo buying office supplies and stamps to send out the articles and short stories I wrote on spec in order to put food on the table.

The lean years were the making of me, though. When I wrote my first adult novel, *Garden of Lies*, the story of babies switched at birth, one of whom grows up rich, the other poor, I knew what it was to go hungry. I knew what it was like for Rose putting on the skirt she wears to work every day, ironed so many times it's shiny in spots. *Garden of Lies* went on to become a *New York Times* bestseller, translated into twenty-two languages. I attribute its success in part to my having suffered.

I've also had my share of romantic ups and downs. More grist for the mill and the reason my fictional characters tend to be of the folks-this-ain't-my-first-rodeo variety. I've been married more than once. At one point, I was married to my agent. His client list boasts some notable names, and just recently I was struck by the realization that I had dined with two of the famous people depicted in the movies *The Theory of Everything* and *Selma*: professor Stephen Hawking and Coretta Scott King, respectively. How extraordinary! I witnessed history and saw it reenacted on film.

I met my current and forever husband, Sandy Kenyon, in a Hollywood meet-cute, which seems fitting given he's in the entertainment business, as a TV reporter and film critic. He had a radio talk show in Arizona at the time. I was a guest on his show, phoning in from New York City, where I live. He called me at home that night, at my invitation, and we talked for three hours. It became our nightly ritual, and when we finally met it was love at first sight, though we were hardly strangers. We married in 1996, and he became the inspiration for talk-show host Eric Sandstrom in *Thorns of Truth*. Though, as Sandy's fond of saying, he never killed a coanchor while driving drunk.

I have many people to thank for the support and guidance I've received along the way.

First and foremost, my husband, Sandy, who's been there every step of the way and who reads multiple drafts of my novels. He's patient, kind, and wise. He understands when I'm there in body but somewhere else in my mind, and doesn't get too upset at having to

repeat himself more than once to get through to me. From him I
learned the true meaning of romantic love, which has enriched my
fictional love stories immeasurably. He's also partly the reason I'm
still walking this earth. More than once it was his hand on my arm,
pulling me to safety, that kept me from stepping into the path of a
moving vehicle while in one of my preoccupied states.

To my children, Michael and Mary, for being the quirky, loving
individuals they are. Whenever I beat myself up for having been
a less-than-perfect parent (which pretty much describes every
single parent), they tell me they couldn't love me any more than
they do. They also both have a wicked sense of humor, which they
get from me. When I was exploring the idea of having another
child, with Sandy, I was told I'd need an egg donor. Which led to
the what-if scenario that would have me giving birth to my own
grandchild (and writing the bestseller that would come of it!), at
which point my daughter remarked dryly, "Mom, would you like
that over easy or sunny side up?"

To friends and family who have made their vacation homes
available to me through the years. Their generosity has allowed
me to go away for extended periods of time to write in solitude
amid serene settings. Bill and Valerie Anders. Frank Cassata and
Thomas Rosamilia. Miles and Karen Potter. Jon Giswold. Thanks
to my friend Jon, I was introduced to the scenic wonders of northern Wisconsin and befriended by the good people of Grantsburg,
which I now consider my home away from home.

To my friends and author pals, who are my cheering section.
Whenever I'm at a low point or feeling blue, they're always there
to offer a hug, a pat on the back, or a word of encouragement. I
wouldn't be where I am today if not for them.

I smile, and brush away a tear, whenever I think of my oldest
friend, Kay Terzian, who had every single one of my titles, in multiple editions, when she passed away. She would always say she was
my biggest fan. I never doubted it.

To my publisher, Open Road Media, and its smart, happening crew led by the visionary Jane Friedman, who saw the future of digital publishing. Special thanks, too, to my editor, Maggie Crawford, who helped shape my most-recent titles and make them better for it. She's living proof of why an author needs an editor.

I am also blessed to have many loyal readers. They range in age from fourteen to ninety-four and come from all walks of life and all parts of the globe. One, a prisoner doing time on a drug offense, sent letters commenting intelligently on my novels, which I was happy to know were available in prison libraries. Shortly before his release, he sent me a Mother's Day card. I had written a few times in response to his letters, but would hardly describe myself as a pen pal, let alone a surrogate mom. I think he regarded me fondly because he felt he knew what was in my heart, which I pour into the pages of my novels. That is the greatest compliment of all and the best part of what I do for a living, worth more to me than fame or fortune.

Thank you for taking this journey with me. If you've enjoyed what you've read, leave a comment on Amazon or Goodreads to help spread the word, so I can keep doing what I do.

Eileen Goudge

ABOUT THE AUTHOR

Eileen Goudge (b. 1950) is one of the nation's most successful authors of women's fiction. She began as a young adult writer, helping to launch the phenomenally successful Sweet Valley High series, and in 1986 she published her first adult novel, the *New York Times* bestseller *Garden of Lies*. She has since published twelve more novels, including the three-book saga of Carson Springs and *Thorns of Truth*, a sequel to *Gardens of Lies*. She lives and works in New York City.

THE CYPRESS BAY MYSTERIES

FROM OPEN ROAD MEDIA

INTEGRATED MEDIA